I break off our kiss, tell myself I'm breathless from Griff and not because I'm scared. Even though I know that's what lives at the bottom of this: I'm terrified. I don't want to lose everything I've been given.

I curl my hands into Griff's shirt. He grins and my heart stutters.

"So I'll see you later then, Wicked?"

The nickname still makes me blush. "Definitely."

Another kiss. This one's hard and fast. By the time my fingers curl into his chest, it's done. He's turning away.

Gone.

Also by Romily Bernard

Find Me

Trust Me

REMEMBER

ME

ROMILY BERNARD

HARPER TEEN
An Imprint of HarperCollinsPublishers

HarperTeen is an imprint of HarperCollins Publishers.

Remember Me
Copyright © 2014 by Romily Bernard

For information address HarperCollins Children's Books,
a division of HarperCollins Publishers, 195 Broadway,
New York, NY 10007.
www.epicreads.com

Library of Congress Cataloging-in-Publication Data
Bernard, Romily.
  Remember me / Romily Bernard. — First edition.
    pages cm
  Sequel to: Find me.
  Summary: "Teen hacker Wick Tate has to decide between right and wrong as she tries
to solve another murder and discover the truth about her mother's suicide" — Provided
by publisher.
  ISBN 978-0-06-222907-6
  [1. Computer hackers—Fiction. 2. Foster home care—Fiction. 3. Suicide—Fiction.
4. Mystery and detective stories.] I. Title.
PZ7.B4551354Rem 2014   2014001887
[Fic]—dc23   CIP
                                                                      AC

Typography by Joel Tippie
16 17 18 19 20 PC/RRDH 10 9 8 7 6 5 4 3 2 1
❖
First paperback edition, 2016

For my parents, who read to us every night with voices

REMEMBER ME

```
         -/  AWF.
       until|9F1:
    -JRRUU\r58"1:
 %p")>(f'  )%p1;
  ,m'    )%p1;
         ^9P.
        19F1:
        5R"s1:
        t//v'
       -"u9;
        ^9P.
       19F1:
       5R"s1:
       )%p1;
       )%p1;
       5R"s1:
    p")>(P+P)%p1pe"r9p'
    p")>(P+P)%p1pe"r9p'
```

Somehow I think I always knew I'd get arrested. I just never expected it to happen during Home Ec. From the looks of it, Principal Matthews agrees. His face is ham-pink and shiny. He seems angry until I see the grin.

"Miss Tate?" he says. "Could we have a word?"

Love it when they make an order sound like a request. I mutter apologies to my group partners and grab my messenger bag from under the counter, pulling the strap across my shoulder. I've been expecting this moment for almost five months now, and I know I deserve it, but I can't help one last glance at the open window across the room.

If I ran full out, I could escape.

"*Now*, Miss Tate."

Or not.

I walk to the nearest of the two officers and bump up

my chin so I can pretend my joints aren't loosening. The policeman looks me over, scowls. I know what he sees—long, pale blond hair; short, pale blue dress—and what he's thinking: trash. He might even be right.

Nice girls don't write computer viruses.

Let alone use them.

The officer takes my bag and, after he glances through it, all of us tromp into the hallway. Just like I always pictured, Detective Carson is waiting. He looks so happy I start to shake.

"Here she is, Detective." Principal Matthews pats my arm and I have to resist the urge to bite him. "Like I said she'd be."

"Great." Carson jerks his head to the left. "Can we use this classroom?"

Classroom? One of the officers prods me forward and I trip, my feet suddenly useless. If I'm not being arrested, then what—

Shit. It's another job. He's going to make me work for him again.

"Um." Matthews rubs the back of his head, looking dumbfounded, which, to be honest, isn't much of a stretch for him. "It's not really protocol."

"It'll only be for a few minutes, and we'd really appreciate the help." Carson's smile goes crocodile wide. "I'll be sure to remember it."

"Oh, good. That's good." Matthews retreats, refusing to meet my eyes. He pats his pockets like he lost something. "We're always happy to be of assistance."

And, to Matthews's credit, he does sound happy, but when he looks at the floor, the roots of his hair are glittery with sweat.

I can't blame him. The detective has the same effect on me.

I follow Carson into the empty classroom, neither of us saying anything until the door clicks closed.

"Well, well, Wicket Tate." He smiles. "You don't call. You don't write. What am I supposed to think?"

"It's not you. It's me." I tap one finger to my lower lip. "Nah, it's definitely you."

Carson laughs. He sits down on a desktop so we're almost eye to eye, a poster of Spanish verb conjugations above his head as he paws through my bag. "I miss this, Wick. You're always such a smart-ass when you're scared."

"I'm not scared of you."

"You should be." He looks up, the amused smile snapped off. "You're not keeping up with our deal. You do what I want now. Remember? Or else you go to jail."

Carson leans closer and I have to push my feet into the floor to keep from running. "I have evidence you hacked to catch Todd Callaway."

My breath dries up. Stupid how after so many months the name can still make me flinch. Todd. My former foster dad and my former best friend's rapist. He almost killed me. What I did to catch him was justified . . . it just wasn't legal.

"If I can find evidence on what you did to Callaway," Carson says, "imagine what I could find on the work you did for that shitbird father of yours."

Odds are, he could find loads—especially if my father and his partner decide to roll on me. I focus on the Spanish verbs so I don't have to meet Carson's eyes. "What do you want?"

"I have another job. It's perfect for you." When I don't respond, the detective clears his throat and continues, "I want to track Jason Baines and I want you to make it happen. Immediately."

He's right. It is kind of perfect. Baines is a mid-level drug dealer who worked for my father. We have history. If anyone could get close, I could—except this is beyond the type of work I usually do. Before, Carson needed an email track here, a credit card trace there. This is way riskier.

"Find someone else, Carson. I do cyberspace. Tracking that fast would require contact."

"Your *point*? Don't play shy, Wick. Baines specializes in roofies." Carson searches my face and, even though I keep my features disinterested, he still sees something that makes his eyes go plastic bright. "He preys on women. That's not too different from the men you used to catch, right?"

Right. Up until five months ago, I ran an online business specializing in catching cheaters and gold diggers. Most of my targets were guys. Most of my clients were women. And yeah, I did it for money—my sister, Lily, and I needed it—but I also did it because those women needed answers. I made sure the men they loved were really who they said they were. I made sure no one ended up like my mom did.

And later, I used those same skills to bring down Todd and save my sister.

But Carson only knows a little bit about the last part and nothing about the first. He's fishing and I play it blank, realizing too late that I should have played it stupid.

"What are you talking about?" I say, twirling a strand of hair around my finger. Carson's mouth thins and I switch the conversation around. "Look, your best bet for tracking Baines is putting something on his phone, only that's no good because I'd have to get close enough to do it and—"

"And it shouldn't be hard since you two go way back. One of my sources says he'll be selling at Judge Bay's Carnivale party tonight."

"You sure?" Bay is a local luminary: rich, well-connected, the kind of guy who uses *summer* as a verb. I know of him the same way most people like me know of him: He presided over our legal cases. "That's pretty bold."

"My source says your new mommy has accepted an invitation as well."

I go very, very still. "You've been watching Bren?"

"Scared now?"

"No." I'm fucking terrified. I shove suddenly sweating hands into my pockets. "You wouldn't dare touch her."

Only, he would, to get to me. My sister and I were adopted by Bren Callaway two months ago in what the papers are calling a fairy-tale ending. Although the description makes me gag, I can't fault the observation. Lily and I went from foster care rejects to looking like poster children for Ralph Lauren. Yeah, Bren was married to Todd, the psychopath who tried to kill both me and Lily, but aside from Bren's seriously crappy taste in men, she's straight out of Disney casting.

She doesn't deserve what Carson would do to her to get to me.

"I want you there." The detective stands, tosses my bag to me. "Do whatever you have to do. I want to be able to follow Baines's movement by tomorrow."

"Yeah, I'm fresh out of magic wands." Then again, I might not be. Baines isn't the only one who can get roofies. I could knock him out, download a tracking app to his phone. There's a certain poetic justice to it. I'm very capable of this . . . and that fact should scare me.

Actually, it does scare me. Thing is . . . if I tag Baines, Carson will go away. Bren and Lily will be safe. I can go on pretending I'm normal.

For a little while at least.

"Make it happen." The detective stares down at me, and even though it's finally healed, my injured arm starts to burn. "You wouldn't want to ruin that lovely new life you landed, now would you?"

"No." And isn't that just the funniest punch line? Here I am with a new life, new start, and I'm already ruining it. Worse, I'm risking ruining it for my sister—and for

Bren—and they deserve any happily ever after life will give them.

I consider Carson. This is probably where I should cry a bit, but I've swallowed my tears for so long they've turned to bone.

I roll my hands into fists. "Maybe you're the one who should be careful. I brought down a rapist you couldn't. The papers are calling me a hero."

Even if I can barely say the word.

Carson's upper lip wrinkles. "That so?"

Above us, the bell rings. School's finished for the day and the hallway swarms with students, their voices swelling like the growl of distant thunder. How long before the rumor of me getting hauled out of class by the police reaches Bren? Or my best friend, Lauren?

Worse, how long before it reaches Griff?

Is it considerate that I want to be the person who tells him first? Or paranoid? I never told him I was working for Carson. He thinks I'm free.

And just like that, my hands are shaking again. "I'll send you a text when it's finished."

"Good." Carson smacks open the classroom door and motions me forward. I'm almost into the hallway when his fingers sink into my bad arm, pinning me against the lockers to hide his grip. "The next time you think about blowing me off, Wicket, you think about everything I could destroy."

I hold my breath, waiting for Carson to twist my arm

until I want to scream. His hold stays light though. It's not punishment. It's a promise.

"Understand?" he asks, fitting Bren and Lily and everything I want into one word.

I nod, but the detective doesn't let go and I shouldn't look at him. . . . I do, realizing too late he isn't focused on me. He's staring at Griff.

Who's headed straight for us.

"Smile for the boyfriend," Carson says.

Funny how I still can. Smiles are so easy when they're for Griff. I smile. Carson smiles. Griff's too far away, but I know his eyes have narrowed.

The detective snorts. "I'm always amazed at the way he looks at you."

Me too.

Carson leans down, his lips so close to my ear the words escape in a hiss: "Think he'd look at you the same way if he knew what you really are?"

He does know. Griff helped me escape my father and Todd. He knows what I was before and he never wants me to go back.

"Think he'd still want you if he knew you were working for me?"

No. Yes. I don't know and it makes my chest shrink tight. This is what happens when you end up with a hero. He expects you to be just as noble.

And I'm not.

Carson releases my arm, his thumb curving across the

spot where Todd rammed in the knife. "I enjoy our little talks. I like seeing everything you've got now, gives me more I can take away. We understand each other?"

"Perfectly."

"Good," the detective says, and swings away from me, cutting left, cutting right as the students surge around him.

"What was that about?"

It takes me a beat before I can finally turn around, and when I do, Griff cups my jaw. His long fingers reach into my hair, streak chills down my spine.

"Todd," I say. The lie is sluggish. I'm looking at Griff and can see only Carson. I shake myself. Another problem with heroes: If you confess your secrets, they will want to save you.

I want to save myself.

"They found some additional information," I add.

Griff frowns. "Anything we should worry about?"

"No." I smile and it makes him smile. He looks at me like I'm perfect.

What happens if that goes away?

"It's under control," I add, and it *is* under control. That part, at least, isn't a lie. I will fix this. I *will*.

Someone jostles Griff from behind and he steps into me, filling my nose with the smell of grass and gasoline and oil paints from his art class. Griff braces one hand above me, shielding me from the crowd. "We still on for tonight?"

I blink. *Dammit. How could I have forgotten?* "Um, yeah, it's just that I have this thing I need to do. With Bren. Can we meet up later?"

"Of course," he says. And kisses me.

I wrap my arms around his neck and he tugs me close, his hands skating over me, dragging shivers across my skin. I feel my heartbeat . . . *everywhere*. Does it make me pathetic that Griff can burn everything else away?

Everything, but this: Would he want me if he knew?

Yes. Of course. No doubt.

Even though I repeat the words, I don't believe in them any more than I believe in the fairy-tale ending I've been given. There's no such thing. Or there wasn't until I met Griff.

Which side of me is worse: the pathetic girl who wants the boy or the pathetic girl who's afraid of the detective?

I break off our kiss, tell myself I'm breathless from Griff and not because I'm scared. Even though I know that's what lives at the bottom of this: I'm terrified. I don't want to lose everything I've been given.

I curl my hands into Griff's shirt. He grins and my heart stutters.

"So I'll see you later then, Wicked?"

The nickname still makes me blush. "Definitely."

Another kiss. This one's hard and fast. By the time my fingers curl into his chest, it's done. He's turning away.

Gone.

I chew my tingling lips and reach for my phone, dialing

a number I haven't used in ages and should have forgotten. Stringer picks up on the third ring. There's no hello, but I can hear his breathing.

"Hey . . . it's me." I lean against the lockers, cradling my bad arm.

"Been a long time, girlie."

"Yeah, it has." Months and months, actually. Before I went into foster care. When Stringer and I were just good earners for my dad. "I need your help."

"What kind of help?"

"Roofies. By tonight."

```
   r.P)tpipe"r*,
 .*(P.P)tpioe"r*p",
 .p(R_)r        *θP)ici
 ¹*  u            *r/&i
                  .it/.
                  .ccah
                  .*θpi(
               ,rfθ*ic'
          .inapt/*r'
       .cθR"ïθo=*
    (P.P)ipi-
  .r*(P.P'
 .URRUU'
 .)">*i
 .p")e
 .θp(θ_
.ait untilïθ*inapt(/*r/&i
 -URRUU\cθR"ïθd*solit/.
```

There are worse things than going to Judge Bay's costume party. At the moment, though, I can't think of any. Things I *can* think of?

How Bren looked at me when I asked to come.

How Stringer looked at me when I bought the roofies.

How it shouldn't be this easy. This is not who I am. It's *not*.

And yet both of them looked at me like it is. Bren was so happy and Stringer . . . Stringer wasn't surprised. I wish he had been.

I keep telling myself I can do this. I will drug Jason Baines's drink. I will wait until he's passed out. I will install a hidden tracking app on his cell.

I will be okay.

But now that I'm at Bay's home, I realize my plan is

super stupid. I had no idea how massive the judge's house is or how many people were going to be here. It's a Carnivale party, which I thought meant feather headdresses and bedazzled bikinis, but I guess when you live in the South, it means resurrecting a tragic Halloween costume.

Seriously. The Tinker Bell to my left looks rode hard and the genie on my right . . . that may not actually be a costume. If Jason Baines is here, I'm going to have a hard time finding him—and if I do find him, how exactly am I supposed to get the roofies into his drink? Which also presumes he's drinking.

I'm going to screw up everything.

"I don't want to be here," I whisper.

"Yes, you do." Next to me, Lauren readjusts her cat ears. I'll be honest, it was kind of awesome running into her. My best friend's family is well-connected, and she often attends parties like these with her mother. I pretty much expected to see them, but part of me still went boneless with relief.

It's probably the same part of me that's responsible for my stupid plan of attack. Or it's the part of me that's gone soft. I used to operate alone. I *still* operate alone and yet . . .

"You being here makes Bren happy—and Bren could use a little happy." Lauren tugs her fingers through her almost black hair, trying to smooth it. Pointless really. The wind is picking up and no amount of Restoration Hardware heaters or outdoor fireplaces is going to hide the fact that it's freaking February.

13

"What if someone asks her about Todd?"

"They wouldn't dare." She says it with such a forceful smile I almost believe her.

Until that smile vanishes.

"Oh shit," Lauren hisses, and I follow her gaze to Mrs. Cross, her mother. She's talking to some guy in a Phantom of the Opera costume, her face absolutely white, her mouth fish-gulping for air. She's on the tip of another panic attack, and just like that, my best friend's melting through the crowd.

I start to follow, stop. Lauren won't want me there. Neither of them will. Lauren and I aren't friends because we like the same ice cream (even though we do) or because we like boy bands (even though we don't). I think we're friends because our mothers are damaged. My biological mom committed suicide. Her adoptive mom is imploding.

I hate it for Lauren, but it's an unexpected windfall. Bren thinks I'm with Lauren. Lauren's consumed with her mom.

Leaves me open to do what I need to do.

I turn toward the house and, like I'm living in some cheesy movie, spot Jason near the bar. He sees me and gives me a tiny nod, dark hair flipping into his eyes. I'm not sure if it's in acknowledgment of how we used to work together or who my father is. Either way, I suddenly know how I'm going to finish this.

I elbow my way to the bar and order a Red Bull, play with my straw and glass until the bartender moves down to get drink orders from a Captain Kirk. There are two empty stools between Jason and me, but I can still feel his gaze crawl up my skin like spiders.

"Can you believe this?" he asks. The question's so quiet I nearly miss it.

"No," I say, and immediately I wish I hadn't. Agreeing makes me more like him and less like the girl I'm going to be.

I keep my eyes on the people around us, fidgeting with my zombie Alice in Wonderland costume. Even if I weren't meeting with Jason, this kind of party makes me anxious. It's where I'm supposed to belong now, but I've been living this life with Bren for almost a year and it still feels borrowed.

In the corner of my vision, Jason shifts. He's in a fifties-style suit, dressed up as a Mad Man, I guess, and as he leans closer, the jacket falls open. "So why're you here?" he asks.

"To see you." I push one hand into my skirt pocket, feel the Rohypnol roll like pebbles. "I have a message. From him."

The dealer goes so still I know I've got him.

"From your dad?" he asks.

For the first time, I dare to fully look at him, raise both my eyebrows in a *Who else do you think, idiot?* way.

Jason smacks one hand against his suit jacket, exposing an enormous gold watch before he fishes out his iPhone. The screen is illuminated with an incoming call. "Give me one second," he says. "I'm working."

"He'll be glad to know." Jason's gaze swings to mine, holds, and I can see nothing but want in his eyes: How he wants my father's approval. How he wants to belong.

How I can use that against him.

So while Jason paces with whoever's on the cell, I put two roofies in his beer. At least, I think it's his beer. I'm almost positive.

After a few minutes, Jason circles back to me, grinning. "Cheers," he says, and clinks his beer—I was *right*—against my Red Bull. He drinks the Heineken in two long pulls. "What does he need?"

"Wait for my friends to leave," I say, and Jason nods.

We watch everyone but each other, and twenty minutes later, I tell him to follow me.

Since most of the party is near the rear of the house, I push toward the front. The number of guests starts to thin and I turn down an empty hallway, skin-crawlingly aware that Jason's only a few strides behind me. I'm trying to look like I'm searching for a bathroom. He's trying to look like . . . I have no idea. I refuse to turn around. With every step, I'm chickening out.

"Where you goin', Wick?" He's closer than I thought and sweat pops up between my shoulder blades.

"Somewhere quiet." I turn to face him. "My dad said this was really important. We don't want any interruptions."

"Good idea."

You won't think so when we get there—if we get there. His skin is shimmery with sweat and his eyes are dilated. The roofies have hit him hard. I have two minutes. Maybe.

I shoulder open the nearest door, spilling both of us into a dimly lit home office. Jason plows into me from behind, closing a fist around my arm. "What did Michael say?"

I shudder. Another name I hate. My father's.

"What's he want?" Jason asks, giving me a shake.

I shove him. Hard. Thank God for the Rohypnol because he spins, staggers, and drops onto a leather sofa wedged under a picture window. I close the door behind us, slump against the wood. My costume is twisted from where he grabbed me and my dark wig is crooked. I pull it off, shake my hair loose.

Jason's face screws tight. "What the hell is your problem?"

"You."

He stabs both hands into the couch, tries to stand, and falls. Horror crawls across his face. "Did you—"

"Give you a little trip? Yeah," I say, knowing he'll never remember it. Like roofie victims before him, his memory of tonight is going to smear into an ugly blank. I come a little closer. "Do you even care what happens to them?"

Them. The girls. They don't have names. Ends up not mattering though because Jason doesn't pretend to be confused.

"No, I don't."

"I do." In fact, I like telling myself that's the real reason I'm here. It's easier than seeing Bren or Lily or Griff behind my eyes. Jason shifts, tries to move, and can't. It's like someone poured him into place. I've seen the look before. I have less than one minute.

"Bitch," he whispers.

Yes. Probably. I wait, counting down the seconds and watching something that might be fear shadowbox behind the dealer's eyes.

"Looks like Lell," Jason mutters, tilts sideways, and passes out.

The hell? On the other side of the office door, people walk by. Someone laughs and I stiffen. Now is *so* not the time to hesitate. We could be interrupted at any minute, but I can't bring myself to touch him. He smells like the peppermints he's always chewing and it makes my throat funnel shut.

Suddenly, I'm not in Judge Bay's home office. I'm back in my bedroom, smelling peppermints on Todd's breath and watching him slice me open. I need to move and I *can't* move.

Another laugh. Closer this time.

Get going.

I drop to my knees, ramming one hand into Jason's pocket. First the left then the right. There it is. I pull out his iPhone and enter the security code I watched him use earlier. The home screen appears and I load the browser, start downloading a GPS tracking app.

Another moment and I'm done. Jason will never know it's there and Carson can watch him whenever he likes. Though it's weird that he even wants to. I can't help wondering what Carson's angle is. Jason's mid-level. Carson's usually interested in bigger fish.

Best not to think about it. I use my dress to wipe any prints from the iPhone and slide it into Jason's jeans pocket. Pushing both hands into the floor, I start to stand and something scrapes the window. I freeze as a shadow glides over us.

Shit.

I drop to the floor, scrambling backward on my hands and knees. I hit the desk and, shoulders rammed against its side, I watch the window. The shadow reappears. There's another scrape, a rattle as the window shakes.

He's trying to get in.

I cover my mouth with both hands, chewing down a scream.

He'll catch me. He'll—he's stopping.

The guy leans close to the glass, staring down at Jason. His head twitches and looks straight ahead. Right at me.

He can't see you. He can't see you. He can only see Jason because he's so close.

The shadow pulls back, looks right, then left. If he goes for help, I'm screwed.

He goes right, disappearing into the dark, and my breath escapes in a rush.

Gotta get out of here. I kick my feet under me, keeping

the window in sight as I move toward the door, grabbing my wig from the floor as I pass. My hands bump into the handle and I hesitate. The outside hallway is lit. If he's still near the window, he'll see me when I open the door.

I swallow hard and press down on the handle, cracking the door open just enough to slip into the deserted hallway. For a moment, there's no one and I can breathe again.

Then I hear voices.

I pivot to my right and power walk into the living room and the crowd. The costume party is in full swing now. A few people look my way, stare. Do they know? I can't tell and cold sweat rolls underneath my costume. I take one step forward. Two. No one starts screaming. No one asks where Jason is. More eyes slide in my direction . . . and stick.

Maybe it's because I'm dressed as a blood-spattered Alice in Wonderland—that has to be a first—but it's probably not. Some people see me as the girl who brought down her foster dad, the child molester. Others see me as the girl who asked for it.

Yet another reason not to stick around. I push through the other guests, heading for the backyard, where I left Bren and two investment bankers. Fortunately, she's still there and the suits are still enthralled with her. Thank God. I've never been more grateful for my adoptive mom's ability to go on and on about diversification strategies.

"There you are." Bren wraps one arm around my shoulders, gives me a tight squeeze. I'm so glad to see her I hug her even harder, have to remind myself to let go before I completely crush her fluffy pink Glinda the Good Witch costume.

"I thought you were going to hang around with Lauren," she says, adjusting the collar of my dress so it's smooth.

"They had to leave."

"Oh." The skin between Bren's eyes creases. "Did you have a hard time finding me?"

I almost burst out laughing. I want to tell Bren no, not at all, because I'm not ten and I can get around, but if I don't want to be Carson's pet, my alternative is cute-and-cuddly teenage girl.

Only I don't like that option either.

"I had a hard time finding the bathroom," I whisper, and everyone smiles indulgently.

Gag. Me. Now.

Bren's attention drifts to my hair, noticing the absent wig. She starts to speak and I cut her off, holding up the dark wig like it's a dead animal. "Sorry. It was itchy."

The guy to my right glances at his phone. "It's almost time for Bay's speech. Shall we go up?"

Shall we? Now I really want to gag. Until I realize Bren is kind of digging his attention. Her smile is white and shiny and . . . unfamiliar. I can't remember the last time she looked so happy.

"That would be perfect," Bren says, gathering a handful of pink tulle skirt. "And if you do decide you want a proposal, here's my card." She passes him a cream-colored business card and the guy pockets it, eyes still pinned to her like she's made of magic.

He doesn't have a clue. I don't mean that to sound like my adoptive mom isn't amazing. She is. But ever since Todd's arrest, most of the town treats her like total crap. They think she should have known what he was doing and stopped it. Thing is, Bren agrees and she's hated herself ever since.

And while I don't regret taking down Todd, I do regret the blowback on Bren. Maybe if I had handled things differently . . . *better* . . . she wouldn't be suffering. I saved my sister. I saved myself.

I ruined Bren's life.

Exposing Todd was right . . . and yet.

"Are you friends with the family?" Guy #2 asks.

A brief pause. Bren always hesitates before she lies. "We've known them for a long time," she says.

But the only reason we even received an invitation to the party is because Bren donated money to Bay's previous political campaigns. They can't afford to snub her even though we can't really afford to contribute anymore. Bren's consulting company is struggling because people around here don't want to do business with her. These guys must be out-of-towners and Bren saw the opportunity. She'll do whatever she has to do to take care of Lily and me.

It's one of the biggest traits we share and I hope she never finds out.

Bren hooks her arm through mine, tucking me close

like I'm everything she ever wanted, like we belong together.

It feels so perfect I smile right through the guilt gumming up my chest.

The four of us follow the other guests up to the main house. Inside, most of the furniture has been cleared away and staff in matching burgundy polo shirts is waving us through, motioning for everyone to huddle closer.

I tilt my head toward Bren. "What's going on?"

"Bay's probably going to announce his intent to run for election again next year. It shouldn't take too long and then we can go home. I only have Lily's babysitter until midnight."

Ahead of us, the judge stands up—probably on some table or chair because he's suddenly two or three feet higher than everyone.

"I want to thank all of you for coming," Bay says, smiling and adjusting his dark suit jacket. I guess he couldn't be bothered with a costume. "I'm sure most of you know what I'm about to say so I'll spare you any more theatrics and, instead, get to what y'all been waiting for—"

I don't know. I'd say *all* of us is a bit of a stretch, but, judging from everyone's rapt attention, I'm in the minority. Bay gestures to the curtain behind him and it starts to slide open . . . and jerks to a stop as someone screams.

Two women crash into me and I stumble. Bren's pulling me away, but I can't stop staring. I can't believe what I'm seeing.

It's a dead woman.

She's dressed like an angel and propped into a sitting position underneath Bay's enormous grinning photograph. More people plow into us, running for the door, and Bren tugs me close, using one palm to shield my face from the sight.

Too late. I close my eyes and the curl of body blooms behind them. The dead girl's dress is torn halfway off, her chest is bloody, but you can still read the words someone carved:

REMEMBER ME.

```
        ..pw p..
     / .8P/ix#8Pic:
   .tii#fi.  '/.r/&&.
 JU\c8'        t//.'
   "           "u#p
               "u#p
              .iose
             .r/&&<
   '!8d.split//
   '.'\nrekcah
              "1i#q.
              lose.
              #<8.
              /.'"\
 .iP..         "u#p"
 .iP.P         .'u#p
 'UU\c8R `.__.split//.
   Pjipipa"r#p".'.
     .inn".."
```

What's worse than going to a costume party? Sitting in a cop car.

Bren was talking to some officer when Carson spotted us and peeled me away to get my "statement." Now I'm stuck here, slumped low in the passenger seat and picking at the upholstery while Carson yells at two EMTs who were called to the scene. There are a lot of hand gestures going on. The detective is not a happy camper.

That makes two of us, I guess.

Carson spins around and stalks toward me, yanking open the car door with enough force to make the hinges creak.

"You had a job to do."

"And I did it. Can I go now?"

"No, you can't fucking 'go.'" Carson chews his toothpick

harder, swinging it from side to side. He's super pissed and I don't care.

Well, I do care, just not in the way I should. I'm not gunning for Employee of the Year—more like Hacker Who Stays Out of Jail. I smile at Carson. He glares at me.

Across the lawn, Ian Bay, the judge's son, catches sight of us and pauses, the red and blue lights from the emergency vehicles twirling over his dark hair. He holds my gaze for so long I look down, pretend I'm hyperventilating. Nothing to see here. Just a scared teenage girl giving her account of the situation to the police. I do *not* need someone from my school wondering why Carson and I are having our second heart-to-heart in less than eight hours.

Carson flicks his toothpick onto the ground. "Who's your friend, Wicket?"

I lick my lips, stalling. I don't know why, but I have always hated the way he says my name. "No idea what you're talking about. He's not my friend."

When I look up again, Ian is gone, replaced by a set of medics pushing a gurney across the grass, wheeling an unconscious Jason Baines toward the street. He isn't moving and guilt pries into all my corners.

"So you *can* take direction." Carson's laugh is a dry bark. "I'm assuming you took my advice?"

I turn my face away. "I hope he wakes up."

"Like it would be a tragedy if he didn't." The detective's tone is equal parts sarcasm and camaraderie—like we're buddies in on the same joke.

We're so not. If he says this stuff about Jason, what does he say about me?

An officer appears at Carson's elbow. "There are footsteps leading around the side of the house, sir. They head east along the flower beds."

My hands go cold. East goes directly past the office, past *me* when I was with Jason.

"Could be one of the guests," Carson says.

"Could be." The other cop glances down at me, hesitant to say more. "However, there's other evidence that suggests it's the killer, sir."

I tuck both hands under my thighs and ignore how my armpits have turned swampy.

"Do not move," Carson says, peeling away to follow the officer.

Not planning to, but thanks for the reminder. I lean over, put my forehead on my knees, and close my eyes. Only I see the dead girl.

Remember me.

Yeah, I'd rather not. I sit up, look around. Hmm. Well, as long as I'm here.

I prop my feet on the curb and go through Carson's glove box. It's been a while since I've been in the detective's unmarked sedan. Looks like they got my dried blood off the dash. Too bad there are the same fast food bags and junk on the floor. Pig.

Heh.

"Wicket Tate?"

"Yeah?" I answer without thinking and regret it once I turn toward the voice. It's another cop, one I don't recognize.

"I have something for you." He thrusts a thin, small square at me, gives it a tiny shake. "Take it."

I shouldn't ease back—makes me look weak—but I do. I don't like this. There's something about the guy's smile that makes the hair on my arms go rigid. "What is it?"

"It's something you should have."

"Yeah, no thanks, I think I saw that after-school special."

"Suit yourself." The cop—Hart, according to his name plate—shrugs and sets the square on the pavement right in between his shiny black loafers and my scruffy black Chucks. He straightens, smiles, and walks off, heading through the rows of parked cars.

Ugh. Now I can't decide whether to be freaked or annoyed.

I'm leaning toward annoyed. Sighing, I look down, toe the square. It's wrapped up like a small, thin present. The bow on top is a little smushed, but the ribbons wave enthusiastically in the chill night breeze.

Crap. Even though I'm pretty sure this ranks right up there with taking candy from strangers, I really want to know what's in there. Why would he want me to have it?

I pick up the present and press it to one ear. No ticking. Doesn't smell funny either. Does that mean it's safe? I have no idea.

I work one finger into the wrapping paper seams and pull the tape away. Underneath, there's a thin line of ribbed plastic. It feels like a DVD case.

I rip off the wrapping paper, find a DVD case. The cover is homemade, one of those white cardboard labels where you write in your title with a marker. Whoever did this one used a thin-tipped pen, making the words hard to read in the dark.

I lean the case toward the floodlights and my stomach bottoms out. The cover says:

June Interviews

And below:

Sia Tate

That's my mom. My *real* mom. She committed suicide four years ago, left my sister and me alone with our drug-dealer father. I hate her. I should pitch the case across the yard on principle.

I should . . . I end up opening it. Inside, there's a glossy DVD and, on the other side of the label, someone wrote:

Enjoy

"Wick?"

I jerk, nearly dropping the DVD. Bren is standing a few feet from me, cell phone in one hand, car keys in the other. "Are you done giving your statement?"

Hell yes I am. I clutch the DVD to my chest and hop up, ready to bolt when Carson reappears. "I'm sorry, Mrs. Callaway. I need to ask Wicket a few more questions."

Bren frowns. "Detective, Wick was with me. She doesn't

know anything more than any of us do about—"

"Please, Mrs. Callaway, the death may be drug related." Carson's eyes swing to me, and, before I realize what I'm doing, I've jammed the DVD under my costume's skirt. "Unfortunately, Wick has a better perspective than most civilians on that sort of thing."

The reminder ripples through Bren. Her eyes briefly close. "Are you okay with that, Wick?" She looks at me. "Do you want me to stay with you?"

And risk slipping up and revealing what I do with my free time? No way. I shake my head, string up a smile. "It's okay. I'll meet you at the car."

Bren nods, turning to thread through the crowd, heading in the same direction Hart took.

"Drug related?" I ask.

Carson shrugs. "Baines was here, wasn't he?"

"He was nowhere near the victim." I hesitate. "Who was she anyway?"

"Bay's assistant, Chelsea Martin." Carson waves one hand like he's flicking away a fly. "I think those words—remember me—are a message. It's Bay's assistant, Bay's house, Bay's party. It's got to mean something for him."

I hate to admit it, but I agree. During those first hysterical moments, Bren had me pulled tight against her, facing away from the dead girl. I ended up staring straight at Bay. I saw him see the body, watched the sight sink into his blood and bones, turn his face green then gray.

The judge didn't look horrified. He looked . . . resigned,

like this had been inevitable.

"I thought it was interesting that he went for his phone right off," I say.

Carson snorts. "Calling nine-one-one is a common practice when you find a dead body."

"Yeah, I just don't think he did." I straighten the hem of my dress and decide I'm pretty badass for sounding fine when my insides have turned to sludge. "He was on the phone too long, talking and talking and then, finally, just listening, even after the medics arrived. If he had been talking to nine-one-one, he would have hung up."

Carson's eyes inch over me. "You see anything else?"

"Not really."

"The girl's BlackBerry was stolen. What do you think that means?"

I shrug. "Could be a lot. Could be nothing."

"I think it's something. Associating with Baines like that, the murder . . . I think the judge is dirty."

Again, I hate to agree with Carson. He's right though. Something's very wrong here. It's more than just having Baines around. Once upon a time, Judge Bay denied every restraining order my mom—my *real* mom—requested against my father. He threw out evidence, postponed hearings—it was almost like he wanted to help my father.

"I want you to take him down, Wick."

And suddenly, Carson's interest in Baines makes sense. The dealer's small. He might lead to something bigger though. Like one of my dad's captains. Like a judge.

The detective puts another toothpick in his mouth, rolls it from side to side. "I can't touch him. Bay did prosecution for years before being elected to the bench. The chief says he's off-limits, but you can. Think of it as a public service."

Destroying Bay? Not going to lie, I kind of like the feel of it. It's been ten years and I still hate him. I hate his tasseled loafers, his slicked-down hair, the way his eyes slide right through people like me.

Well . . . people like I used to be.

Underneath my skirt, my fingertips dig into the DVD case and I almost—*almost*—ask Carson if he knows that Hart guy. Something holds me back though. The detective would want to know why I want to know and then I'd have to explain. No thanks.

"Bay's out of my league," I say finally.

"That so?" Carson's attention swivels to something behind me, a muscle jumping in his jaw. I turn, see Bren sitting in her Lexus, waiting for us to finish, ready to take me home.

Makes my throat close up tight.

"Pretty car." Carson's not looking at me, but I can hear the smile in his voice. "Think she'll be able to hold on to it after everything that's happened?"

No. *Yes.* Of course.

I stand. "Bren was always the brains behind their company. She'll make it work."

"Won't work if everyone keeps shunning her. Your new family is so interesting to me. Like, you ever wonder how she got your adoption papers to go through so fast? 'Cause I do. I think that's very interesting and I really wonder what would happen if I did some digging? Think I'd find anything that would make her look even worse?"

I try to swallow. Can't. There's no way he'd find anything on Bren . . . right?

"You can't save everyone you love, Trash. Doesn't work like that. In fact, I can make *sure* it doesn't work like that. Find out everything you can on Bay or I'll destroy you and make sure Bren gets the blame. Think how that would go: First she didn't recognize her husband was a monster; now her adopted kid is breaking the law. Bet they'd take your sister away from her."

I bet they would. I look at Carson, and, in the swirling blue lights, his grin grows monstrous. It pushes chills up my arms.

"Leave her alone," I say. "I'll do it."

Bren and I drive home in silence . . . or in silence as only Bren can do. She keeps tapping the steering wheel with her fingers, jiggling her left knee. She's vibrating, and I'm afraid to say anything in case it makes her spin apart.

"It's so horrible," Bren says at last. She smoothes one hand against her pink skirt, forcing it to flatten. "Bay's a good man."

I snort. Can't help it.

"He *is*."

"I'll have to take your word for it." And I will because, suddenly, I'm not in Bren's car. I'm standing over my mother as she cried. Bay was never good to her. The man's an ass, but if Bren thinks he's . . . wait a minute.

"Bren," I say, and have to push each word from my tongue. "How *did* you manage to adopt us so quickly?"

A pause. "Bay helped."

"Why would he help us?"

"I . . . paid him. It was worth every penny."

I focus on the houses beyond the window so I don't have to see how Bren's watching me. She's waiting for a reaction and I only have this: Carson will find out.

And Bren will suffer.

My skin goes cold, clammy. "That doesn't make him good."

"It does for me." Bren turns the car onto our street, knee jiggling harder. "I'll get an appointment with your therapist tomorrow, and we'll pick up a notebook so you can catalog everything you're feeling."

Yay! Feelings! I concentrate on picking at my battered wig so I don't groan. Bren's a big believer in therapy—especially after the Todd situation.

"There are some very good books out there on dealing with post-traumatic stress," she continues. "I'll get a reading list from Dr. Norcut."

There's a beat of silence and I can't tell whether Bren's paused for my response or just trying to catch her breath. I think she's going for reassuring, but her list sounds more like a plan of attack.

"I'm okay, Bren. Truly." I fork one hand through my hair, rub my right temple, where my migraines usually start. "I don't have PTSD or whatever."

"You don't know that." We maneuver around the baby-sitter's Honda and park in the garage. Bren shuts off the car and touches her fingertips to my cheek, searching my face for any signs I'm about to freak.

I smile like I'm fine, like the corner of the DVD isn't digging into me.

My mom. *My*. Mom. It's a heartbeat in my ears.

"What if this starts to bring back . . . everything else?" Bren asks softly.

"It won't."

"Wick, you've been doing so well. I think this could really set you off, and after everything that happened to you and everything you're still dealing with, we need to be prepared."

I stare out the car window, gripping the DVD case even harder because Bren's not talking about Todd and she knows nothing about Carson. She's worried about my mom's suicide and whether I'll obsess over it because I saw a dead body.

And even though Bren means well, I'm suddenly, savagely irritated with her. I wish people would stop examining me for damage.

"What happened tonight wasn't suicide," I say, taking a shaky breath and letting it out bit by bit. "It's not like what happened to my mom. That girl was murdered."

Bren flinches. "I want you to talk to Dr. Norcut tonight. This can't have been good for you."

Good for me? She makes the whole thing sound like we're discussing my vegetable intake. It's stupid . . . until I realize there's guilt seeping under her determination.

"What happened tonight wasn't your fault," I whisper.

"Maybe not. That doesn't mean it was good for you though." Bren pops open the car door, and under the garage light, the smudges under her eyes turn black. "I think you need to talk to someone."

"I'm really tired. Can we do it later?" *Or like, maybe never?* I hold Bren's gaze, trying to look equal parts pitiful and hopeful. I don't want to stoop to a quivering lower lip, but . . .

"Fine. We can wait for morning." Bren rubs one hand over her face. "I need to pay the babysitter and check on Lily. Try to get some rest, all right?"

I nod, reaching for the door handle.

"Wick?"

"Yeah?"

"You're not getting out of this. I'm calling Dr. Norcut's emergency line tonight." Bren grabs her purse, heaves it onto one shoulder. "God help that answering service if they give me any shi—*problems* about making you an appointment too."

Norcut's answering service always gives her problems when she calls. In fact, they give her so many problems that I start to tell Bren it's a waste of time. Too late. She's already out of the car, charging into the house. Honestly, she should just wait until the psychiatrist's assistant gets in on Monday. If she calls tonight, she'll be on the phone for hours . . . which might not be a bad thing.

It might even be great because I'd have all the time I

need to go through the DVD.

Tucked into the waistband of my skirt, my mother's name begins to burn.

Upstairs, I turn on all the lights, make it look like daytime in my bedroom. I shouldn't, because Bren always notices and I always refuse to explain. We both know why though: Todd came for me in the dark. Admitting I'm scared—even to myself—is embarrassing.

Turning off the lights is worse.

Considering Bren thinks I'm headed for a nervous breakdown, I should probably do something to look more on board. Maybe turning off one light or screwing the grates onto my air-conditioning vents. That would be progress.

Except I don't think I can manage either.

After discovering Todd installed video cameras in my room's vents, I took down the painted metal grates. They've been lying in my closet for months. It's comforting to be able to look up and see the air-conditioning vents are still empty.

Maybe I'll screw them on again . . . later.

I toss the DVD case onto my desk and power on the computer, waiting for it to return to life. Because I run a metric ton of firewall and antivirus software, my system takes longer than most to boot up. Usually, I don't mind, but tonight it feels like the longest four minutes of my life as I change out of my costume and into yoga pants and a sweatshirt.

Once I'm logged in, I slide in the DVD and start a scan program, checking to see if any viruses are waiting for me, then, while the program finishes the check, I open Firefox and search "Officer Hart Peachtree City."

There's a loan officer . . . a technology officer . . . but no *police* officer by that name. The back of my skull prickles. Could he be new? Possibly. Then again, I was at a costume party. Maybe he was in dress-up? I decide I'll have to look into new officer hires and switch windows, closing my search page and opening the local newspaper's website.

Sure enough, there's a human interest story about Todd's family and how devastated they are, how they wish Bren wouldn't divorce him in his hour of need. I've never met my former foster dad's parents and, frankly, I'm not feeling the lack. Instead, I go straight for the comment section.

Hidden behind anonymous handles, our neighbors are letting it rip. Some are siding with Bren. Some are showing support for Tessa Waye, Todd's first victim. I'm interested in the ones who are out to blast my adoptive mom.

Like BrownBear47, for instance. According to BB, Bren is a coward and a fool and is destined for bankruptcy. How nice we live in a country where everyone can have an opinion.

It's even nicer that I can take that opinion down. Takes me a bit to log in as the website administrator, but I block BrownBear's ISP address. She—somehow it feels like a she—won't be getting on the newspaper forum on her home computer any time soon. And just in case she decides to use another computer, I lock her out of her account as well.

Am I petty? Probably. Is it satisfying? Definitely. Does it help Bren? Not sure. Not going to stop.

I've just finished deleting the last hater when my anti-virus program flashes. The DVD's scan is done. No viruses found. A table of contents pops onto my screen. There must be twenty different files. I swallow, take a deep breath, and pick the first one.

The image shifts, revealing a thin woman sitting at a metal table, and even though I knew I was going to see my mom, it still feels like getting punched. It's her dark hair, her lean cheekbones. It's *her* and I expected that, but my stomach still hits bottom. For a second, I think I'm going to be sick.

The video opens with a close-up, then jerks back for a wider shot. For about ten seconds, no one says anything as the camera gets adjusted and a fluorescent light above them flickers. My mom touches the side of her neck, snags her fingers in her hair, and suddenly, I remember the way it smelled. Vanilla. All her clothes smelled like vanilla. For months after she died, I would sit in her closet and bury my face in them.

Until my father caught me and burned them.

"I only have an hour and then I have to be home." Again, another punch. I haven't heard that voice in four years. How could I have forgotten how she made her vowels slide?

My mom stares straight into the camera with glossy, plastic doll eyes. "Now isn't a good time."

"Then you'll have to be fast, won't you?" A man's voice

emerges off camera. I don't recognize it. He must be to my left—my mom's right—because her eyes follow the sound and her mouth flattens.

"There's nothing new to report. He isn't involving me."

He? Who's he? What's she reporting? I lean a little closer to the screen, and even though I can hear her fine, I turn up the volume.

"What are you doing to encourage him to involve you?"

My mom winces. The camera zooms in as she covers her mouth—her *bruised* mouth—and suddenly I know who "he" is. My dad. They're talking about my dad. What kind of interview is this?

"I've asked to help," she continues, her gaze wandering around the cramped room. "I told him I would be willing to work. He was . . . uninterested." Her hand drops to the table, revealing a pale forearm marred by dark finger-prints. "I did try, Detective."

My hands curl. Detective. Work. She's collaborating with the police. I crank the volume again, trying to identify the guy's voice.

"Then you should try harder," he says. "You know how to handle him, Mrs. Tate. I know you do. You wanted him in the first place. He's your husband."

My mom's eyes lift to the camera, stare straight at me. "I wanted him to save me. There's a difference." She swallows. "I have to go."

The camera wiggles, the screen goes black . . . and white letters appear.

See What They Did To Her?

My breath dries up. What. The. Fuck? I minimize the video and click on the table of contents again, scrolling through the list. So many interviews. I watch them all and realize this wasn't just a onetime thing. My mom was a police informant.

And "see what they did to her?"? Who's "they"? The police?

Outside, a tree branch shakes against the glass, and even though I know who's there, I still stiffen. I turn to look, somehow convinced it's Todd who's about to crawl through and finish me. It's only briefly though because his smile is white in the dark. It's not perfect, but it's mine.

I throw open the window and Griff spills into the room, turning the air heavy, thick, into something I can't inhale.

I have to gulp.

"You came," I say, digging both hands into his T-shirt, pulling him close.

He angles himself over me. "Always."

```
#_)Xptwait until#fin;
lit//.".URRUU\c8R"%8;
kp".
kp".
_)3;
lit//.".URRUU\ca.
;Hi\c8R"%8d=split//.
                 ".-"u#p
                    8P/1.
                    '%maj
                    %8d=
                    ine"
r#p"               pine'
'lit/.             8"%8d
kp".'u.,      .#')3pir
".-"u#p"]=(P,P)ir
   %t#p(q_)='
```

We sit in my too-bright bedroom, listen to Bren pace downstairs, and I tell Griff everything. Well, almost everything.
I leave out Jason entirely . . . and some of Carson. The
secrets thump in my teeth and toes and I ignore them. It's
just the trouble with heroes again. If I tell Griff, he'll want
to save me. Better yet, he'll want to save Bren and Lily.

And he'll want to do it honorably.

Tell the police. Confide in a teacher. Speak up. It's not
that Griff's a Boy Scout, but he uses his skills for the greater
good. I don't want to save the whole world. Just mine. I'll
play by Carson's rules to do it. Griff won't.

He'll look at me differently because I will.

There's enough said about me at school and on the
newspaper blogs. I'm not going to add to it. So instead I
concentrate on the assistant's death. At first, Griff keeps

rubbing the muscle between my thumb and forefinger. After I tell him the details about the body, he stops.

"Are you okay?" he asks.

Funny. With Bren, I never thought about it. I just said what she needed to hear. With Griff . . . "No. I mean yeah. Yeah, I'm rattled. I think I'll be okay though."

"I think you're wonderful."

The words surprise me and my heart twists hard. Griff often says things like that, and, every time, they make me melty. Sometimes I wish they didn't. I'm not sure what to do with the girl he turns me into.

Then Griff smiles that smile I crave and I lean into him, pressing my lips against the corner of his and scooping handfuls of his polo shirt. It's so soft and thin I can feel his heart's bird-wing beat. Griff goes rigid, but his hands ease around me. Ever since Todd, we're so careful—and even as careful as we are, when his hands push up my rib cage, I flinch.

"Wick?"

"Sorry. I'm . . . sorry . . . just . . . it was a bad night. I'm sorry."

He pulls back, disappointed. I am too. Then again, I'm also relieved . . . which is disappointing . . . and disconcerting. How can I be afraid to be with him?

And even more afraid to be without him? Once upon a time, I wasn't afraid to be without anyone. I only needed Lily. Now . . . Carson's right. I have too much that can be taken away.

Griff closes my hand in both of his. "It'll get better. You're still recovering."

Recovering. Like I'm broken, and I'm not. I look away, eyes falling on my computer.

See what they did to her?

It's something Griff and I would agree on.

"It gets worse actually." I untangle myself from him, swiping the DVD case from my desk. "I need to show you something."

I hand it to Griff and his mouth twists. "Isn't that your mom's name?"

"Yeah. I was waiting to give my statement to Carson. This cop gave it to me. He even wrapped it like some sort of messed-up birthday present. There're a ton of interviews."

"What would the police want with your mom?"

"I think she was informing on my dad."

"Willingly?"

"Don't know. I watched all the files, and from what I saw, she didn't seem super thrilled about it and there's a message at the end of the first interview. It says 'See what they did to her?'"

Something shifts in . . . out . . . of Griff's features. "What?"

"Something's wrong here." His green eyes go dark. "One of the cops just gave you the DVD? Which cop? Why?"

"Never met him before. His name was Hart."

"Hart? That doesn't sound familiar." Like me, Griff helps the police from time to time. Unlike me, he actually wants to be there. His cousin works in narcotics, and thanks to Griff's help, they brought down my dad, catching him with so much evidence he won't see the light of day for years. Griff testified that I had nothing to do with any of it.

It's a lie Carson still doesn't believe.

"Are you sure he was a cop?"

I shrug. "I did a quick internet search and didn't find anything, but he had the right uniform. I guess that could be stolen or bought. It *was* a costume party." The more I think about it, the more my brain clings to how his shoes looked next to mine. They were shiny black loafers, not government-issued black boots.

"It doesn't make any sense," Griff continues. "Why would he give you something like this? Why would someone put a message at the end?"

"No idea." That should bother me more than it does, but right now, all I can think about is my mom. All those years we stayed. . . . I thought it was because she was too afraid to leave. I hated her for it. What if she had no choice?

"It doesn't change the fact that she was working for the police," I say.

"The same way you are?"

I go still, feel the question fall through me until it hits bone. I thought he didn't know.

"Tell me you aren't working for him, Wick."

I focus on the white zombie makeup slicked on top of my hands. The more I rub to get it off, the worse it smears. "How did you find out?"

"Rumor. Carson's closing cases left and right. He's the department's biggest rising star, making connections no one else has ever thought of. It's like he's psychic . . . or he has a really good hacker."

I nod, take a deep breath. "I've been doing odds jobs for him for a few months now."

"Jesus, Wick. *Why?*" Griff's pissed, edging away from me, and I follow . . . stop. In the space between us, the words I need seem to come more easily.

"He knows I was involved in my dad's stuff and with Todd. He says he'll dig into me and he could find enough to put me away too."

"By agreeing to work for him you're practically admitting guilt!" Griff pushes ink-stained hands through his dark hair. "He'll just use you and arrest you later!"

"And give up the glory he's getting? I don't think so. Carson could bring down a corrupt judge on this one. He'd be a freaking legend around the station." I'm trying to sound light and I'm failing. The words are bitter, but they're also true. "Carson needs me. It's not like I have much of a choice. It isn't just me he's threatening to hurt. It's Bren too. Lily."

We both go quiet. After a moment, Griff clears his throat, looks toward my window. "So do you have a new job?"

Funny. I can tell he's already guessed the answer.

"Yeah, Carson wants me to investigate Bay. He thinks the judge is dirty and he wants my help proving it."

"You know this is blackmail."

"Yes." I rub my temples with both hands. Every time I close my eyes, I see the dead girl . . . and then Judge Bay's face. He wasn't just horrified. He was scared. Why do I keep snagging on that?

"So when does it end?" Griff asks.

It doesn't. The rest of the world thinks I brought down Todd by physically fighting back. He attacked me, I fought him off. He took my sister, I tracked him down. The truth is . . . a little more complicated.

I hacked to find Todd. I broke the law. Even though Carson doesn't have proof yet, he can search hard enough and long enough to eventually find something.

What would that do to Bren? Worse, what would it do to Lily? My sister is so sweet. She wants to fit in. She wants to be loved. She wants everything to be okay.

It's my job to make sure it will be. If working for Carson will keep the detective from unpacking my past and ruining Bren's and Lily's futures, I'll do it.

Griff studies me. "It could end if you found something on him."

A laugh skids out of me, stops. I've never worked like that. Not with my dad. Not later with his partner, Joe. Not now. I've never fought back. I'm not brave. I've always just tried to disappear.

"It might not be hard to do," Griff continues. "Think about it. If he's willing to blackmail you, what's he done to other people? You could find something and use it as leverage."

I stare at Griff. *Leverage?* What a pretty way of saying blackmail. Pretty and not like Griff at all. Am I rubbing off on him?

Leverage. I roll the idea around. He's right. I've been so caught up in damage control I didn't think about how to turn this. I could. My new life is worth everything to me.

And Carson's career is worth everything to him.

"As for your mom?" Griff shakes his head. "There's something wrong here, Wicked. Really wrong. Why give you the interviews now? What's the angle?"

Another good point. Getting the DVD is problematic. If the Hart cop wasn't actually Peachtree City Police, then who is he? And how does he know me?

"Going after Bay is dangerous stuff." Griff pulls away again, putting more space between us, and I sit on my hands, tell myself the knot in my chest is not panic.

But in my head, Carson's smile slides wide and I hear him ask, "Think he'd still want you if he knew you were working for me?"

"You've got to find a way out of it," Griff says.

I nod, agreeing because I should, not really because I do. Finding dirt on Carson . . . getting a copy of my mom's interviews . . . they're interesting problems—interesting *and* scary. Tracking down Bay? That one feels perfect. The temptation is hot syrup warm against my teeth.

Griff turns the DVD case over and over in his hands. "I really don't like it."

"Yeah, agreed."

49

"No, really, Wick. It feels like . . . a trap."

"I know."

"Doesn't sound like it."

I snake my head around to face him. "What does *that* mean?"

"It means you don't sound freaked. You sound . . . interested."

And he sounds hurt. Worried.

"Well, I am a little bit interested," I say. The words are defensive and guilty and they piss me off. I shouldn't feel, sound, or even *be* guilty. "I have every right to be 'into it.' It's *my mom*."

Griff won't meet my eyes. "Promise me you'll look for leverage on Carson."

"Gladly."

"Whatever this is, it's bad. You have to stay away from it."

"I will." It shoots out so fast I don't realize until seconds later that I'm lying.

Hours later, I wake, choking on a scream. Sunlight pours through the windows, casting yellow squares across my bed. My hands are fisted in the sheets and my T-shirt's soaked through. I'm alone though. I'm okay.

I *am*.

Except I can still feel Todd's fingers twisting into my hair.

I lean off the side of the bed, check the floor. Empty. I squint at my room's air vents. The grills are still down. Empty. Closet's wide open—I leave it that way all the time now—it's also empty.

Like always, so stop acting like a spaz. Stupid how I can't. Maybe that's normal. I almost died and I almost killed Todd. Maybe whatever's left should be a little broken.

Don't think about it. But if I don't think about Todd, I

start thinking about Griff, and that's no good either. I stare at the window he used last night and my throat closes.

"Wick?" Bren's voice floats up from downstairs. "Breakfast is ready!"

"Coming!" I stick my hand behind my headboard, feel my jump drive pinned to the wall and the DVD taped just below it. Relief rushes through me. Not like they would've gone anywhere since last night. It's reassuring to touch them though. Turning off the lights I left burning all night, I get dressed, and by the time I hit the stairs, my hands have almost stopped shaking.

In the kitchen, my little sister and Bren are making breakfast. The whole lower floor smells like waffles and cinnamon.

"Wick!" Lily rockets off the bar stool, a blur of pale blond hair and bright pink T-shirt. She hugs me hard. "Mom told me what happened."

Mom? I stare. Lily's talking about . . . Bren?

"Yeah, it was pretty awful," I say, ignoring how Bren is now watching me, dissecting my words for emotional cracks Norcut would need to medicate. I think about smiling at her and then think again because I have no idea how that would be interpreted.

Besides, when did we start calling Bren *Mom*? This feels huge, but I sit down like I barely noticed, digging into the scrambled eggs Bren sticks in front of me so I don't have to face either of them.

If Bren is now our mom, where does that leave our real

mom? Do I tell Lily about the DVD?

My first instinct was to show her. Now I wonder if I should. It's been four years since our mom jumped. Bren is more her mother than our mother ever was. Maybe Griff's right. The DVD said: See what they did to her? Well, yeah, I see it. Doesn't change anything. Maybe I should leave it alone.

I don't know if I can.

"Did you take your meds?" Bren asks me, sliding another waffle onto Lily's plate.

"Yep."

She beams and I have to fight a smile. I kind of hate that Bren sets the bar so low. Then again, it's nice to be able to make someone so happy. These days, Bren thinks it's a whole new me: no migraines (meds), new hair (blond), and fancy car (gift).

Bren pours more waffle batter into the iron. "I spoke to Dr. Norcut's office. You have an appointment for Monday morning—before school—so it won't interfere with anything."

Whoopee for me. "That's great. Thanks."

Bren double-checks the timer on the waffle iron. "What do you have planned for the day, Wick?"

"Government project I need to finish. I have to go down to the courthouse to take notes during some of the trials and put it in a report."

Which is a convenient excuse to get a closer look at Bay. He's supposed to be working today. Thanks to government cutbacks and overloaded dockets, the court system runs Saturday court once a month. Bay should be putting in a full load today. After last night, I'm not sure if he will be. Hopefully, I'll get lucky.

Bren's spatula hovers above the waffle maker. "Like at the courthouse with the criminals? Is that safe?"

I smile. Sometimes it's touching how much Bren worries. Other times, I wonder if she thinks I'm an idiot who will wander into the first panel van marked "Free Candy." "I'll be fine, Bren. If anyone kidnapped me, they would return me. Promise."

I'm shooting for a laugh. Bren just stares me down.

I sigh. "It's a project the juniors do every year. I'll call you when I'm leaving."

Bren's face creases into a smile and she looks at me like I've just done the most amazing trick. "Okay, just be careful, Wick."

"Always."

The Peachtree City Courthouse shares the same low-slung building as the library. I park by the long-dead fountain and wait in line to get through security—security pretty much being a metal detector and a single overweight cop sitting on a plastic chair, his thumbs jammed into his straining belt.

"Purpose?" Body by Budweiser asks me.

"Research for school." I hold up my laptop and he passes it through the scanner. No bombs. How very unsurprising.

Triple B gives me back my computer without a second glance. It always amazes me that no one realizes I don't need a bomb to do damage. Whatever though. Makes my life easier.

According to the online schedule, Bay should be in the first courtroom, and just as I push through the courtroom doors, he's taking the bench. Considering what happened last night, he looks pretty good—hair's helmeted into place with gel; his eyes snap around the room like he's ready to get started.

Or like he's looking for someone.

It's just past nine a.m. and I have my pick of seats. I head toward the front, staying near the wall so I'm close to Bay, but far enough that I have some privacy. Very few people notice me—probably because I blend better now than I did in my previous life. If I had known Ralph Lauren clothes were an excellent cover, I would've used them.

Then again, if I could have afforded Ralph Lauren clothes, I probably wouldn't have been hacking in the first place.

While the prosecuting attorney presents the DUI case they're about to try, I work on accessing Bay's Black-Berry. It takes me a few minutes before I can pick up his cell remotely—gotta love it when someone's logged on to a public WiFi—and start working through his in-box. Work stuff . . . work stuff . . . dentist appointment reminder . . . calendar invitations . . . more work stuff. Bay's campaign manager sent a list of last election's top donors, and, surprisingly, Lauren's parents are in the top three. Other than that, there's nothing.

Until I get to the very bottom.

Almost a week ago, Bay received an email confirmation from Barton & Moore Security detailing his recent order. From the looks of it, the judge has gone all out: security cameras, motion detectors, and panic buttons in the bedrooms. He's seriously freaked and that's a serious problem for me.

It doesn't say anything about beefing up the family's internet security, but considering it's Barton & Moore, they'll have something in mind for that as well. I scroll down, skimming the rest of the email for anything else that's going to make my life harder, and that's when I see it. The entire email chain between the security firm and Bay started with a single email sent to Bay's personal account. The sender used a Yahoo! email address and there's no subject, just two words that make my skin prickle:

Remember Me

Same words that were carved onto the dead girl's chest. Within two minutes of receiving the message, Bay had forwarded it to his contact at Barton & Moore. Interesting. Apparently, whatever he's supposed to remember upset him.

As I watch, another email comes through. Barton & Moore again. This time, they're confirming security guards will be arriving tonight. Understandable, considering the murder.

It doesn't explain why the whole security upgrade started a week ago though, well before the death.

Unless Bay suspected something like that might happen.

To my right, someone slides down the bench and turns in my direction. I watch the figure from the corner of my eye, and when it starts to edge closer, I minimize Bay's inbox and pull up a Word document.

"You working on Farenstein's report?"

Ian Bay. I turn slowly to face him and he's closer than I would like. Much closer.

"Yeah, I am," I say, and have to arrange my features so I don't look so confused. Ian is a weird hybrid at our school. He's too clumsy to be athletic, too knife-faced to be good-looking, but I guess money gives him a pass because he hangs around the popular kids.

Actually, I should say he *tries* to hang around the popular kids. I don't think many of them actually like him.

"You working on the report too?" I ask.

"Already finished it." He nods in his dad's direction, a fringe of dark hair falling across his forehead. "Kind of the family business."

Yeah, no shit. But I smile like that's a brilliant observation on Ian's part and that makes Ian smile wider.

"So I've been seeing you around more, Wick."

Huh? I've been around. Ian and I have attended the same schools for the past five years. I watched him lose his mom to cancer, heard about his dad getting remarried, and his older brother, Kyle, running off with some chick. I know about him the way everyone around Peachtree City knows about him . . . and me, I guess. There are rumors. People talk. But dead moms and dysfunctional families are everyday news. It's Ian's dad who makes it special, makes *him* special. Anyway, it's highly unlikely he hasn't seen me.

Then I notice the way Ian's eyes inch over my hair. Usually, it's purple or pink or, more recently, Kool-Aid red. Right now it's blond.

Like the girls I see him following around at school.

Suddenly, the way Ian was staring at me last night and the way he's staring at me right now start to make sense.

Can I throw up?

I try to scoot sideways, run into the end of the bench. "I guess I've been getting out more."

"Yeah, must be hard going around town with your mom and all."

I stiffen. My mom. This time, the word means Bren. "Why would it be hard?"

"Well, you know, because of . . ." Ian lifts one shoulder, eyes rolling in his head because I'm supposed to get the implication and play along.

And I'm not.

"No, I don't know." I stuff my laptop into my bag, tug the strap onto my shoulder. I want a copy of that Remember Me email, but not enough to risk it with the judge's kid sitting next to me. "Bren has nothing to hide."

Ian blinks. "Oh, yeah, agreed. I mean, of course. I wasn't saying—"

Yes, you were. I edge around him, make my way to the rear of the courtroom and head for the parking lot exit. I'm barely into the hallway though before Ian's stepping on my heels.

"Look, Wick, sorry. I didn't mean to say it like that." He grabs my elbow and I round on him, fist clenched. Ian shies away, shrinking into the wall, and, to my right and left, people start to stare.

Dammit.

"Don't grab me," I whisper.

"Because of . . . ?"

My mouth drops open. Because of Todd? I'm suddenly sorry I didn't punch Ian right in the ear. "Because it's rude."

And yes, because of Todd.

"Oh. Right. Sorry." Ian's cheeks go My Little Pony pink, and even though I'm irritated with him, I start to feel bad. It's not like he's a threat. We probably wear the same jeans size. Besides, most people probably wouldn't have a problem with their elbow getting touched.

Which, technically, makes *me* the freak.

Sigh. I need to apologize.

"Look," Ian says. "I wanted to ask if we could partner on that computer lab project."

"You're not in my class."

"I know. I'm in Mrs. Lowe's fifth period. She's okay with it if you're okay with it."

I stifle a groan. Why the hell would our teacher say that? No *way* do I want team up with Ian Bay. Not only is there the whole *I'm investigating his dad* thing, there's also the problem that two geeks are easier to target than one.

I fly under the radar at school, avoiding anyone who

might toss me in the Dumpster (don't ask). Ian tries to fit in. He follows the popular kids around, hoping they'll eventually warm to him. It should disgust me, the way he begs for their attention, but . . .

I heave an enormous sigh. I hate when people pity me, but right now, that's all I feel for him. "Are you sure you shouldn't partner with someone else? I mean, we would have to write the report after school instead of during class and, with everything you have going on . . ."

"That's kind of the thing." Ian rubs the back of his hand against his nose, making him look like an overgrown kid. "I don't really want to be home right now and I'm pretty much bombing that class. I thought it was going to be way easier and, you know . . ." He shrugs, stuffing both hands into his jeans pockets. I think he's trying for nonchalant. It's coming off as pitiful.

I will be a total idiot if I agree.

So why can't I force myself to say no?

Because I understand what it's like to not want to go home. Because I understand what it's like to be buried.

Because I am that total idiot.

"Okay, fine." Even though the agreement emerges in a snarl, Ian's eyes go bright. "Email me at this address and I'll send you my notes." I scribble my personal email onto a piece of scrap paper and pass it to him. He pockets it.

"Thanks, Wick."

"No big deal," I say, turning to leave, and, thankfully, Ian doesn't follow me. I make it to the parking lot by myself. Where I see Griff leaning on my car.

It kicks the air right out of me.

"Hey," he says, peeling himself up.

"Hey." I unlock my car door, grip it with both hands so I don't reach for him. I am not going to be that desperate.

Even if I'm scared I already am.

"How did you know I was here?" I ask.

"Bren told me. I wanted to apologize. For last night. I get it."

He doesn't. I can see it in the line of his shoulders, how they tense at the words. He's faking.

"It's okay." I'm nodding too hard, can't seem to stop. "I understand. You were just upset."

Griff's eyes spear mine. "You don't have to make excuses for me."

I do because that would mean the alternative is Griff not understanding the situation—not understanding *me*.

"So." He shifts from foot to foot, studying the thunderclouds gathering on the horizon. "How did it go?"

I hesitate, still hearing the way he said I was enjoying the job. "It's not going that great. I was able to get into Bay's personal email. It's going to take some more digging."

Griff nods. "You'll need another computer."

"Oh! Yeah, no problem. Do you need yours?" I go for the laptop and Griff's hand circles my arm.

"No, no, it's just, you'll need something faster—like what you had before."

I scowl. "I don't think PD's returning mine anytime soon."

In one of Carson's earlier attempts to trap me, he talked

Todd into giving him my computer, told my foster dad it was for my own protection, and the detective still has it. The thought of forensic computer specialists going through my hard drive gives me serious terror sweats.

It's not that I wasn't careful, I was. I *am*, but all it takes is an undeleted keystroke, a partially remaining file. Used to be I had to worry about what I'd done. Now I have to worry about what I've missed.

Back then all I could think about was how I had to catch the man who was stalking my sister. I would have been dead in the water if it wasn't for Griff. He gave me the laptop I used to trap Todd.

Griff's right though. I do need something else. "Problem is," I begin, "my old builder won't touch me anymore."

After Todd was arrested and the newspapers hailed me as a hero, my builder freaked and went underground. He said there was too much attention surrounding me. I figured his paranoia would pass. It hasn't and that's kind of left me up the creek.

I know it sounds weird. If you're into coding and computers, you should be able to build a decent system, right? Not so much. Software hackers, people like me, do software not hardware. Yeah, I know how to build a basic computer with off-the-shelf parts. The problem is what I want—what I *need*—requires a specialist.

Griff nods. "I know your guy went under. Thought you could use mine instead."

"You have someone?"

"Yeah." Griff edges a little closer and his hand—stained with faded blue ink—cradles my jawline . . . my cheek. His thumb grazes my lower lip and we both swallow. Hard.

"That would be amazing, Griff. I really appreciate it. Thank you."

Jesus. Could I sound any stiffer? I want this thing between us fixed and I don't know how to do it. Do I kiss him and apologize? Or do I just kiss him?

Maybe it's because of the DVD or maybe it's just because this is my first boyfriend, but I keep thinking about how my mom tried to fix things with my dad. She did it wrong. I wanted to do it better.

And I'm not.

"I want you to be safe," Griff says. "My guy is . . . a bit of a dick. He's good though. Really good."

I nod, sounds fine to me, but there's something about the way Griff offered his builder that makes me think he kinda sorta wants me to say no.

"Are you okay?" I ask, hoping he hears the *are we okay?* hovering underneath.

"Yeah. 'Course." Griff shrugs, watching his fingers trace across my skin. His touch is so light and it makes my stomach feel liquid and heavy. "It's just that, when I thought about being with you . . . this isn't how I pictured it."

I force a smile, lean into his hand.

That makes two of us.

```
P,P)\pipe"r#p","u#p"
he/ ##P/iw##P>rloss#
                &<#,_
                /."\
             \ xir
            .(#q#
            clos•
           •r/&&'
          ,lit/
         ,r#p","
         'r#p"•'
       d=spl
      ,e"r#
      pe"r
     >/1x'
    \map
    \8d=
```

Griff follows me home, leaving his bike at my house so we can head to Five Points in the Mini. The clouds above us have turned the pale cream of baseball leather, promising better weather to come, but traffic is slow. It takes us almost an hour to reach downtown Atlanta, and when we finally turn down the last side street, I'm sure Griff is screwing with me.

"This is it," he says, motioning to the squat building on our left. Usually computer specialists work out of storefronts or their houses and we're turning in to an abandoned restaurant that looks like something out of *The Walking Dead*.

"You take me to the nicest places," I joke, negotiating around an enormous pothole. I'm trying for funny. Griff doesn't even crack a smile. His eyes are pinned to the caving-in front awning and the man in a hoodie standing under it.

"Is that your builder?" I ask, and Griff shakes his head, mouth set.

"No."

We park and get out, Griff coming around to my side before I can even shut my door. "Hey, I have a confession," he says. "I had to tell him who you really were."

I stiffen and Griff sweeps his hands down my arms. "He doesn't take new clients, but I knew he was a fan of your work so . . ."

I force a smile. "It's okay."

Only it's kind of not. I'm careful to keep my hacking life separate from my real life. Griff's one of the few people who knows both and he gave me away. As soon as I think it, though, I smother the thought. Griff did this to help me with something he doesn't even want any part of.

I close my hand around Griff's and squeeze, following him across the parking lot. Up under the restaurant's awning, the hoodie guy starts to pace. The closer we get, the harder his feet stab into the sidewalk.

"What do you want?" he demands, voice creaky and rusted, a box lid unused to opening.

"Looking for Milo Gray," Griff says, easing sideways so I have to peer around him. "He here?"

"Maybe." The guy moves toward us. This close, his eyes are an ashy gray like whatever's inside him is burning its way to the surface.

Homeless. Maybe high. He doesn't look well. His skin is the color of overcreamed coffee and his clothes are stained and rumpled. The stench is enough to make my eyes water.

"Who are you?" He's talking to me now and it makes Griff stiffen.

"Wick," I say.

He mouths my name, twitches, and Griff's breath stalls. I curve my hand around his forearm. *It's okay. It's okay.*

Then suddenly it's not.

The guy lunges at me and I duck, stumbling back and lashing out with my fist. I connect with his throat. He coughs hard and goes to his knees.

"Hey!" Another voice—a guy's—comes from my left. I jerk sideways and the newcomer lunges forward, ripping past me to crouch by the guy. He nearly gets flattened for his efforts though. The man leaps up and takes off.

Leaving the new guy to round on me. He surges forward, shoving me into the restaurant's wall. "Who the hell are you?"

"Wick Tate." I start to knee him in the groin and he twists sideways, swearing. "Who the hell are *you*?"

"Milo Gray." His hands loosen and he moves back a step. "World's greatest builder."

"Who was that?" Griff asks. Outside the restaurant, the storm has regrouped and rain bleeds down the dusty windows in veins.

Milo studies Griff. "No one that concerns you."

"That's because it was your dad, wasn't it?" Both boys pivot to stare at me and I pretend to straighten my shirtsleeve so I can cradle my throbbing arm. "Attached earlobes. It runs in families, right? So maybe he's your dad or really older brother?"

"Dad." Now Milo's studying *me*. His eyes linger and I shiver. Griff's guy doesn't look like a techie . . . he looks like some sort of surfer boy: dark hair, dark eyes, worn black T-shirt stretched across a gym-sculpted chest, and tribal tats curling up his forearms.

"You didn't tell me she was going to be in danger if I brought her here," Griff says.

"And *you* didn't tell me who she really was. You said you were bringing me Red Queen, not . . ." Milo's attention never swerves from me. Slowly, the side of his mouth quirks up. "So what should I call you? Wick? Or Red Queen?"

I try to smile. Can't. My face has gone tight. Red Queen is one of the aliases I use online and, generally, my best known. "Wick's fine."

"You got it . . . but how do I know you're *the* Red Queen? How do I know you're the one who came up with the Pandora code?"

"Well, if I could just borrow a computer . . ."

"No way you're touching my gear." Milo's tongue taps the corner of his mouth. "Tell me about how you nailed Walker Internet Securities."

I flinch. It was probably some of the best work I ever did

for Joe. I meet Milo's gaze and refuse to think about what Griff must be thinking . . . or about the shame heating my face. "So their CEO was way paranoid; getting into the company's systems was impossible. They'd thought of everything . . . except for their cable boxes. They were running this old version of BSD, which meant I had my pick of vulnerabilities. After a few directory traversal attacks, I was able to access every internet and wireless device in the office." I force myself to breathe. "By using an XSS vulnerability in the HTML firewall log I was able to install a malicious JavaScript packet that would look for various password and configuration files and, if found, send them back to me. When the CEO viewed the firewall log the next morning, the XSS had launched, and we ended up with the company's enterprise-wide root password." I shrug. "Pretty much full access to passwords, source codes, credit card numbers . . . I also set every channel in his cable box to Disney."

Milo's eyes flicker. "Say it again, but this time, do it in a breathy voice."

"Pervert."

He grins, his teeth werewolf white against his darker skin. "I've been following you for years. Never thought we'd meet. Or that you'd be . . ." Milo's gaze climbs down me. It should feel dirty, only, somehow, it's more like he's assessing me in terms of my jobs. And he's impressed.

It's kind of flattering.

Maybe more than kind of.

"I worked for Group Eight," Milo adds. "We were all big fans."

G8? Huh. That was a tightly run outfit. They did good work until the Feds brought them down. I remember really liking how they . . . crap. No way am I admitting I've been admiring Milo as well.

"Are we going to talk computers or not?" I ask.

"I thought we were," Milo says, motioning for us to follow him through the restaurant. The main dining room is filled with dusty tables pushed up against each other, the chairs long gone. Milo pops behind the counter and through the kitchen—unused as the dining areas—and into what must have once been a storage room.

Long stainless steel counters line the walls, snake nests of Ethernet and power cords spilling from their tops. I'm picking my way through the tangle, trying not to trip, when the wires pinned to the wall catch my eye. I stop dead.

"Are those *explosives*?"

Milo looks over his shoulder, gaze following mine to the small red boxes attached to the wall. "Yeah. It's a hobby of mine. I rigged the whole place. Supernova in, like, fifteen seconds. Eighteen, tops."

"Jesus!"

Milo smiles. "I'm even better."

Next to me, Griff clears his throat, his hand finding the small of my back. "How do we know your dad won't return for a second shot?"

"We don't. . . . I don't think he will though." Milo pulls out a couple of chairs shoved into the corner and offers me one. "He's not dangerous. It's just, like, an episode. He gets them sometimes—especially when he's off his meds.

"Look, your little girlfriend is fine." Milo smiles again. This time though it's forced, lips pulled up with strings. He glances in my direction, catches me staring at him. "See something you like?"

"You wish," I say, turning a small circle to take in the room. There's dead takeaway piled in the trash can and the floor doesn't look like it's been vacuumed in weeks. Typical. Computer geeks are such slobs. If his mom shows up, the cliché will be complete.

Well. Almost complete. Milo's computers are pristine. The desk is wiped clean, no food within spilling distance, the cords are neatly tied together—even the screens are dust free. It shouldn't matter, but I like him a little more because of it.

"So." Milo drops into a roller chair and spins it to face me. "Talk. What kind of system do you need?"

Eyes on Griff, I give Milo the quick run-down on what I need and who I'm up against, and when I finish, the builder lets out a low whistle.

"So to get to your guy, you have to go through Barton and Moore? That's a high-end target."

I glance at Milo. "Too high-end for you?"

He smirks. "Not at all. I'll do it."

And there's something about the way Milo says it that makes the whole thing sound like fun. I grin because, for this really weird second, it feels like I get Milo—really get him—and it's so strange and funny I turn to Griff, expecting him to laugh like I want to laugh.

But when our eyes meet, I can tell he also sees the thing between Milo and me and he doesn't find it funny at all.

"Eight grand," Milo says, waiting for my response.

I blink. That's a lot of money. I have it—I've been stockpiling cash for a couple years now in case Lily and I had to run. I just . . . "Fine."

"Good." Milo scribbles something down on a notepad and, ripping the page off, hands it to me. "Wire it to this info. You don't show up when I call, I part the machine out, understand?"

"Yeah." I start to go and Milo jumps up.

"I'll walk you out."

"Think we can find the way," Griff says, and there's something threaded underneath his tone that makes me pause.

It makes Milo laugh. He follows us and we're almost to the door when I notice the low-slung table near the wall. It looks like computers come there to die. There's a soldering gun in one corner and parts are strewn everywhere, some of them snapped into pieces . . . except for a black box smaller than my fingertip.

"What's this?"

"Sniffer." Milo passes it to me and, even though I don't want to be, I'm impressed.

I fit the sniffer against my palm, testing the weight. "Did you make it?"

"Like duh." Milo rolls his eyes and plucks the transmitter from my hand. "It's specifically designed for

BlackBerrys. You pop off the bottom of the handset's charging station, attach this baby, and away you go. It copies me on emails, internet usage, texts."

My heart bumps into my throat. It's perfect. This could get me close to Bay without actually *getting* close to Bay.

Only it's not perfect because I'd have to get my hands on Bay's BlackBerry charger.

"Does it work?" I ask.

"Of course it works." Milo turns over the transmitter, pokes it with one finger. "Well, it should work. I haven't had a chance to test it. Everyone I know has either iPhones or Androids. I need to get close to a BlackBerry user."

Again, the proximity problem. I look at Griff, feel the familiar squeeze deep in my chest.

"How much?" I ask.

Milo's face wrinkles in confusion. "For this? It's not for sale. I'm trying to figure out how to scare BlackBerry so they buy the patent from me."

"What better way to do that than by showing them it actually works?"

Milo goes still. "A thousand."

"You're high."

"If only." Milo shrugs. "Six hundred."

"I'm already buying an entire system from you."

He smiles. "Five."

I stare at him, waiting, and Milo smiles wider. "Fine." He drops it in a plastic baggie and tosses it to me. "It's free—only because I like you and I want details of how well it works."

"*If* it works."

"*When* it works."

Outside there's a crack of thunder and the lights flicker once, kick-starting the low hum of generators in some other room. We must have lost power.

"Storm's getting worse," Griff says. He's watching us without meeting my eyes. "Let's go before the Mini ends up floating."

"Okay." I follow him, and Milo trails after me. The rain's coming down in sheets now and Griff takes my keys, promising to drive my car close so I can duck in without getting totally drenched. I start to say it doesn't matter and I don't mind, but he's already off and running.

"So sweet," Milo says as Griff sprints through the rain.

Yeah, he is. I want to smile and try not to. Even though I've only known Milo less than an hour, I can already tell he'll wreck the nice gesture. Sometimes Griff treats me like I'm breakable—something I should hate. When it's Griff doing it though I just end up feeling special. Wanted.

Lucky.

Milo steps in front of me. "You could do some serious damage with the hardware I'm going to build you."

"I'm not like that."

"Why not?"

It should be another smart-ass question, only Milo sounds genuinely interested.

"Because it's wrong." I wait for his response and, when it doesn't come, I glance at him, realize he's staring at me. "What?"

"Everyone is capable of damage."

"Well, I'm not like everyone."

Milo jerks up his chin like I've just taken a swipe at him. "Everyone is everyone."

"Not me."

"Not yet."

I roll my eyes and it only seems to make his curiosity grow. Milo draws so close I can smell the mingling scents of cologne and computer plastic clinging to his clothes.

"What is this then? Like a girl power thing? You only use your powers for good?"

"No, I use my powers for money. I just don't destroy people." Well, that's sort of a lie. I *have* ruined people. After I turned in my findings, I'm sure some people were never the same.

That's not to say that I did it for funsies. Those guys deserved it. I'm not getting into that with Milo though.

"You've been given a gift, Wick. Why aren't you using it?"

"I *am* . . . just not like that."

"If I had your talent, I'd rule the world." Milo watches the Mini's headlights draw closer. He opens the restaurant door and a cold, wet wind nudges under my clothes. "You're special. Why are you hiding from it?"

I tuck my jacket around me, getting ready to run for it. "Bringing people down wouldn't make me special."

"No, the fact that you *could* makes you special. I'll be in touch soon. Pleasure doing business."

In typical Georgia fashion, it's stopped raining by the time we get home, but the sky is still marbled with purple-gray clouds and I'm worried about Griff getting drenched if he rides his motorcycle home.

"I could drop you off at your house," I offer as he pulls us into my driveway. Griff parks and turns to face me. "You could pick up your bike tomorrow."

"It's fine. I don't melt if I get wet."

"But I do?" I'm grinning, even though a little piece of me remembers Milo's comment and bristles.

"Of course you do." Griff traces his hand through my hair, his fingertips resting on my pulse like he wants to hold my heartbeat. It. Just. Kills me.

Sometimes when we're touching, I can't even hear my thoughts. Part of me thinks that's dangerous. The rest of me *knows* it's dangerous. Look what happened to my mom. Look what happened to Tessa. They fell in love and it consumed them until there was nothing left.

I always thought I would be different. When it comes to Griff though, I may not be different at all.

"You'd totally melt," he murmurs, raising chills across my skin. "Wicked Witch of the West–style."

I laugh. Can't help it. I love that about him. Whatever tension I'd sensed at Milo's is gone now. Maybe I even imagined it.

Griff's hand drops. "What are you going to do with the sniffer?"

"I don't know yet." It's not exactly a lie. I really don't know how I'm going to make this work. I just know I will. The transmitter's in my pocket. I can feel it, and knowing it's there makes my stomach unclench.

We climb from the car and I give him a lopsided grin— the best I can do at the moment. "They're good to have around, Griffin. Maybe I'll turn over a new leaf, go totally stalker girlfriend, and use it on you."

He laughs, looks at me like I'm wonderful, and when I look at him, I feel wonderful. That's Griff's gift. He looks at you like you're the only girl in the world.

Like you're his reason to exist.

"Well, I guess you could be into shoes or whatever," Griff says, smiling, and then, just as suddenly, scowling. "I'm sorry about the name thing. I didn't want to tell him who you really are."

"No big deal. Red Queen isn't my real name anyway."
It's not like that's who I am. Well. It is, but I'm changing that.

"It's just that he's a friend," Griff continues. "Sorta. I trust him. It was the only way he'd take the job. Milo doesn't really need the money."

"Seriously? That place is gross."

"I know, right?"

We both laugh.

Griff looks at me sideways. "I miss this."

"Miss it?" My sudden laugh dies. "We never stopped."

"It just feels like everything's different now."

"It's not."

"I know. That's still the way it feels."

I lift my face for a kiss and he leans down, grabbing me with both hands. I hook my fingers into his belt loops and angle us closer.

It makes him kiss me harder. He feels so good. Perfect even.

His mouth moves over mine, urging me on, and I can feel that familiar hunger crawling through me, threatening to take me apart as his lips trail across my lower lip, along my jaw, and find that impossibly sensitive spot on my neck.

"I gotta go," Griff whispers against my skin.

"Okay." It's not, but I pretend it is. I pull back, smooth my hair until you can't probably (hopefully) tell we've been kissing.

Griff watches me and, when his eyes meet mine, they're darker than they were before. Hotter.

"See you at school?" he asks.

"Yeah. Sure."

Griff waits for me to open the front door before he starts his bike. He lifts one hand in the air, pulls into the street. I drag myself inside and barely have my shoes off before Bren's calling me from the kitchen.

"Wick?"

"Yeah?"

"There's a package for you. I put it on the hall table."

Package? I drop my bag on the floor, kick it next to Lily's yellow backpack. There are about forty different catalogs smeared across the table. Most of them are for gourmet food or cooking tools, the rest are for kids' toys Lily and I are too old for.

"Do you see it? Is it from one of the colleges we looked at?" The oven slams and something, dinner probably, clatters onto the counter. "Don't forget they're supposed to send you more information."

Forget? How could I possibly forget when you remind me every day? It should irritate me, but more and more Bren makes me smile.

As promised, the package is at the table edge. It looks too small for glossy college brochures and for a second I don't want to touch it. Something's wrong here. There's no return address. The label is computer printed. It looks clean . . . I know it's not.

And in my head, I hear Todd breathe my name.

I press my shoulders against the wall and tell myself to stop it. This isn't like what happened before.

"Wick?" Bren sounds closer this time like she's approaching the hall. "Did you find it?"

"Yes! Thanks!"

Get moving. I work my fingernail against the tape, then lift the box lid.

"It's not the college stuff," I yell, bracing one hand against the table to keep my knees from crumbling. "It's that study guide I ordered."

Only it isn't. It's another DVD.

How can she look even thinner? I sit at my desk, knees tucked under my chin, as the interview progresses. It's like watching one of those stop-motion videos. In every new interview, she looks smaller.

Even more scared.

It's the only thing that feels familiar about any of this: her fear and my . . . hate? I pull my knees closer. It used to be hate. Maybe it still is. It would have to be, right? I hate her for jumping. I hate her for leaving us with him.

Mostly, I hate how our love was never enough, how his was somehow better because he withheld it.

I can't think about that right now. I minimize the video, calling first the city police department and then the county's, asking the receptionists if I can speak with Officer Hart. Even though I've blocked my cell from showing on their caller ID, I'm still twitchy, ready to hang up if Hart answers—only he doesn't because no one's heard of an Officer Hart at either location.

"In fact," the last receptionist says, "we've never had *any* officer by that name. Sorry."

She disconnects and I stare at my computer screen, my breathing high and wheezy. I should toss the DVD now. No Hart at either location? Then who is he? This is some sick game. I should . . . I hit the play button.

"You have to let me go." My mom's at the same table. Someone's given her a wilted sandwich and she's pulling it apart. The gesture is so Lily it cracks me. "You have to let me stop."

"When you've given us what we want."

"I've tried!"

"Have you?"

"I—I—" A sob hijacks her answer, but they keep pushing her, setting my teeth on edge.

Or maybe it's just from her crying. I have to force myself to sit through it and no matter how much I adjust the computer's volume, bass, or treble I still know the sound of her. Coming through a set of speakers or overheard through the walls of my once-upon-a-time bedroom, I know her.

And, suddenly, I miss my mom so much it makes my throat go thick.

"What else do you have, Mrs. Tate?"

It's a new voice. Male. I rerun the video so I can hear it again. Even though I've been around a shit ton of Peachtree

City cops, I don't recognize this one. For the next four minutes, it's nothing more than her soft sobs and their urgent words. I can't make out anything . . . then the video ends. Black screen. White letters.

See How She Was Used?

Bile touches the back of my mouth.

I turn the monitor off, lean my forehead against the edge of the desk, and focus on how my bare feet press the hardwood floor. I don't understand. What's the point of this? Why is someone sending me these?

To make me feel bad?

No. Obviously, no. That would be stupid.

Then what? What am I supposed to learn? "See what they did to her?" "See how she was used?" Is this supposed to show me how I had it all wrong? She wasn't a coward for refusing to leave . . . she was what? Brave for staying? That doesn't feel right either. There's nothing brave about letting your husband terrorize your kids.

And who's doing the interviews anyway? My instinct says Carson. It's not his voice though—no matter how many times I try to convince myself it is. So that leaves . . . the Hart guy?

Hell if I know. I don't think I heard him in the video. Then again, we only spoke for what? A minute? Would I recognize him without seeing his face? Not likely.

How did he send the new DVD anyway? How's he know

where I live? I grab the ripped-open box from my bed and study the postmark. Anyone could have mailed this. Maybe Hart was just a onetime messenger.

But if that's the case, who's he working for?

I rub both hands over my face and notice the time. Jesus, it's late. I'm going to look like death warmed over tomorrow and I have a chemistry test I need to study for.

Frustrated, I open my desk drawer, pull out the homework I should be doing . . . and my eye catches the sniffer.

As long as I'm on the subject of people I don't know shit about, I might as well take care of Milo too.

I open another browser window, spend a few minutes wiring money to the builder's account. Thank God my clients paid me well. I've saved everything I've earned from the past few years in an offshore account, making it easy to move funds around. After I get the wire transfer confirmation, I email it to the address Milo gave me. Then I open Google and type in his name. It doesn't take much time to find out the builder went to Westminster, an überpricey private school on the north side of Atlanta, and based on the graduation date from the Facebook alumni page, he can't be older than twenty.

Other than that? There's nothing else—not exactly unusual for someone like him, and it'd be disappointing if his father weren't a completely different story.

According to two online newspapers, Simon Gray used to work for the NSA. Then, following a total nervous breakdown, bounced between mental institutions and jail.

The arrest reports are pretty much all the same: loitering, resisting arrest, drunk in public.

Rinse. Repeat. End up living with Milo.

Interesting. I can't quite reconcile the swaggering techie with someone who has this kind of backstory and I'm not sure if that says something about him . . . or something about me.

I look at the time again. Three a.m. No point in going to sleep. Might as well stay up and watch the rest of the interviews.

The thought makes my stomach tilt.

Maybe Griff was right. This is bad stuff and I should never have looked, but now I did and I don't know what to do. All I can think about is my dad's addicts, how I never understood why you would return again and again to something that would make you bleed.

I guess I have my answer now: How can you *not*? I push play again, watch my mother's face come to life. For the first time, there's a case number at the bottom of the screen. Coincidence?

See how she was used.

My mom stares into the camera and recites her week with my dad. He's brought home some druggie. The girl is sleeping on our couch. He's doing something in the garage. She's not sure what because he locks the door every time he leaves.

My mom catalogs everything in a flat voice, like this is all no big deal, and I catch my mind wandering, trying to figure out *which* week she's referencing. This was important enough to tell them and yet I don't remember it. How much was she hiding from us?

They get to the end of the interview and the officer tells her she can leave. The camera leans to the left, presumably as someone gropes for the off button.

"One last thing," she says, and the camera stops rocking. They're waiting on her and she milks the moment, stretching the silence. "There's someone following me. It's not my imagination. I think someone knows and if that's true and *he* finds out . . . he'll have me killed."

The screen goes black.

There are no more interviews.

I don't remember falling asleep, but when I finally wake up, it's early afternoon. I check the DVDs (still hidden) and pad downstairs, fixing myself a sandwich while Bren watches me from around her magazine.

"Wick? Are you okay?"

"Migraine," I whisper. It's not that far from the truth anyway. My head is thumping. All I can think about is how that *can't* be everything. There have to be more interviews.

Only there aren't—no matter how many times I sift through the DVDs' files, I don't find anything.

Lily and Bren go to bed around ten, but I can't settle down and end up doing homework until after four. The good news? I'm now ahead in math and chemistry. The bad news? None of it drowned out the loop in my head: no more interviews. No more information.

At this rate, I'll have to wait for another DVD and that's what? Another two days? *Maybe?* How am I supposed to sit by?

I swallow and my throat clicks. Answer is: I don't.

I have a case number now. And was that a mistake? Or was it deliberate? The thought makes the base of my skull prickle and I push the idea under until it stops kicking. Bottom line, I have a case number. I could use that.

I just need to get into the police department's system.

I close the interview menu and open my browser. I haven't done this sort of scam since I worked for Joe and my dad and it takes a little setup. First, I check the Peachtree City Police Department's home page, writing down a few detectives' names. Then I head to the Fayette County home page, where I double-check the IT director's name. Yep, it's still Bill Bearden.

Bill hits the city blogs from time to time because he's spearheading a modernization movement within the county government—new databases, new computers, new electronic filing systems. It's about as exciting as drain hair except the Peachtree City Police Department has been taking part—I've heard Carson's bitching—and that means I might have an in.

All I need now is a Peachtree City government phone number. I click the browser on my cell and surf through a few different phone spoofing sites until I get the one I want.

The premise is pretty simple: scam your friends and family by changing your phone number. Well, you don't actually change your number. You just change the way it appears on your target's caller ID. You can make it look like you're phoning from anywhere: Santa's house or your ex-girlfriend's. In this case, I'll be calling from Bearden's county office.

I plug the IT office's number into the app and add Bearden's name to appear above it. Down the hall, an alarm blares. Bren's awake. I hit send.

"Peachtree City Police Department," a receptionist says. "This is Molly. How may I direct your call?"

"Hi!" I go a little bubbly, hoping Molly equates perky with nonthreatening. "I'm Drea Thomas. I work with Mr. Bearden's group over at the sheriff's office. We're working on that case file database you've been hearing all about."

The pause is so long I think she's about to call my bullshit. "Oh, yeah. Right. What can I help you with?"

"I'm verifying some log-in information." I clear my throat, acting like I'm looking over whatever paperwork is supposed to be in front of me when all I really have is the three names I copied from the department's website. "Is Detective Thompson still rthompson? Password—"

"Oh, I don't know." Molly takes a sip of something, swallows. "I'd have to ask one of the supervisors and they're not in yet. Can you call later?"

I wince. Definitely not. Odds are, a supervisor would ask more questions, and phishing scams work best on people who don't. "Yeah, it is pretty early, isn't it?"

"Disgustingly."

I eye my bedroom door, listening for footsteps in the hall. "Hey, look, I'm really sorry to ask this, but Mr. Bearden's going to be here soon for our morning staff meeting and I've gotta have this verification for him. Do you think you could look it up for me? I'm really sorry to ask. You know how he is."

I hold my breath, knowing I'm pushing it a bit. I'm preying on two things here. One, people are usually willing to help coworkers. Two, she knows what Bearden's like or she's willing to pretend she does.

"I just want to make sure it's right for your officers," I add, forcing a smile into my voice even though I'm cringing.

Molly sighs. "Believe me, you do. They are such babies when stuff doesn't work. Hang on. I've got keys to the IT guy's office. The chief makes him keep a printout of everyone's passwords in case they forget."

I stuff down a squeal when Molly puts me on hold. When she says "everyone" is it possible she also means—

"Okay." Molly grunts into the receiver as she settles into her chair. "You still there?"

"Yep. I have Detective Thompson's log-in as rthompson and his password—" I hesitate again like I'm looking up the information when, in reality, I'm making up a variation on the log-in Carson used (and I overheard) months ago. "Password is 865203A."

"No, that's not right. His password is 594370LA."

I scribble it into my chemistry notebook. "And Chief

Denton's?" My tone spikes and I dig my thumbnail into my thigh, hold it. If she gives me the chief's log-in info, I could access everything: my mom's case info, my dad's, *everything*. "I have pdenton and 962185G."

"You're way off. He's 433785GB."

"Wow, we had it completely wrong." Head buzzing, I write the password above Thompson's information.

"You better make sure you check the others before the database goes live."

It isn't already? I want to ask and can't. A real employee would know that information. "Oh, yeah, definitely. We're staggering the launches though. County stuff will be up before the city's probably."

"Are we still up next week?"

I grin. "Barring any problems, you should be. I'm going to put these correct passwords in now and I'll verify the others later. Thanks *so* much, Molly. You have totally saved me."

I click off just as someone knocks at my door. Bren sticks her head inside. "Hey, you're up already." Worry tints her expression. "Insomnia again?"

"No, just . . . eager to get the day started."

"Well, let's get going then. I don't want you to be late for your appointment with Dr. Norcut." She nudges the door wide so I can follow her and I do. One more week. I touch the passwords and feel something inside me settle and go still.

———————◆———————

Maybe I should've pretended to be sick. As if discussing Chelsea Martin's death with Dr. Norcut wasn't fun enough, I get to hear about it all over again at school. It's a different girl, different circumstances, but as I walk through the hallway, I feel like I'm in the days after Tessa Waye's suicide . . . which then brings me to my mom and her suicide . . . and then to how terrified she sounded on the recording.

I spend a couple minutes at my locker, swapping my books around. I didn't do my history homework, and if there's a pop quiz, I am so hosed. I flip open my notes, checking to see if I can fake my way through any of it, and hear a disgusting, guttural hocking noise to my left.

I jerk right. Hard. Fast.

Not fast enough.

A wad of spit rolls down the side of my neck, disappearing into my collar. Gagging, I scrub my sleeve against my skin. It comes away sodden, a sticky mass glued to the fabric, and my stomach heaves into my mouth.

"Whore." Someone laughs and I look up in time to see Sutton Davis and Matthew Bradford blow past me, slapping each other on the back. Used to be I was just Freak. Thanks to Todd's attentions, I'm now labeled Whore and Slut.

"Ass—" I start to yell, and stop. Two teachers have arrived on the scene and they're giving me the stink eye. Amazing how they missed the star lacrosse players being total douche canoes, but they're ready and waiting for me to mess up. I slam my locker door extra hard just as

Lauren appears at my side.

"What's wrong?" she asks.

"Nothing," I mutter. I don't want to explain. Unlike me, Lauren is popular. She brushes the description off. It's true though. If you call her on it, she'll just say our classmates want to be around her because she doesn't want to be around them. She'll also say that when I avoid them I look scared.

I say when I avoid them I stay out of Dumpsters and don't get spit on.

Well. Usually don't.

Anyway, it's one of the few things we disagree on and I can't really argue with Lauren's results; the tactic obviously works for her. We've been best friends ever since she moved here almost a year ago. She knows about my hacking, my mom, Carson, pretty much everything. It still amazes me she sticks around.

Lauren leans one shoulder against the locker bank. "Can you believe this? You'd think Chelsea was all they had to talk about."

"It probably is." I turn my sleeve over and paw at my neck again. There's something about Lauren's tone that makes me curious. "Did you know her?"

"Sort of. My parents supported Bay's last run for office. His team was at our house a few times for parties—fundraising things. She was going to write my recommendation letter to Duke. . . . Are you itchy or something?"

I drop my hand. I'm going to have to bleach myself

before I feel clean. "Or something. What was Chelsea like?"

"Uptight. Driven."

Interesting. Coming from Lauren this is pretty excellent praise. Above us, the first bell rings. We need to get going, but when I glance up and down the hallway, Griff's nowhere in sight and my stomach squeezes tight all over again.

"You coming?" Lauren asks, turning to head toward her first class. I hesitate and then follow her, telling myself it's fine. Really. Griff must have had something come up.

But it feels off.

"Chelsea was close to finishing law school," Lauren continues. "Working for Bay was just a stop along the way to something bigger."

We turn down the science hall and Lauren slows, dragging out our time together before she has to turn in to her English class. "I know the newspaper is speculating that it was personal. I agree. A few days before she died, I saw Chelsea talking to that detective who was always sniffing around you. She looked upset."

Part of Carson's charm. "Wonder what he wanted."

"Exactly. Because, thing is, once I started thinking about it, I realized I've seen the detective and Chelsea together before—when I was dropping off campaign stuff for my mom at Bay's office. Chelsea looked really unhappy. What could he possibly have wanted to talk to her about? Do you think he knew something was going to happen?"

"Miss Cross, Miss Tate." Lauren's English teacher

walks past us, her Band-Aid-colored panty hose rubbing together. "Don't you have somewhere to be?"

Lauren rolls her eyes and leans closer to me. "Hey, look, I'm going to be out of school for a few days—maybe a week."

"Your mom again?" Lauren sometimes misses school to care for her, but it's been months since she's had to.

Lauren nods. "Yeah, but maybe this doctor will actually be good."

Unlike all the others hangs between us.

"Anyway," Lauren says. "I'll see you later?"

"Definitely," I return, and sit through my morning classes in a blur of Chelsea Martin. Why would Carson want to talk to her? Had to be because of her connection with the judge. As his assistant, she would see everything. It would make her an excellent resource.

Griff said I should think about how Carson was willing to use me and how he might be willing to use other people. Could that extend to Chelsea?

Like someone flipped a switch, the word *leverage* strings across my brain in Christmas lights. If he was pressuring the judge's assistant and she ended up dead . . . maybe there's something I could use against him. In the middle of calculus, I start to grin, and even though I should be thinking of Chelsea, I'm now thinking about my family, about Griff.

He's right. If I could get leverage on Carson, we could go free.

———◆———

I go straight home after school. There aren't any other "study guides" waiting for me on the hall table and the whole house smells like vanilla. Like complicated, delicate desserts.

Which means something's happened and Bren's upset.

I edge farther into the kitchen, trying to quietly assess the situation. There's a Julia Child cookbook lying open on the counter, about twenty ramekins of something buttery scattered across the island, and both ovens are going. Yep, Bren's upset.

I am *so* not good in these situations.

Bren sniffles and I flinch. There's no way I can leave now. I force myself into the kitchen, hop onto a bar stool. "Hey."

"Wick!" Bren swipes at her eyes. "You scared me!"

"Sorry." And I have to bite my lip to keep from repeating it. There's something I need to say here and I don't know what it is. My adoptive mom isn't crying, but she has been. Her eyes have red smeared around their edges. "You okay?"

"Yes. No." Her gaze searches the ceiling, comes down to meet mine. "I will be. I had to stop by Lily's school today and I ran into another mother."

It's the way she says "mother" that makes me wince. I know where this is headed and I want to tell Bren to stop, to not tell me because I don't want her to have to relive it. Only there's no way to say that without sounding bitchy.

Or maybe it's because it feels like exposing her marriage's rotten underbelly is something else I've done to her.

I've lied. I've hidden things. I've pretended to be someone I'm not.

She didn't deserve any of it.

"She was *so* nice," Bren continues. "We talked for a few minutes because her daughter cheers with Lily. She had already invited me to come to lunch with some of the other moms and I thought she was lovely until they called my name . . . and she just . . . shuddered. She looked at me like she finally realized who I was, *what* I was, and she was horrified."

"It wasn't your fault." It was mine.

No. It was Todd's.

"I trusted him," Bren adds, the words piling together in her rush. "I loved him. I should have kept you safe and I didn't."

"It turned out okay. No one got hurt."

"You did."

I start to say that ten stitches and a concussion isn't really getting hurt—it isn't permanent—but then Bren will bring up the nerve damage in my arm. No matter how many times I tell her it's fine, she doesn't believe me. It's the only lie I've ever told I couldn't get her to buy.

"You were worth it," I blurt. It's true. Maybe we *do* have a fairy-tale ending because in every fairy tale there's always a villain and ours was Todd.

I'd sound like a lunatic if I say that, so instead I add, "Please stop blaming yourself."

"I can't . . . you should probably know . . . child services is making a few inquiries."

My heart double-thumps. "Why? The adoption papers are final."

"Apparently, there have been some complaints? I don't know what they call it. Accusations? There's a social worker who may want to talk to you about my . . . skills."

Not if I get to Carson first. I know what this is. It's a reminder, a warning of what's to come. He's screwing with her to remind me to hurry it along. I will fix it for her. I will make it go away. I will make all of it go away.

I want to tell her and I can't.

We stare at each other until Bren turns to the oven—either because she can't look at me anymore or she just wants the conversation to end—and watches her soufflé through the window. "You remember Lily has a cheer competition this weekend, right?"

No, actually, and I'm pretty sure that makes me a rotten sister, but I'm grateful for the conversation turn. Heartfelt confessions always make me feel like a fat man's sitting on my chest.

"Yeah, 'course I remember. It's downtown or something."

"Birmingham." Bren straightens, checks the cookbook. "Would you like to come?"

Under different circumstances, yeah I would. Lily loves cheering and she loves it even more when I come. I just can't afford the time away, not if Carson's going to play these games.

"I wish. I have a history project that's really kicking my butt." I pause, knowing I'm pushing it with what I'm about to ask. "Do you mind if I stay home?"

"We'll be gone for the whole weekend." Bren's statement curls up at the end, fitting in *Are you sure?* and *She'll have every light in the house on* behind the words. I should probably be offended. All I can think about is the windfall. Two whole days. It might be all it would take. A smile slings across my lips.

"School's important." Bren touches her fingers to the cookbook like she's reading the text, but her eyes never move. "You can come to the next meet. . . . Are you sure you'll be okay alone?"

She picks her way so carefully through the question, it sounds practiced, like this was expected. Maybe it was. After Todd's attack, all Bren wanted to do was keep Lily and me close to her. If she had her way, we would both be home-schooled now and travel everywhere with her. She's trying really hard to give us space.

I'm manipulating that.

I scrape my fingernail against the counter, not meeting Bren's eyes. "Yeah, I'll be fine. I have a few school things that I can take care of while you're gone."

"You sure?"

"It's no big deal."

I slide off the bar stool, stop dead. "Bren? How did that work? When you paid Bay to push through our adoption papers?"

Now she's not looking at me. "I worked with his assistant, the girl who died."

There's something to that, a taste behind my teeth I can't name . . . yet.

"You know you can't say anything about that, right, Wick?"

"I won't. I would never." I hesitate. We have nothing left to talk about, but I feel bad leaving her.

"Are you going to be okay?" I ask.

Bren goes so still I know she's about to lie. "Of course, sweetheart, everything's fine."

And we're both so good at this, I almost believe her. I go upstairs, turn on all my lights, text Carson to call off his dogs, watch my window *and* my air vent.

Until midnight, when Griff climbs in from the dark.

"What are you doing?" I whisper. I can't stop my smile though, and when Griff sees it, he grins.

"Your light was on and I wanted to see you."

It makes everything in me do a stupid wiggle dance. "See me for what?"

"Midnight picnic."

"What?"

"You heard me." We're kneeling on the floor beneath my window, knees almost touching, and Griff nudges closer, mouth brushing mine. It makes the skin on the back of my neck prickle to life.

"Sneak out with me," he whispers against my lips.

I nearly laugh. Hells no. There's no moon tonight and two of the streetlamps are dead. Problem is, if I say no, I'd have to explain. How do you say "I'm afraid of the dark" without sounding like a two-year-old?

"I dare you." His words curl through me, hit bottom.

"You're on."

Griff blinks, smiles. I've surprised him. I've surprised myself.

I shove my feet into sneakers and go to my bedroom door, listen for Bren. I'm pretty sure she went to bed ages ago.

"We'll be back in an hour," Griff says. "She'll never know."

I follow him to the window; take a steadying breath as I look down into the shadows.

"You want me to go first?" he asks. "Catch you as you come down?"

I'm not sure which is worse: Griff thinking I'm afraid of falling or Griff knowing I'm afraid of the dark. I roll my eyes. "What? You think this is the first time I've snuck out of my bedroom?"

He grins and I kick my legs over the sill, digging my sneakers into the nearest tree limb. It holds under my weight and I scramble to the ground in only a few seconds. Maybe not the most graceful thing I've ever done—

Griff drops down next to me, chest skimming my arm, heat rolling off him. If I lean forward, we could kiss.

"Nicely done, Wicked."

My mouth goes dry. "Where are we going?"

"You'll see."

Ends up, not very far. Griff takes me to the kiddie park near my house, where we sit on the swings and eat cold

Chick-fil-A sandwiches. I twirl my swing in circles, noticing how the shadows suddenly don't feel so smothering. Maybe it's Griff. Maybe he chases away my dark.

"What brought this on?" I ask.

A pause. "This is the kind of stuff I always wanted to do with you."

I dip my eyes away from his, end up looking at the curve of skin above his collar. It makes my mouth go hot.

"What do you want, Wick?"

You. But I don't say it because that's not what he means. Griff is talking about school and college and life after college. He's talking about all the things he has figured out.

And I don't have a clue about. I can't think that far ahead. I wasn't supposed to have this life. Tates don't go to college. They go to jail.

Or the morgue.

I shrug, look away. "What do *you* want?"

"To keep drawing. To afford painting. SCAD. For food stamps to be part of someone else's life. For . . . it isn't hard, Wicked. Tell me what you want."

"I don't know what I want yet," I say at last, pressing one hand against my forehead. I can feel a migraine coming on. Stress. The space behind my eyes is beginning to thump. "I'm just taking things as they come. It's hard to plan anything with Carson in the middle of it."

"Then let's take him out of it." Griff hesitates. "What if we tell my cousin? He could help us bring a case against Carson."

"And take me down in the process. Worse, it'll take Bren

down." Saying it aloud makes guilt squeeze me breathless. "My *sister* will go down."

I'll be alone. It's brief and brilliant, blazing across my brain in a language I didn't think I understood. When did I become that girl?

"They won't go down," Griff says, edging closer even as I'm straining away. "We'll figure it out. We'll weather it together."

We. Not them. I shake my head, can't stop.

Griff makes a strained noise. "Bren and Lily will be fine. They wouldn't want this for you."

"I don't want any of this for them. It's my burden, Griff." What I really mean is it's my fault. I want to fix this for them. I also want to fix it for me.

"I'll minimize the damage, Wicked. I did it once."

He did. Carson tried to catch me helping my father and I would have gone to jail for sure—*if* I'd been caught. Griff erased all my digital fingerprints from the files I gave my dad and his right-hand man, Joe Bender. They went to jail. Griff saved me.

No guarantees I'll be that lucky the second time. "There's more at stake here than just me, Griff."

Besides, even if I could take Carson down . . . I want to finish Bay first. Two for the price of one.

"Think about it," Griff says. "It's your decision."

Funny how three little words can make me feel so warm. So do these words: I will save myself. I will protect Bren, and by protecting Bren I'll protect Lily.

I look at Griff and smile. "I don't know what to do with you."

Now he's smiling. "I have a few ideas."

For the rest of the week, I spend my afternoons watching Bay's house from the shelter of the woods. In some ways, this is stupid easy because my hiding spot is well hidden and, more importantly, no one at home misses me. Griff is finishing an art project for his college application port-folio. Bren and Lily have their own things going on in preparation for the cheer meet. Ian . . . well, Ian is still bugging me about our project, but I've managed to put him off. Everything's working.

Sort of.

Because I haven't made any headway. For *days*, all I get to watch is the guards and the Bays go about their business—come home from school, eat dinner, walk around the backyard; it's every bit as thrilling as it sounds.

Then, on Sunday, I get a break. Just after lunch, one of the guards reaches into his pocket, pulling out a cell phone. He messes with it for a moment, waits, and then shows it to his partner. They both stare at the handset. The guard on the left shrugs and turns for the car. I sit up straight. What the hell?

The second guard fiddles with his phone—I think he's texting—then follows the first. They climb into the sedan and drive away. This makes zero sense. The Bays have been gone all weekend. I even saw the emails between Bay and the security firm. The guards are supposed to be here until the family gets home sometime tonight.

I shift, pressing one shoulder against a tree. This is too good to be true.

Which makes me suspicious.

And also eager. Because if I skirted the woods, I could run around to the rear of the house and use the rose trellis to climb onto the back porch roof. According to the last email I saw between Barton & Moore and Bay, the second-floor windows still don't have functioning alarms. If I jimmied the lock, I could sneak into the house and install the sniffer without interruption. It would be a round of brilliant good luck.

Then again, who's to say someone wouldn't come home and catch me? The idea turns my blood slushy. That won't work.

Screw it. I'm going. I pull my hoodie tight over my hair. With one eye on the house across the street, I follow the tree line around until I'm in the Bays' backyard. Still half in the trees, I wait, watch. There's nothing. The house is completely still. If I'm going to do this, I better do it now.

Breaking from the trees, I hustle across the lawn, heading for the rose trellis. I thread my hands through the prickly vines and test the wooden frame's sturdiness. I think it will hold. I *hope* it will hold.

Hoisting one foot up, I jam it into the space where wooden slats are nailed together and start climbing. Hand over hand. I make it to the roof's edge in less than fifteen seconds and heave myself up, rolling to my feet, ready to pry the window open.

Except I don't need to. The window is cracked open.

Another squeeze of unease. This is too easy. Something's up. I wait another beat, listening for any sounds coming from inside or out. There's nothing. So why do I feel watched?

I stare hard into the trees behind me, look carefully to either side. Nothing. I'm alone and paranoid.

Screw it. I'm going. I shove the window farther open and slide through, hitting the carpet with both feet. Again, there's nothing. The house is completely quiet.

Get in. Get out. Get in. Get out. I cross the room and crack the door. The hallway is empty. I edge forward, glance around. The Bays' upstairs is open to the downstairs, and from my position in the upper hallway, I can easily see the floor below. Kitchen looks clear . . . living room directly below looks clear . . . I ease to the handrail, craning over the side to peer down at the keypad near the front door. No flashing lights.

It's not on. I dash for the stairs, feet soundless on the thick carpeting. Down the first five, turn on the landing, down another five. Wait.

Still nothing.

I take a deep breath and hustle across the main living room. Thanks to the party, I know exactly which door off the hallway to pick. The handle turns noiselessly in my hand and I'm in.

Bay's study. It smells like orange cleanser and polished wood. The curtains are drawn and it takes me a moment to locate his BlackBerry charging station in the shadows. It's tucked to one side of the cherrywood desk, power cord neatly fed through a small hole in the desk's shiny top. Turning the charger upside down, I pop off the cradle's bottom, then by pushing the charging pins out, I am able to slide the sniffer in, attaching the charging pins to the back of it. Now, whenever Bay puts his phone on charge, the phone will connect with the sniffer and I'll get a direct feed of his texts, emails, and pictures.

Resecuring the bottom, I replace the charging station, wipe my fingerprints, and glance around the room. It's really tempting to do a little digging. *Really* tempting.

Until I hear a thump.

It's so muffled I almost miss it, but my heart rides right into my throat, and for a terrible moment, I'm frozen.

Get out. Get. Out. I fling myself at the study door, peer outside. Nothing. I'm just spazzing. There's a good reason I stay on the other side of the computer. I can't handle this stress. Time to blow this Popsicle stand.

I'm easing my way up the last steps when I hear it again. Another thump.

Slowly, I turn, see a shadow slide past one of the open doors farther down the hallway.

I am not alone.

I spin around, running for the window and trying to be quiet. I'm just not quiet enough. It's not that I hear someone behind me.

I just somehow know he's there.

My heart is behind my teeth now, but I have just enough brain cells left to ease the window down with sleeve-covered hands and run for it.

Or, rather, slide for it.

I push my way down the roof until my feet are dangling off the side, twist, and grab onto the rose trellis. Then I scramble. My feet hit the ground and, just as they do, I hear the window above scrape open.

I freeze, shoulders pressed against the siding. Whoever was down the hallway is now above me on the roof. I can't run the way I came because it would take me directly across the yard. I'd be seen. Can't stay here though. I can't—my eyes latch onto the woods. That'll work. I'll run for the woods. If I go around the side of the house, I can reach the trees. They'll provide coverage.

Hopefully.

I take off, coming around the side of the house at a dead run. Behind me, the rose trellis shakes and something heavy hits the ground.

Shit. Shit. Shit. I speed up, running past the end of the Bays' house and straight into the surrounding woods. I keep a good pace as I push farther in. The underbrush isn't very thick and the ground is soft from the recent rains, muffling the slap of my Chucks. I veer to the right—need to get closer to the road—and duck behind a fallen tree, curling myself into a tight ball. I wait, listening. At first, it's quiet.

Then come the footsteps.

They're steady, but farther off, like the person went straight when I went right. I press myself into the dirt, willing my breathing to slow. No good. Fear is mixing with exertion and I can't get enough air. I cover my mouth with both hands and the movement turns my head just enough to see the wedge of space between the standing trunk and the fallen tree.

There's someone coming through the afternoon-darkened trees.

It's a man. He's moving quickly, head casting from side to side like he's looking for something he lost.

He's looking for me. I press closer to the ground even as he draws farther away. I can't make out his face. He's tallish . . . with baggy clothes . . . and . . . crap. The shadows make it almost impossible to gauge anything definite.

Who is he?

Not Ian. Not the judge. Who else would want to be in that house besides me?

My skin goes cold. The killer.

No. Why would he come back? I flatten myself into the dirt, waiting. He walks left, then right, then disappears behind a thicket of trees. I fling myself upright and run for it. The road shouldn't be much farther. If I can get that far, I can reach my car. I'm out of here.

And then the ground gives way.

I pitch forward, sliding, sliding. My shoulder crams into one rock and my head glances off another. Light flashes behind my eyes as the force spins me around. I end up half buried under a mound of dirt.

Get up. Get up. I thrash, spilling more dirt. Somehow I've fallen into a ditch and the ground is crumbly from all the rain. I can't get traction until—*finally*—my feet hit rock and I push myself up, wiping dirt from my eyes. My fingers come away wet, bloody.

This isn't a ditch. It's a giant sinkhole. I'm at least eight feet below the surface, my legs partially buried in the soft, dark dirt. The ground behind me feels firmer and, somehow, the ground above me is intact, curving over me like a roof.

I wiggle. Something pokes me in the side. Shit. I reach around, knowing even before I touch my cell that I've crushed it. The screen is deeply cracked and it won't power on. So much for calling for help. I'll need to dig myself out, but there's too much dirt on my legs. I can't move, and this time, it isn't footsteps that alert me he's close. It's the way the birds go silent.

A shadow casts across the hole. He's standing above me, looking down, and I go utterly still. I can't tell if he can see me. My lower body is completely buried. The rest of me?

I press into the dirt wall. Maybe with the overhang, I'm okay. Unless he comes around the other side of the hole; then I *know* he'll spot me. I won't be able to get away.

I wait. He waits. Small clumps of dirt drop from above, and for a single, hysterical second, I think he's going to fall through the overhang and land on top of me. Then his fingers close around the edge of the hole. They curl into the dirt so I can see the pink tips and I know he's leaning in.

He's coming in for a closer look. I bite my tongue, taste mud. More dirt clumps fall and then his fingers pull away. He's moving. Back and forth. Back and forth.

He's pacing.

Then he stops. Something cracks and I jerk. There's a rustling, dragging sound. Ragged shadows arc across the hole's opening and a large branch lands across my buried legs.

Panic surges through me. What the hell is he doing?

He begins to whistle. Another crack. Another branch.

Why's he covering up the hole?

Crack. Branch.

Holy shit, he's going to bury me alive.

I swallow, dirt coating my tongue. *Get a grip. He's not burying you. He's covering you. He's hiding the hole. Why? Because I'm in it? Can't be. He doesn't realize I'm here.*

The whistling—light, tuneless—recedes again and I start working my legs up and down, pushing at the dirt with my sneakers. I can't let myself get pinned like this. Maybe if I ball up, I'll have a better chance of getting my feet under me and shoving my way out.

I wiggle harder. My left knee pops loose, punches through the mud. I draw it close and keep working at my right leg. It's so far under all that dirt. I don't know how—

Another branch lands on me and I stifle a whimper.

Only maybe I didn't stifle it enough because he pauses. The long shadow slides across the hole again and I press one hand against my mouth, convinced he can hear my breathing. That's when I notice how the mud's been smeared.

By dragging my leg to me, I left a long line in the dirt. Did he notice?

Waiting. Waiting.

He moves. The shadows retreat and I heave my right leg out, pull my knees under my chin, and tuck myself into a ball.

Another branch. He starts pacing again . . . stops . . . retreats.

Leaves.

His footsteps recede and I exhale hard, waiting for him to be far enough away that he won't hear me crashing through the tree branches. A minute passes. Another. The sun's lowering in the west, inching me into darkness. I should wait—

Screw it.

I kick my feet under me and start pushing. The limbs snag on everything—my hair, my clothes. I shield my eyes with a forearm and the branches dig into my skin until there's blood.

I keep pushing—even more freaked now than I was in the house. Why would he cover a hole? Surely if he knew I was in there . . . I swallow hard. I don't want to think about that. But I know something's wrong.

And, somehow, I know he'll be back.

I balance both feet on the lowest branch and push up. A branch claws my stomach, ripping my T-shirt, and I manage to scramble a little higher. The ragged ledge is almost within reach. If only my freaking phone worked!

I brace my feet on a branch's bend. One foot slips and I flail, clawing both hands into the soft earthen walls. My fingers catch and I drag myself higher, vowing I'll drive straight to Carson's. He's off tonight. He should be there.

Except . . . shit. My *car*. I left it by the road. What if someone reports it? That would place me in the local area of the crime.

Worse, what if *he* finds it? If he found out who it was

registered to . . . I shudder, forcing my hands to dig deeper into the dirt. I hit something hard.

Tree root? It curls around my fingers and I jerk back, exposing the long, delicate bones of a hand.

Vomit surges into my mouth. *That's what he was covering up? A body?*

I kick harder, powering onto the forest floor in jerks; then, crouching, I press both hands onto my knees and try to catch my breath. In. Out. In. Out.

A fucking body!

I push to my feet and take off at a dead run. Even so, it still takes me almost twenty minutes to reach my car. I keep stopping, leaning against trees to listen. Nothing. No one's following me. I'm alone.

Or maybe not.

Because when I break through the woods and emerge on the street, someone's already been there. My car is still parked up on the curb, but there's a line of footprints—orangey-red and heading out of the woods—leading to the driver's door.

They're the same color as my filthy fists and clothes.

I take a few steps closer, tell myself that, possibly, this doesn't matter. When it rains in Georgia, everything turns orange-red. It's from all the clay. Maybe it's someone out for a walk, a jogger cutting through.

Then comes the low, lilting whistle and my heart rams into my throat.

He's *close*.

And that's when I notice how the footprints don't go past the car. They go around it. They circle the vehicle and walk back to the woods.

He checked my license plate.

He's going to figure out who I am.

I drive straight to a gas station—ignore the attendant's stares—and buy a GoPhone, dialing Carson's cell from memory. He doesn't pick up.

I sit on the curb next to my car and try again. Still doesn't answer. He probably doesn't recognize the number. He's waiting for a voice mail that I'm never going to leave. Too risky.

Kind of like staying here. I scan the gas station's parking lot again. Empty. So why do I still feel exposed?

Maybe it's the head injury. I've had so many by now I'm going to end up stupid. My left eye is swollen, but still open enough for me to realize my vision's gone funny, blurry. I probably shouldn't be driving.

I dial Carson's cell again and get his voice mail. While I'm listening to his message, I count the bubbles of light drifting in the corner of my vision. Six. Six is a nice number.

Or not.

I disconnect and lurch to my feet, bracing one shaking hand against the Mini's hood. Good. I haven't passed out or started screaming.

Now where to?

Home. I angle myself into the car and start the ignition. I need to get home and check the security system and locks.

What if he's already there?

I shift the car back into park and redial Carson. This time, he answers on the second ring.

"*What?* Who is this?"

"It's me."

"Why the hell are you calling—"

"I need you to get to Judge Bay's house." I lean my head against the steering wheel and close both eyes so the bubbles disappear. "I just found a body."

I hang up with Carson and go straight home, check the alarm system, check the locks, check the windows.

Everything looks good.

It makes me smile until I realize of course they would look good. If he slipped unnoticed into the Bays' house, why should our place be any different?

The thought makes tears prick my eyes.

Bren and Lily will be home tonight. How could I

endanger them like this? How could I have screwed up so badly? I nearly got caught. I touched a *body*.

I hold on to the kitchen counter and take three deliberate breaths. I'm overreacting. There's no need to panic . . . yet. I know he has my license plate number. I don't know how long it will take him to trace it—depends on his skill set or his connections and either one could take a while.

So for now, I'm good.

I just don't know for how long.

My legs give out and I end up on the floor, slumped up against the bottom cabinets. Dimly I'm aware that I'm leaving dirt everywhere. I need to change, but I'm scared to go upstairs. I'm scared he's already here, waiting for me.

I tuck my knees under my chin. Oh, God, I am in so much trouble. Not just me. Bren. Lily. If he traces me to my sister—

There's a soft whump as the garage door turns on. My stomach rolls. The garage. I didn't check the garage. I scramble forward, land on both knees as my mud-slicked feet shoot out from under me.

The door scrapes open.

"Wicked?"

Relief turns my bones mushy. It's Griff. Holding a pizza. He stares at me so long I think he's going to turn around and leave. Then, suddenly, he's at my side. His arms are around me and I shouldn't plaster myself against him—I'm muddy, bloody, maybe even crying—and I can't let him go.

"What're you doing here?"

"I finished early. I wanted—the *hell*, Wick? What happened to your head?"

"I . . . fell. In a hole."

"What?" Griff's face wads up. He touches his fingers to the cut above my eye. "Wait. Back up. Start from the beginning."

I can't. I have no idea what to say. Everything I can think of will only piss him off and I'm not even sure I know where the beginning is. When I caught Todd? When Carson said I wasn't finished?

"Jesus, your skin feels like ice." Griff wraps his hands around mine. He's right. The thought of telling him the truth has hollowed me, left nothing but chill.

"I was working the job," I say at last.

"Same one as before?" Griff's rubbing my arms now, hard. Bits of dirt scatter onto the floor. "Tracking down Bay?"

"I broke into his house to plant the sniffer."

Griff's hands stop.

"Someone else was there—someone who wasn't Bay or Ian. I ran and he ran after me." The words are hurtling out of me now and I have to put both hands on the floor to keep myself from collapsing. "I don't know who he is or what he was doing there. I think he's going to figure out who I am. He found my car. Saw the license plate."

"And you thought he was coming through your garage door. You thought I was him."

I nod.

"Did you check the house? The security system?"

More nods. It's all I can manage.

"You need to get out of those clothes. You want help up the stairs?"

Do not say yes. Do. Not. Say. Yes.

"Yes."

Griff looks away, his jaw flexes once. "You want me to wait outside the bathroom while you shower?"

My fingers curve into the kitchen tile and I have to concentrate on breathing so I don't think about what I want to say and shouldn't.

Doesn't matter because all that comes out is, "Yes."

I start to stand, but Griff tucks me into him, lifts me so I'm pinned against his chest. "Griff, please, it's not—"

"It is."

Griff stalks up the stairs, puts me down outside my bathroom, and goes inside to crank the hot water. Steam fills the room and I follow him, lean against the vanity counter, shivering, as he piles fresh towels near the shower door.

"I'll get you some clean clothes and try to wipe up the mud downstairs," Griff says, drying his wet hands on the backs of his jeans. "You don't want Bren finding it. Move, okay?"

I stare at him. *Move?*

Oh, because I'm in his way. He wants to leave.

I want him to stay. I put one hand on Griff's chest, feel his heartbeat. I take my other hand and lock the door.

Griff retreats a step. "What're you doing, Wick?"

Wick. Not Wicked. Which is what this is, isn't it? I want Griff. I want his mouth, his hands. I want him to hold me so I stop shivering.

"I—" I kiss him. It's not pretty. He's too tall. I have to tug him down to me, and when I do, he hesitates and I nearly sob. Please don't let me have damaged this too.

"Please," I breathe. His hands find my jaw, my cheeks. He smoothes back my hair, and my skin warms like always. How can everything be so wrong and he stays so perfect?

"God, you're so—" Griff groans against my hair and the way his voice turns rough feels like want.

I tug at his shirt, yanking it over his head and leaving muddy handprints across his chest. I'm not being careful.

Neither is he.

His hands work my jeans loose. They crumple at my feet and he lifts me out of them. We stumble into the shower together and I yelp when the hot water hits my skin. Griff pivots, pins me to the wall. His fingers knot in my hair, angling my head for another kiss.

His mouth covers mine and I'm gone. My arms loop around Griff's neck and he lifts me to meet him, pressing my shoulders into the wall. I love this. I love how he takes me out of me, until the water hits the dirt and suddenly all I can smell is mud and decay and I gasp.

"Wicked." Griff loosens his grip and I stare dumbly at him, hearing a whistle in my head that makes my body go cold. Water sluices down his face, tiny droplets catching in his eyelashes. "Slow down."

I can't. He's begging me to stop, but his hands are telling me how I'm wanted, how I'm powerful.

Like what happened to me didn't really happen.

I choke on my sob so it doesn't emerge in a scream. Tears crowd my eyes and I push away from him.

I'm not going to cry. I'm not going to cry.

I'm already crying.

In front of Griff. Oh, God.

It's coming out in big, ugly gasps now, bending me in half and driving my knees to the tile. I can't stop. I'm crying for Chelsea and for me.

Because I don't want to do this anymore.

I end up sprawled at Griff's feet, and when he gathers me

close, I want to die. This is not how I want him to see me.

This isn't how *I* want to see me. Griff holds my head against his chest so our breathing comes down together. It's almost enough to make me feel like I've survived it.

Until the GoPhone vibrates on the counter.

I fumble with a towel before picking it up. The screen is smeared with mud, making the incoming call barely legible. Carson.

Griff sees it too. "Whoever it is can wait."

"It can't—it's Carson." Now I'm the one who retreats, shuffles around to separate our clothes. When I pass him his T-shirt, all I can see is how my muddy fingers made the fabric look bloodstained.

Griff catches my hand and something wordless snakes between us. He wants to talk. I want to disappear. I can't believe I fell apart. Well, I *can* believe it. I wish I hadn't.

Because it feels like I just changed everything.

The phone buzzes again and Griff looks at me, the air between us wrapped with everything he will not say: Don't answer, don't put Carson first, don't do this. And I have to and I'm not and I have no choice. It looks like I'm putting Carson first and I'm not. I'm putting Griff and Lily and Bren first by keeping Carson at bay. I should explain that.

I angle the phone against my ear instead. "Yeah?"

"Where are you?"

"Home. I had to check the security system."

"We have to talk."

"Tell him to screw off." Griff moves toward me and,

without thinking, I shy away, stopping myself too late.

"Wick? Are you there?"

I keep my eyes trained on Griff. "Where do you want to meet?"

"My house. In an hour."

I should probably pretend I have no idea where Carson lives. Definitely shouldn't reveal I scoped his place once because I thought it might be useful information.

"Fine," I say, and disconnect, tossing the phone onto the bathroom counter. I stare at it so I don't have to meet Griff's eyes. "I have to meet Carson. His house. It's a few minutes from here."

"I'll go with you . . . if you want."

Of course I want. I should be ashamed of how grateful that makes me. I start to tell him anyway and stop. Instead, I pull up my chin.

"I'll clean out the Mini," Griff says, studying the wall above my head. "If it's half as muddy as you—"

"You don't have to protect me."

"I couldn't if I tried." He walks out, leaving the bathroom door wide open.

Run after him. Apologize.

No way.

I scrub one hand over my swollen eyes. He makes it sound like I enjoy this shit, like I go looking for it. It's not like that. It's *not*.

I open my mouth to tell him it's not about what I might ruin. It's about what I *will* save. Too late though—Griff's feet have already hit the stairs. I'm alone. This isn't the happily ever after he signed on for, but this is who I turned out to be.

Carson doesn't live in Peachtree City proper. He's probably fifteen minutes outside the city limits. It's a small house at the end of a long dirt road, bordered on three sides by thick trees that rise up like broken teeth. The odds of anyone seeing us are next to nil. Even so, Carson still makes us park the Mini well behind the house.

Griff pulls the keys from the ignition, and as he reaches for the car door, I reach for him. "Griff."

He's already walking away, the lines of his shoulders sharp under his faded T-shirt. Carson waits at the door and, silently, we all pile into the living room, where Carson collapses on a swaybacked couch and helps himself to the bottle of Jack propped on the coffee table.

"Classy," Griff says.

Carson pauses, plastic Solo cup at his lips. "Don't be a smart-ass. I'm only here long enough to shower and get something to eat."

"That's getting 'something to eat'? I must be doing it wrong."

"Again, don't be a smart-ass." Carson's voice rises and, next to me, Griff tenses, his feet push into the floor. It makes Carson smile.

He switches his attention to me. "Tell me how you got in."

"Rear window. Second floor."

"How'd you get out?"

"Same way."

Carson scrubs one hand along his jaw. "What I don't understand is why the security guards left. I sent two officers up to Atlanta to question—"

"It looked like they were called away."

"Go on."

I grip the couch cushions under my knees, suddenly very, very aware of Griff watching me. "I was on the bike path. It looked like one got a text or maybe a visual voice mail. He showed it to the other and they left."

Carson swirls his drink around as he thinks about that. "So what does that mean?"

"It means your killer has someone on the inside of the security firm," Griff says.

"Or," I counter, "it means we're dealing with another hacker."

Both of them look at me. Carson's interested. Griff's . . . shuttered.

"Security firm like that," I say slowly, trying out the words. "They don't make mistakes. Their people don't just wander off. They get orders. They're told what to do, and whoever told them was someone they trusted and knew."

Carson sits up. "Or they *thought* it was someone they trusted and knew."

"Exactly. Getting into Barton and Moore's main computers would be really freaking hard. Getting into a supervisor's cell phone and accessing his people from that cell phone? Easier."

"Anything else?" the detective asks.

"What about the . . ." I close my eyes. Open them. I'm afraid of what I'll see in the dark. "Bones I found? How did you explain it?"

"Body was reported by an anonymous tip." The detective digs around in his jacket, pulls out a plastic baggie. Inside, there's a dark square of something and Carson flicks it onto the coffee table, where it lands with surprising weight.

It's a wallet.

Carson pushes the baggie around so I can see the girl in the dirt-stained license smile at me. "You know who that is?"

I shake my head. The plastic is so stained I can't make out much of the face, only the long blond hair.

"That is—*was*—Kyle Bay's girlfriend, Lell Daley. You uncovered her body."

Next to me, Griff stiffens. Even through my jeans, I can feel how his muscles stand up like rope.

Carson leans off the side of his couch and sifts through a box of files on the floor. He pulls a set of folders onto his lap and flips through a few, flicking a couple of pictures onto the coffee tabletop. "According to her mother, the girl"—Carson taps the face of a girl with honey-blond hair, her skin almost Crayola orange from fake tanner—"eloped with Kyle Bay a few years ago."

I recognize Kyle at once. Dark hair. Deep-set eyes. There's a sneer at the corners of his mouth like he's trying—and failing—not to laugh at you. It's so much like his dad I scowl.

"They were both eighteen so it's not like anyone could do anything," Carson continues. "Mrs. Daley was thrilled with the marriage."

"The Bays weren't?"

"That would be my guess. The real question is, when did she die? According to her mother, she eloped four years ago."

"Somehow I don't think she made it that far."

"Agreed."

We watch each other for a moment and Carson breaks first, reaching for the bottle again. He doesn't pour another drink, but he studies the liquid like he wants to.

"So if Lell's body is in the ground," I say. "Where's Kyle?"

Carson toasts me with the bottle. "Isn't that just the question of the hour?"

"Is Kyle a suspect?" Griff asks. He hasn't spoken in so long that Carson and I both blink like we'd forgotten him.

"Pretty much my number one suspect," Carson says. "Kid's been gone for years and now Bay's getting emails about remembering and the assistant who hated Kyle turns up murdered."

"Kyle and Chelsea didn't get along?" I ask.

"According to Ian, they didn't. You sure you were the

only other person in the house?"

I rub damp palms against my jeans. "Why?"

"Because Ian Bay was attacked today and he says his brother did it."

The room is suddenly stuffed with silence. "How bad is he?" I ask at last.

Carson shrugs. "His face is pretty trashed and he's scared, but he'll live—he's already home again. He said his brother jumped him. They fought. Kyle knocked him out cold. You must have interrupted them."

My stomach lurches. So that means . . .

"It must have been Kyle who followed me," I say slowly. "I fell in that sinkhole and he covered it not knowing I was down there."

Carson goes still. "Do you think you could identify him?"

"No, not really. I only saw him from a distance. He was tall . . . had baggy clothes."

"Brilliant, Wicket. That narrows it down. What happened?"

I quickly sketch the details: sinkhole, mud, a whistle that makes my skin crawl, and the footsteps that circled my car. I study the veins standing up on the backs of my hands and tell Carson everything: how I've screwed myself, how I've endangered my sister, how I've endangered my mom.

As soon as I say the *m* word, I cringe. Which mom? What was I thinking?

If Carson notices, he doesn't say anything. In fact, he's

so quiet I finally look up and, out of everything I expected to see, I never thought he'd be smiling.

"What?" I demand.

"Maybe we can use this to our advantage."

Carson sounds so hopeful my heart should lift, but the way he's smiling makes my skin go cold.

"This is excellent," he continues. "Really excellent. Welcome to the side of good, Wick. You're finally going to help do the right thing."

"What?"

"Aside from Ian, you're the only other person who's seen Kyle alive. He'll track you down. He'll have to. So we make that work for us. I'm going to use you. As bait."

Griff puts his hand on top of mine. "You can't do that."

Carson laughs. "You sure? Because I don't think she has a choice. She blew it. He saw her—has probably traced her car by now. She's a loose end."

He's right. I stare at the carpet, not sure I can even say what I need to say because he's right and now I have to live with it.

"I could protect you, Wick," Carson says, and I can hear the smile in his voice. It makes his words slide like butter. "But you'll have to do what I want."

Someone from Carson's team calls, and while he's on the phone, Griff and I leave. I need to get home, call Bren from the house number, and tell her I broke my phone. I'm worried she's been texting me and, since I haven't responded, my adoptive mom will be convinced I'm dead in a ditch somewhere.

It's kinda funny how close to the truth that almost is.

Griff and I walk silently to my car, making it to the end of the dirt drive before he finally turns to me.

"Bait?"

My hands tighten on the steering wheel. "Don't."

"Wick—"

"Don't! Just don't. I have this. It's fine." I focus on the road, acutely aware of Griff's gaze sliding up and down me.

"You didn't know her, did you?"

"Lell? No. Did you?"

"Yeah. Sort of. She lived a few doors down from us. Her mom liked to party with my mom." Griff stretches his legs out, plays with a loose thread on his jeans. "I haven't thought about her in years. I must've been one of the last people to see her before she . . ."

Died. Say it. I can. Why can't he?

We make a left onto the main highway and I force myself to be quiet. I want to ask for more details, but Griff still seems to be working through his memories. He's staring out the window, wandering through cast-off moments he never thought he'd have to remember.

"Her trailer got robbed," he says at last. A cop car passes us and we both sit straighter, watching the rearview mirrors. Griff because he's trying to see if it's his cousin. Me because, well, I'm me.

"I remember my mom dragging me over there so she could see Lell's mom." He sinks into the seat. "I think her name was Reichelle. Anyway, I remember Reichelle just crying and crying and Lell was, I dunno, *smiling* like she was okay with all her stuff being broken and stolen."

Griff shakes his head, cracks his knuckles. "I thought she was as crazy as her mother. Later, when we all found out she ran off with that rich kid, I thought I knew why she didn't care. He was just going to buy her more stuff. It was probably freeing to lose it all."

"Really? I think that's weird. Don't people usually get attached to their things?"

"Yeah, and after a while, it owns you. If you lose it all?" His voice tilts and there's a wistfulness that I've never heard in it before. "You get to build it back up."

"Do you really think she thought they were going to run away?"

"Oh yeah." Griff sighs heavily as we turn into my neighborhood, staring down the gas lanterns as we pass the entrance. "I was barely around her and I knew all about her rich boyfriend. Maybe she already knew they were going to run. Maybe to her, she already had a light in the dark. She thought he was her savior and he killed her."

I park the Mini in the garage and reach for Griff's hand, missing it by a mile. "Griff?"

"I'm going to check the house." He jumps out of the car, slams the door behind him.

"I'll come—"

"Don't."

I do. I push past Griff and he grabs my arm. It's nothing . . . or it should be until Griff's fingers dig in, hitting damaged nerves. My vision ripples.

"Griff."

He drops me like I burned him. "Shit! I'm sorry! I'm so sorry."

"It's fine. Don't worry." I laugh, but it's shaky. "Remember me? The girl whose dad kicked her around? I've been through way worse. I'm durable."

"You should never have to worry about that with me." Griff's smile is bitter. "I'm . . . edgy. I'm sorry, Wicked."

They're always sorry after they hurt you. The thought slithers from the dark and, just as quickly, returns to it, lying in some unused corner to wait. I'm being ridiculous. This is Griff. Not my dad. Not Todd.

I reach for him again and he sidesteps me, goes upstairs to check the bedrooms, leaving me to circle through the downstairs, noting how everything is fine. Perfect even. The lamplight has turned the rooms peach and gold, like we're living in a jewelry box. Knowing Bren, that's probably on purpose.

Except for a tiny smear of dirt still on the kitchen floor, the house is as immaculate as ever. I'm wiping up the mud when Griff walks into the kitchen.

"It's empty. You're safe."

"Thanks." The word's so small I don't think he even hears me.

Or maybe he does, because Griff pauses, hovering as if he wants to tell me something. I step closer and Griff shakes his head, once, like he's clearing it, and says, "I should go."

"Okay." He's out the door now and I sit on the floor listening for his motorcycle long after the sound has disappeared. After a bit, I make my way upstairs and, out of habit, my hand brushes the painted-over mark from where I crashed into the wall as Todd chased me. Between the lighting and the dark paint, you can't see the dent unless you feel for it, but it's there.

In my bedroom, I collapse into my desk chair,

reminding myself that at least one good thing came out of this: The sniffer was installed. I should be able to start working on Bay tonight. The thought is such a relief it takes me a beat before I realize my laptop is on . . . and I never leave it running when I'm not around.

Slowly, I straighten and look around my bedroom. Nothing's been moved. Nothing's been touched.

But suddenly it feels like someone's been here.

Bren takes the cell phone accident better than I expected. It's probably side effects from the mini-vacation to Birmingham—her voice is the lightest I've heard it in weeks—but she tells me it's okay and these things happen. She's even generous enough to offer me one of her old cells. It's completely lovely and makes me feel way worse.

Tears are dangerously close to the surface now and I know I should get off the phone before I blurt how I screwed up everything . . . and yet I can't seem to make myself—hearing Bren's stories about their trip feels like a lifeline.

I wait for them with every light on in the house. And when Bren and Lily finally come up the driveway, I pretend that this is who I really am: a girl whose little sister grabs her for a bear hug, a girl whose adoptive mom grins and waves the moment she sees her.

It feels so good I almost believe it.

"What happened to your face?" Lily hisses, one arm snagged around my neck.

I resist the urge to touch the cut with my fingertips. It looks better than it did. I found some concealer in Bren's bathroom and touched up the edges, thinking about my mom the entire time, how she used to do the same thing after my dad went after her. It was all very, *Maybe she was hit in the head. Maybe it's Maybelline.*

"'S no big deal," I say. "I tripped and fell."

Lily's scowl doesn't last. She's too flipping happy and wants to show me a trophy that's almost as tall as she is. She bounces through the house, alternating between dancing and doing moves from her routine, giving me a play-by-play of the tournament.

I don't remember ever loving anything that much. It makes me feel even worse.

I spend time with Bren, helping her unload the SUV while Lily runs upstairs to shower. Used to be, I needed my sister around to make small talk with my adoptive mom, but we've gotten better.

At least for the three seconds before Bren sees the cut on my face.

"What. Did you. *Do?*"

"Slipped. I have to remember to pick my feet up." Along with Stand Up Straight, Pick Your Feet Up is one of Bren's favorite discussion topics and never gets old.

For her.

My adoptive mom must really be tired though because she sighs and follows me into the house, muttering about ordering takeout. While Bren studies the Pies On Pizza menu pinned to the fridge, I drag Lily's suitcase upstairs.

Only to find my sister in my room.

Lily's facing my bed and I don't even make it through the door before my stomach sinks two inches lower. Something's wrong. "Lil?"

She turns around and heat rolls up my neck.

Lily holds out one hand, the two DVD cases fanned against her fingers. "What are these?"

There's a rushing in my ears—my blood's humming like bees. "Why were you snooping behind my bed?"

"Because I wanted to borrow one of your jump drives. I have pictures I want to download." Dull red climbs Lily's cheeks. "What *are* these?"

"Police interviews."

"With Mom's name on them?"

I swallow. "Yeah. They were . . . given to me." Even though that's true, the words sound lame and Lily's pale eyes narrow. "She was informing on Dad, working with the police against him."

"Were you going to tell me about them?"

"I couldn't figure out what to say." It's true. It's so true. I can't decide what I think of it myself. How am I supposed to explain it to my sister?

"You say, 'I have videos of Mom.'"

"Do you want to watch them?"

Lily jerks her head side to side. "No way. I don't care. I don't get why you had them and didn't tell me."

I can see her hurt, feel it—because we both know the sister code. You can lie to yourself, lie to your parents, but you never ever lie to each other. "Lil, I'm sorry. I really didn't know what to say. She had this whole secret life and I had no idea, did you?"

Nothing. I wait for Lily to digest the revelation. I can't tell if she does. Her features stay hard. "Did you hear what I said?" I ask.

"Do I look like I care?"

"I . . . how could you *not* care?"

Lily throws the DVDs onto the bed. "You're going to mess everything up, Wick. What if Bren finds them?"

"What if she does?" *Crap, what if she does?* How would I explain how I got them? How would I explain what I was doing with them? I glare at my sister and try to look like I've already thought of all these things and, more importantly, thought of ways around them.

It doesn't work. There's a lump in my chest and it's scaling my throat with claws. I'm not going to feel guilty about this. I'm *not*.

"Don't you care why she jumped?" I demand.

"No." And for a moment, Lily looks so sad I think she's lying . . . until I realize that sadness is for me.

"It's more complicated than we knew, Lil. Let me show you some of the interviews."

"No. She left us, Wick. She left us with *him*. I hate her for that."

"She was sick. She wasn't thinking—"

"She was selfish."

I gape. It's not like my sister's comment is anything new. We heard it plenty of times after our mom's death. Counselors, teachers, parents. Everybody had an opinion. It just feels new coming from Lily, like I've just been gouged open.

"You can't forgive her, Wick. I don't want Mom finding these."

"Bren's not our mom."

"Fine, she's *my* mom." Lily glares at me. "Blood doesn't excuse anyone. You don't get a get-out-of-jail-free card because you're related. Family is who you choose—not who you got stuck with because you share a gene pool. Bren doesn't have to care for us. She *chooses* to. She went to *find* us. She's not like . . ." Lily flails one hand and I can't tell if she's batting away our mother or groping for her name. "She left us, Wick. She. Left. *Us*."

The words should not sting. They shouldn't. I taught them to Lily. I repeated them and repeated them until she believed them—because I believed them. Now? Now I don't know.

Once, Lily had been the one to tell me how our mom would never have left us, and she might have been right.

I ruined that.

I've ruined everything.

"Get rid of them," Lily says. "I don't want Bren finding them. She's fragile right now."

Fragile? That's a Norcut word. I cross both arms. "You're

not the only one who cares about her."

"Doesn't look that way."

"So in order to care about Bren, I have to pretend all of this never happened?"

Lily shrugs. "It happened and it doesn't matter anymore. You used to tell me to think of the future. What happened to *you*?"

Carson . . . Todd . . . Griff.

Now I can't figure out what my life would be like if any of them hadn't happened.

I'm not sure I would trade it. Looking at my sister though, I know Lily would. She used to be the other side of me, but we're no longer the same.

And I keep making decisions that take us farther apart.

"Promise me you'll stop, Wick—if not for her then do it for me." Lily's eyes are saucer round, her fury dissolving into fear. "Please?"

"Of course." The words are instant and inevitable. I agree to anything when it comes to my sister . . . so why do I sound rusted? Like some part of me just broke.

"Wick? Lily?"

Bren. For a stomach-churning moment, I'm convinced she heard us.

"Can you both come down here?"

Lily bolts for the door and I'm hot behind her. We clatter down the stairs, skidding to a stop on the landing as my heart rides into my throat.

Carson's standing below us, beaming at me like I'm the good guy.

Or like he is.

"Girls," Bren says, arms clamped tight around her middle. "You remember Detective Carson, don't you? I know you do, Wick. Lily?" She searches my sister's face. "Do you remember?"

Lily nods, serene as some ceramic doll . . . as long as you don't notice how her hands are clenched.

"There have been some new developments," Bren continues. "Some possible leads in your father's case. He's going to monitor the house for the next few weeks. Make sure we're safe."

"It's all going to be fine," Carson says.

All I hear is *you'll have to do what I want.*

I stare at the detective and know I'm never getting out of this.

Still, he's keeping up his end of the deal. I should feel safer now.

Funny how I don't.

It feels like I've only been asleep for minutes when my new
phone vibrates, skittering around on top of my nightstand.
I slap my hand around until I find the cell, hold the screen
a few inches from my face. It's a text from Griff.

morning, wicked

I text

can't wait to see you

And I can't.

Another text message.

What do you have for me?

Ugh. It's a number I don't recognize, but I know it's
Carson. He's using a burner phone.

A body isn't enough?

A few seconds pass and my phone buzzes again.

Maybe your social worker should pay you a visit.

I start typing a text illustration of a hand giving Carson the bird. I'm barely into my tenth dash before the next text comes through:

Maybe I should let him have you. Or them.

My heart heaves. *He's just screwing with you. Stick to your part of the agreement and he'll stick to his.*

Thing is, Carson *would* sacrifice Bren and Lily, and no matter how much I try to ignore this, it simmers under my skin.

I roll to my side, deleting the texts and opening my phone's email app. Thankfully, it's only the usual school bulletins and sports practice schedules. Nothing that can't—crap. There's an email from Ian. He's finished the notes for our project and wants to meet.

I start to blow him off and decide against it. I might as well get this over with so I send a quick message asking Ian to meet me after school tomorrow. Then I switch to the sniffer's email folder. All of Bay's information has been feeding directly to my in-box, making it easy to see everything at a quick glance.

I scroll through the items, wincing at the two texts telling poor Ian to "get the fuck back here." I guess the kid really wasn't kidding when he said he didn't like to be home. The emails between father and son aren't much warmer either. Bay must have sent Ian ten different college applications—all expensive, Ivy League types—with orders for Ian to "get to work."

Wow. If I were Ian, I'd pick the school farthest from Bay

and focus all my efforts on that one.

I linger a moment more on the other emails, checking the sender names . . . and that's when I see it. There's a single email pinned between a scheduling request and something about an upcoming hearing.

It's from Dr. Norcut.

I push myself upright, kick off the blankets. I had no idea they knew each other. I stab the email with my thumb and it opens in another screen.

```
Mr. Bay,
We've had our differences in the past, but
you and I both know how important it is that
we find Kyle before the police do. Please
consider stopping by my office. I have a few
thoughts on where we might find him.
Dr. Allison Norcut
```

Huh. It probably *would* go better for Kyle if he offered himself for questioning. Of course, if you killed someone, you probably wouldn't want to do that.

It kind of sounds like Norcut thinks he did kill someone. Or might have. Or . . . wait . . . is she intending to turn Kyle over at all? Or is she offering to help cover it up?

I reread the email and still can't decide. By finding Kyle before the police do, could they get him out of the country? Definitely . . . right?

Actually, I have no idea. I do know if Bay can look the

other way while my dad tortures my mom, he'd have no qualms with trying to get his kid out of a murder charge.

I punch the forward button, plug in Carson's personal email address. If the detective wants something, he can have this.

Even with two coffees in me, Monday is still an exhausting blur. Go to class. Get homework. Go to another class. Get more homework. All I really want to do is crash, sleep for a week, and then smooth things over with Lily and Griff.

Of course, in order to do that, I'd have to know how.

A lie. I do know. I just have to give it all up. Drop my mom's interviews in the trash. Find something on Carson. Too bad I haven't managed to do either.

Staying late at school doesn't help much either. Ian was supposed to meet me to finish our project, but he never shows and I end up doing most of the work myself. Mrs. Lowe kicks me out of her classroom at six and it's a relief. The hallways are quiet except for the hum of a floor polisher somewhere in the math wing. I'm almost to my locker when the dance team comes giggling toward me. I shuffle out of the way heading for my locker and something catches my eye.

I should say *someone*. Milo's walking straight toward me, pretending not to notice how the entire dance team is staring at him with open mouths.

"What are you doing here?" I whisper-shout.

Milo grins. "Well, Wicket Tate, as I live and breathe."

"Very funny. Seriously, what are you doing here?"

"I wanted to see what you did all day. I can't believe you're actually *going* to high school."

As opposed to hacking the school's systems and giving myself straight As? I try to look superior, like the thought never occurred to me. It isn't working though because Milo's grin slides wider and my face gets hot.

Really hot.

"It's called being honest, Milo. You should try it."

"Why?"

Two more girls walk past us, eyeing him and giggling. Milo smiles at them and they giggle louder, hurrying down the hallway.

He turns to me. "Where's your skinny gargoyle?"

"Why do you care where Griff is?" I ask.

"Maybe I don't." Milo holds up a large shopping bag. "Maybe I'm just here to play delivery."

I should probably be more concerned that Milo had zero problems getting onto campus with what could have been a bomb, but all I can think is: *My new computer. Gimme. Gimme.*

I grab the bag with both hands and Milo laughs. Ignoring him, I pull out a sleek, compact desktop CPU, inhaling its plasticky, canned air scent.

God, I love that.

"That was a seriously fast build!" I slide the computer into the bag and pack the wrapping carefully around it. "Thank you! You didn't have to bring it to me."

"Yeah, I did." Milo smiles at another pair of girls. Wait. No. They're the same ones. They're just coming back for a second look. "You have cops at your house."

Does everyone know where I freaking live? I take a steadying breath, put two fingers to my suddenly jumping right eyelid. "Why were you at my house? You said you were going to contact me for pickup."

Milo shrugs, flashes me that same *I'm sexy and I know it* look. "Curiosity. I wanted to see where you live. I've been watching your work for years. Never suspected you were a girl until Griff brought you by. Gotta say, I was shocked."

"You sound like a sexist asshole."

"Thank you!" Milo props one hand against the lockers, the long sleeve of his shirt slipping down to reveal the edges of his tattoos. He leans a little closer, crowding me, and I back up, my shoulders nudging into the lockers.

This feels like flirting and it shouldn't.

"Well, um, I appreciate you bringing it by, but you might want to get going. You're not a student and I don't want to have to explain what"—I flap one hand—"*this* is."

Because it isn't really anything and yet Milo's looking at me like it is.

I hoist the shopping bag between us. "Thanks again," I say, swerving around Milo and beating feet for the parking lot.

I don't make it three steps before I realize he's following me.

"Side note?" I turn around and he keeps coming. He doesn't stop until our tennis shoes are nearly touching. "I don't appreciate being stalked."

"Yeah, probably not."

"Is that supposed to be an apology?"

Milo touches his fingers to his mouth, eyes pinned to me. "I could think of another way to show you I'm sorry."

My ears go nuclear. "Does that line usually work for you?"

"You tell me."

"I have a boyfriend. Remember him? Your *friend*?"

"Just because you do business with someone doesn't make him your friend."

"Nice," I say, and spin on my heel, power walk to my car.

"Okay, look." Milo strides along next to me and, somehow, that pisses me off even more. He's as tall as Griff, and no matter how fast I walk, they can both easily keep up. "Sorry. I crossed some boundaries. I shouldn't have said that. Any of that. I'd probably be a little freaked out too after what happened with your foster dad."

I want to be pissed. Freaking papers. Freaking Milo. Then again, it isn't like I didn't research him too and, shockingly, he does sound sorry, but as soon as I glance at him, I know it was a mistake. Milo's dark eyes go suddenly bright.

"'Cause your foster dad stalked you, right?" he continues. "And then you had to rely on pure dumb luck to catch him. Isn't that the story in all the papers?"

"Yep," I agree, and even though he couldn't possibly

know the truth, Milo grins like he enjoys it when I lie.

I jam my car keys into the lock and lean the driver's seat down so I can put the computer on the floorboards. Milo bumps one hip against my car, staring down at me.

"You sure you know what you've gotten into?" he asks.

I throw a jacket on top of the bag. "I think I have a pretty good idea."

"You working with your dad again? Is that what this is?"

I don't answer. The only thing worse than working for your career criminal father is being blackmailed into working for a career cop. Let Milo think what he wants.

He searches my face, eyes lingering again on my mouth. "It's a terrible thing to have power. No one knows how to use it."

"You say that like you're the one person who does."

"Hell no. I think you could."

I don't know what to say. Milo being earnest is far more distracting than Milo being . . . Milo. "I'll check the hardware tonight. Thanks again for the work."

"I want to help."

I don't answer. I open my messenger bag, digging around for a folder that should be there and . . . isn't. Crap. I left my project folder in Mrs. Lowe's classroom.

"I want to help," Milo repeats.

"Why?" Wrong thing to say. Not "I don't need help." Not "I work alone." *Why?* Because I'm an idiot.

"How about because it's the closest I'll ever get to being a superhero?" he says. It's a joke and yet it comes across as serious . . . interested.

"Um, yeah, I'm good. Thanks." I peel away, heading for the school, and this time, he doesn't follow. But just as I think I'm in the clear, he calls:

"Then how about because I can get you into Dr. Norcut's computer files?"

"Yeah, I thought that would get your attention." Milo's tennis shoes scrape against the pavement as he approaches me. "That sniffer works brilliantly, if I do say so myself, which I do."

"You were checking the sniffer I bought from you?"

"Well, technically, you didn't buy it. Why do you care?" Milo's trying for defiant, but there's an undercurrent of worry beneath his words. He's expecting me to pull a hissy and I'm pretty freaking close.

I take a breath, blow it between my teeth until there's nothing left in me. "In what *universe* did you think I would be happy about you screwing with my job?"

"The same universe that has cops outside your house and you digging into a judge's personal life. Who's this job for anyway?"

I stare at him, waiting for him to realize I'm never going to tell.

"I can help get you into her files," Milo says, the words pickup-line smooth. "I did all her networking. It was a few years ago when I was still freelancing. I left back doors in case I should ever need them."

Something cold coils in my stomach. *Keeps his fingers in everyone's business, doesn't he?* I grab my phone, check the time. "I have to go."

Milo deflates a little. I'm not sure what he expected from me? Squealing? A kiss? I don't appreciate his interference.

Then again, if I play this right, Milo could be helpful. I try not to think about what that would make me though. Something similar to Carson, I suspect, and the thought leaves me a little sick.

"If you really want to help," I say, "I want to know if anyone's been hired lately to do work against Barton and Moore. Can you ask some of your contacts?"

"Sure. Why?"

"I want to confirm a hunch. I'll keep your other offer in mind, Milo. Thanks." I take off before he can respond, focusing on my project, on my homework, on *anything* except for how I can feel Milo's gaze—heavy, hot—between my shoulder blades.

I slide back inside the school, hit the stairs two at a time, and by the time I reach the second floor, I'm repeating how I've got this, I'm okay . . . and maybe that's why I don't hear the voices.

By the time I do, it's too late.

Matthew Bradford, Sutton Davis, and Eric Williams have pinned Ian to the floor outside the bathroom, Ian's polo shirt rucked up to expose a fish-white belly.

"Leave him alone." I sound pissed and I am, but I have to stab both feet into the tile to keep from running.

All four boys stare at me. Matthew breaks first, nudging Sutton with his elbow. "Should we take out the trash?"

Both of them smile.

Sutton and Matthew move toward me in slow motion as, behind them, Eric wrenches Ian to his feet, the white showing all around Ian's eyes. Sutton and Matthew split, approaching me on either side.

"Don't touch me," I say, and Matthew cocks his head, eyes narrowed.

"You know you want it. Everyone knows all about you and that foster dad of yours." He takes two steps closer, and on the other side of me, Sutton lunges. Instinctively, I shy backward and crash into Matthew's chest. He wraps one arm around my torso, twists both of us around, and shoves me through the bathroom door.

I land on my hands and knees, palms skidding across the black-and-white tile. I sweep my legs under me, ready to jump to my feet, and something heavy knocks me down again.

Matthew. I can't breathe. Too heavy. Too—I jam my elbows backward and connect with his knees.

"Bitch," he mutters, and flips me. My shoulders hit

the floor and his hand circles my throat, tightening until I can't gasp.

I claw his face and Matthew jerks out of reach. His eyes dip lower and his other hand follows. It creeps along my skin with spider legs.

"No!" I stamp both feet into the floor, kicking myself up and unseating him. "Stop!"

"Say please." His words are singsong, and when I don't respond, his fingers snag the bottom of my T-shirt, pulling it up and exposing skin that suddenly burns.

"Stop it!"

"I will if you say please."

"No."

Matthew's smile promises mayhem. "*Say* it," he hisses, taking a fistful of my jeans now, touching me like he owns me and I'm here with him instead of floating above us. I'm here and not here as, somewhere very far away, Ian whimpers and I swallow and Matthew's horrible smile blurs as I watch some other Wick say, "Please."

"Look at you." He pushes to his feet, leaving me curled on the floor. "You sound almost like a real girl."

Laughter. I roll onto my side, putting my back to them. No good though. Their gazes crawl across me like fire ants.

Do not cry. Do not *cry.*

I open my eyes. Ian's a few feet away. His shirt is gone and he's staring at me, face puffy from crying and Kyle's beating. The skin by his hip stands up in ridges, the imprint of a sneaker.

A toilet flushes and Matthew steps around us still laughing. They're all still laughing. I can hear it long after the bathroom door slams shut.

"Are you okay?" I whisper.

"Yeah." Ian swipes a forearm across his eyes, the skin along his cheekbone a stinging purple. "My brother used to beat the shit out of me all the time. That was nothing." He glances toward the stalls. "I think . . . I think they stuffed my shirt down the toilet."

I crane my head and, sure enough, water's spilling onto the tile from the third stall. The whole bathroom will flood. I tuck my arms around me. It's hardly cold, but my skin is sprayed with chills.

"We should go," Ian says, struggling to stand. He sways once and steadies himself. "I don't think they'll come back, but, you know, if they do . . ."

If they do, it'll go far worse for us. I don't think either of us can say the words, but we understand. That's weird to me. It's weird that he gets it. I thought money protected you from this stuff. I thought it could make you belong.

Ian offers me his hand, not meeting my gaze. I recognize that feeling too. Shame. Right now, I'm lit with it. I'm plastic in acid, dissolving in it.

Ian tugs me to my feet, turns away, but not before I see how his ribs are spotted with circular scars.

"What happened?" I ask.

"Lit cigar and my brother's game of cry uncle . . . I never did."

He gives me a shy smile and I smile back. I think we're both fighting tears. "Want to make a run for it?" I ask.

"God, yes."

I stick my head into the hallway, listening. "Okay, I think it's clear."

We hustle toward the parking lot, swiping our stuff from the floor. Thank God, Matthew didn't pitch my keys in the trash or something. I pocket them, waiting for Ian to scrape together his spilled homework.

"Ready?" I ask.

Ian nods, opening his book bag and pulling out a fleece jacket. "I'm sorry I was late for our project stuff," he says.

I snort. "You want to talk about that *now*?"

"We could finish it at my house," Ian continues. We're through the double doors now, almost around the bend to the parking lot, and he's so close I can smell his Trident gum. "I've already done the first two sections. It shouldn't take too long to finish everything, right?"

"Ian, that asshole rolled me around on a *public* bathroom floor. I'm not doing *squat* with our project. I'm going home to scrub myself with a Brillo pad and—oh, shit!"

The parking lot is so empty it's easy to spot the Mini. It's even easier to see what they did to it. "Bitch" is scraped across the driver door in huge, looping letters and "trash" is carved underneath, spilling across the quarter panel in one long arc.

"Nononononononono!" I sprint into the parking lot, Ian chasing after me.

"Wick! Wait!"

I don't. I skid to a stop next to the Mini, kneeling to run my hands along its sides. The gouges are deep. There's no buffing them away. "My car," I whisper, feeling wobbly. It was the nicest thing I ever had and they destroyed it.

The computer!

I check the backseat and, thankfully, nothing looks disturbed.

"Why do they hate you so much?" Ian walks around the car in a slow circle, taking in the damage. He lets out a long sigh when he sees the other side and I know I don't want to look.

"No idea." I'm lying and Ian probably knows it. They hate me because of Todd and Tessa and how everyone thinks the trashy girl probably wanted Todd's attention. Bren may have changed my life, but she will never change who I am to these people. "They're not too fond of you either."

"Yeah. True." Ian looks toward the road, thinking. "They might not hate you as much, you know, if you stayed down more. If you didn't fight back so much."

"So let them stomp all over me?"

Ian shrugs, bends down. "This yours?" he asks, handing me a Droid cell phone. Definitely not mine. One of the boys must have dropped it. I should repay the favor by breaking it into a million little pieces and returning it.

Except that's nowhere near equal to what they just did to my car, to me, to Ian. People like Matthew Bradford and his friends don't just wreck our stuff. They wreck *everything* for people like us.

Stay down? My hand circles the Droid, tightens.

Ian scuffs his shoe against the pavement, watching me. "What're you going to do, Wick?"

I smile at him. "Call my mom's insurance company."

And then I'm going to make Matthew Bradford, Sutton Davis, and Eric Williams pay.

If finding "bitch" keyed on the side of your car is bad, driving it home is worse. Everyone points, looks at me. I stare straight ahead and pretend I don't notice, but my face is seventeen shades of red and my neck . . . well, I glanced once in the rearview mirror to check and once was enough. The skin hurts, but it'll heal. It's not even *that* bad.

And yet I'm still shaking.

I want my mom. It's weird actually. She's been gone for over four years, but the need is so sharp-edged, it feels like I lost her yesterday. I swing around the officer parked by our house. I don't stop to say hi, but I know he gets a good look at the Mini. By the time I'm turning in the driveway, he has his radio ready. Great. It's one more thing I can explain to Carson.

I park my car alongside Bren's, killing the engine as my

adoptive mom walks into the garage. She stops dead, gaze pinned to the Mini.

Then to me.

"What happened?" Bren demands.

I hesitate. There's no getting around the truth even though I brainstormed lies the whole way home. It's not that I want Matthew and his cretins to get out of this. I just want to deal with them on my own and yet now, looking at Bren, feeling Matthew's hands branded on my skin, feeling sudden tears prickling my eyes . . . I want to tell her everything and I want *her* to fix it. I want someone to save me because I'm too damn tired to save myself anymore.

Griff once said Bren would help me, that she'd never want me to handle Carson alone. If that's true, I'd have to tell her.

I edge a little closer. "It was keyed by some kids at school."

"Which kids?"

"Matthew Bradford, Eric Williams, and Sutton Davis." I pause, waiting to see Bren's face flush red in anticipation of the ass kicking she's about to deliver, but it never happens. When I say the boys' names, she flinches.

"*Alan* Bradford's son?" Bren asks.

"I guess."

Bren swallows, swallows again. "I have a breakfast meeting with Alan day after tomorrow. He's the only person who's returned my calls in weeks and—and—are those *bruises*? What happened to your *neck*?"

"Matthew Bradford," I whisper.

Bren makes a strangled noise deep in her throat. "I don't understand. Did he . . . touch you?"

Are you stupid? Of course, he freaking touched me! I try to work my mouth around something to say and, suddenly, understand what she means. "No, he didn't touch me like that."

*He just humiliated me. He made me feel like trash. He made me—*I inhale hard against the tears. If I start crying now, I won't be able to stop.

Bren's shoulders go slack and she rubs her forehead, eyes still locked on my neck. "Do you want to make a statement? Do you want to go to the police?"

Yes . . . no. I'm tripping over her tone. This is Bren. *Bren.* Shouldn't she be making me? I don't understand. Her tone is worried about me . . . not angry with them.

"I'm not sure," I say at last.

"Wick, if he hurt you, we have to go to the police."

She sounds stronger this time, but still not herself, and as I stare at her hand (shaking) and how it plays with her nonexistent pearls (when was the last time she wore them?), I start to see everything else: how her cardigan hangs looser . . . how there are smudges under her eyes . . . how I wasn't the only person Todd took things from.

Oh. I blink. Her tone is worried because Bren needs Alan Bradford. *We* need Alan Bradford.

"I'm sorry," I say. The apology is so fast it feels greased. It's only afterward that I catch myself because why should I be sorry? What's more, why do I *feel* sorry? I feel like this is somehow my fault, like I've let her down.

I get my bag and new computer from the backseat, carefully tucking my jacket around the bag. This conversation is uncomfortable enough without explaining why I'm dragging around a CPU.

"Tell me what happened," Bren says.

I don't want to anymore. "Matthew and his friends were bothering someone. I intervened and they . . . Matthew." I pause, waiting for her as hope—I just didn't realize what it was until now—drains from me. "It's no big deal. It was roughhousing, stupid stuff really, and it just got out of hand. They probably thought keying my car was funny."

Our eyes meet, and for a very long time, all I can hear is my breathing.

"Why couldn't you just get along with them?" Bren asks.

I freeze, positive I heard her wrong. "I'm sorry I . . . *what*?"

"Why couldn't you just get along with them?" Bren hunches in half, arms wrapped tight around her torso. At first, I think she's holding herself back . . . then I realize she's just holding herself up. That's how much I've disappointed her.

That's how much I've failed.

Heat chases up my neck. "I can't get along with them because they're assholes."

"You could have ignored them. You could have *pretended* you liked them."

I recoil. "It doesn't matter if I pretend. They don't care.

They hate me. There's nothing I can do about it."

Bren's eyes go hollow. "There's always something you can do about it, Wick. This is survival. You have to learn to play right with the right people and you better learn it now because your future will depend on it."

Depend on them? I . . . can't. The realization slams me in the stomach. If that's my future then I don't want it.

I stumble from the car, dashing upstairs and slamming my bedroom door. How can she not understand? I throw my messenger bag onto the floor and set the computer next to my desk, dropping into the chair beside it.

Is this what life is? Just letting people use you? Bren acts like it's okay because she knows it's happening, like she's in control. She's not. None of us are.

See how she was used?

I sit straight. They're not my words, but they feel like mine. They're crawling out of some corner I've always kept hidden. Until now. I pivot to face my old computer, powering it on and opening my chemistry notebook. Forget Lily and Bren. If they want to pretend bad things don't happen, fine. Doesn't mean I'm going to.

I flip to the page with the passwords and log in to the police department's employee site, using Detective Thompson's information first.

It doesn't work. Small, red letters appear to the side of the password box saying "User already in use." I glance at my phone. It's almost nine at night. What are the odds Detective Thompson is working this late? He might be. I don't know the guy personally. Maybe he's a workaholic.

Or maybe someone else is in the system like I am.

I tap my fingers against the side of my keyboard. Whatever. I'll try the other log-in. I enter Sheriff Denton's info and another menu opens. I'm in. Thank God for Molly the Receptionist. The main dashboard is set for accessing closed and open cases, tickets, and court appointments. Gotta love when people are organized.

I click the Closed Case link and use the search function to type in my mom's case number. It takes the system a beat, but the file populates with some case notes and a summary of contents for her evidence box. No video files though.

I open the Content Summary link and scan the list. Okay, here we go. In addition to witness statements, there are also "recorded interviews with victim." No mention of how many though. I've received almost forty video files at this point. Could there be more?

I hit the back button and skim through the case notes. Someone named Lawrence Haralson was lead detective, and a quickie Google search reveals he's retired and living in Alabama. Detective Sams, his partner, now works for the Atlanta PD.

Let's see what else. . . . I scroll to the bottom of the notes, stop. Haralson and Sams weren't the only people present during the interviews.

So was Bay.

My fingers . . . toes . . . face go cold. Numb. Bay knew. He was in on it. Did Carson know? Is that why he picked me to help him? I place both hands on my desk, leaving smeary prints on the wood.

Well, that explains why Bay always denied my mom's restraining order requests. It would have taken her away from my father, away from a case that would have padded his résumé.

I almost laugh. No wonder Carson doesn't like him—they're the same.

Enough of that though. What am I going to do? I start to pull off my jacket and it's the weight in the pocket that reminds me.

The Droid.

I can suddenly breathe. While I don't know what to do

about Bay, I *do* know what I'm going to do with this. I mash the power button, waking the phone from sleep mode. No security code. Candy, meet baby.

Dropping onto my bed, I surf through the phone's settings until I get to its name: Matthew's Phone. I have the sudden urge to giggle. It's Bradford's cell. Oh, this is going to be *good*!

I switch to the contact lists. Girls from school. Guys from school. Other names I don't recognize. Nothing useful. I check his email and it's a little more interesting. Might be fun to infect his parents' computers with a virus. Something nasty. If they think the email's coming from Matthew, they'll click without thinking.

Promising. Still not grabbing my interest though.

What about text messages?

I flip through another set of screens. Ah, yes, someone's a disgusting pig. I scroll through the conversations. Matthew's been sexting with his girlfriend. I wonder if his mommy would be bothered by that? I check her email address and realize Matthew's mom works for a restaurant chain known for its Christian values. That could be fun. I wonder if her coworkers would be bothered by Matthew's texts?

Her work email is listed under the contacts. Maybe I could send an email blast of darling Matthew's requests. Again, promising, but I want this to hurt.

On to the video files. He has four or five. The first few are worthless—just Matthew and his friends goofing around. The last one makes me smile.

Bingo.

For exactly four minutes and thirty-six seconds, Matthew Bradford, Eric Williams, and Sutton Davis pass the phone around, filming themselves drinking.

And smoking.

I replay the video, peer a little closer at the screen. That's not just smoking. That's pot.

I can't help my grin. Holy shit, this is going to be good.

The guys are still in their lacrosse jerseys and they're passing a bottle of Jack back and forth. We're not talking HD clarity here, but every time they turn around, you can see the names printed across their shoulders. So much for their reputation as good boys.

I watch the video twice more, and each time, the knot in my stomach twists harder. This is going to be awesome.

I take my new computer out of the bag and spend a few minutes hooking it up to the rest of my peripherals. It'll still need updates before I'm fully functional, but I'm more than ready for this little job. I plug in the last cable, noticing Milo burned some sort of symbol into the plastic casing. It looks like the Cheshire cat's smile from *Alice in Wonderland*, the toothy grin after the cat has disappeared.

I like it.

After the CPU powers up, I plug the phone into the USB and wait for the video file to download. In terms of what to do, I have a few options. Honestly though there's only one place that's perfect for such a windfall: our high school's YouTube channel.

I settle into my chair and start working on obtaining access to the school's account.

Next morning, I wake up late again and Bren drops me off just before the first bell rings. We don't talk much on the ride over. I fiddle with the scarf around my neck. Bren switches radio stations. She pulls into the school's drop-off lane, and just as I'm about to slide out of her car, Bren grabs my hand, holds it tight.

"I'm sorry for yelling at you, Wick. I completely screwed up. I feel terrible."

"I'm sorry about the car."

"It's not your fault." Except I know she thinks it kind of is. If I weren't such a freak, if I weren't such an outsider, if I weren't so . . . *me*, this stuff wouldn't happen.

"It's not your fault," Bren repeats, and I smile like I believe her. "I know you said you don't want to make a statement, but I'll support you if you change your mind."

I shake my head. No need to change my mind. "I appreciate the ride, but I can drive the Mini like it is. No big deal." It's totally a big deal. I'm just not going to admit it. Thankfully, though, Bren shakes her head. "Okay . . . I could walk then."

"You're *not* walking. What would people say?"

"That I like to exercise?" Or that after her husband went to jail Bren had a hard time making ends meet. I know that's what she's thinking. Worse, I know that's what the neighbors are thinking too. It's weird to live in a world where not having an extra car for your teenager is considered poverty.

Wish I could acquaint her with what not having enough money really means.

Then again, no I don't. I would never want Bren to worry like that. She'd probably stroke out. She's annoying, but she's mine.

"I really am sorry, Wick. This mom stuff . . . it's a lot harder than I thought."

"It's okay. Really. I'll see you tonight." I close the car door, head through the school's front entrance and make a left for my locker. I put away the books I was supposed to use for last night's lab project and pull out my English notebook.

"Did you hear about the video that was uploaded to the school's YouTube account?"

Ian. I try to look surprised though it doesn't really matter. He's watching the hallway behind me and picking at the scab on his lower lip. *Does he know?* "No, I didn't. What happened?"

"Someone put up a video of Matthew, Eric, and Sutton drinking and smoking weed. It was at an away game last month. They've been expelled."

My hand hovers on top of my history book. Did I just have a twinge of guilt? Because I am not going to feel guilty. I'm *not.* "How did they know it was at an away game?"

"Dunno. Stuff behind them, I guess. Because they were drinking and doing drugs at a school function, they were automatically expelled." Ian looks at me, waits for a response.

I stare right back at him, feeling Matthew's hand around my neck.

Under my shirt.

My stomach heaves. I turn to my locker, throw books around until I can breathe again.

"You look really tired today," Ian says.

"Gee thanks."

"You should probably wear more makeup."

And you should probably learn some damn manners. I nearly say it, but, looking at Ian, I can't. He's too freaking pathetic. He's too . . . lonely. It's written in his skin, in the way he slides closer to me, almost vibrating because someone's talking to him.

The ache in my chest is unexpected and unwelcome and I can't make it go away. There are jocks and populars and nerds and kids like Ian who are so desperate for attention they'll hunt it anywhere, making themselves so annoying no one wants them around.

"Look, Ian—"

"Wick!"

I turn, smiling before I even seen him. Griff weaves through the hallway, eyes pinned to me, and my grin falters. He doesn't look happy. He looks . . . pissed.

Griff knows.

We take the long way around to my English class. Griff walks as close to me as he usually does—only this time he doesn't touch me and all I want is to grab his hand.

I grip my book bag's straps instead.

"I know you did it," he says at last.

I start to lie, but this is Griff and, even if I wanted to, I think he'd see through it. "They attacked Ian and me in a bathroom *and* they keyed my car. They had it coming."

Griff jerks. "Attacked?"

"They keyed my car," I repeat. It's easier to say anyway. I'll tell him everything else later. When I'm ready.

"You could have filed a police report, gotten the school to give you the security cam footage."

"Only I was parked near the science wing and that camera hasn't worked since we were freshmen."

Griff winces, nods. He's still not meeting my eyes though. "I can't believe you didn't call me."

"I—I—" I didn't and the realization feels like someone dropped me. I was so busy being pissed, so focused on bringing Sutton, Matthew, and Eric down. I just didn't . . . think.

Or maybe I did, because the next realization drops me harder, faster: I was scared he would look at me like Bren did.

Like he might be doing now.

My stomach rolls into my throat. I walk faster, but can't outrun Matthew. He's nowhere near and yet I can smell him—citrus gum and sweat and the bleach from that damn bathroom.

Griff drifts a little closer to me, keeping pace. "How did you get the video?"

"Bradford dropped his phone. It was the video or the sexting. I preferred the video."

"What are you trying to prove?"

"That they can't keep pushing us around."

He gapes at me. "So you got them *expelled*?"

Not intentionally. I'm glad I did though. The satisfaction is a warm, red rubber ball deep in my gut. Those boys were bullies. They hurt people. It's about time someone returned the favor.

"I don't regret doing it. I'm glad they're screwed."

Griff passes one hand through his hair. He's speechless and I'm not sure how I feel about that. I hate it . . . but I'm not ashamed. Griff doesn't understand what it was like.

"You talk about saving people, Griff. You don't actually do it. I did."

"This isn't saving people. This is revenge."

"And now they won't hurt us anymore. They're expelled. How is that *not* saving kids like us in the future?" I stare at Griff—*my* Griff—and it feels like I'm looking at a stranger. He doesn't understand. How can he not understand?

I fidget with the strap on my book bag. "If you don't act, all your talk is just words, Griff."

The late bell rings and I look up, catching Griff staring at me. He shakes his head. "I gotta go."

He lopes off without kissing me, and for the first time, I don't mind. Well, I don't mind as much. I was right to upload that video. I *was*.

Deep in my bag, my cell buzzes. I want to ignore it, but almost anything is better than thinking about Griff being mad at me and how I'm mad at him.

I jam my thumb against the answer button. "Yeah?"

"I love it when you sound all pissed off. It's sexy."

"What do you want, Milo?"

He laughs. "You really want me to answer that?"

"No." It's the usual teasing, but there's something floating underneath his joking tone that makes me stiffen. Milo is seriously excited.

"Actually, it's more what *you* want, Wick. The guy who called off those guards? I found him."

"Will he talk to us?" I should have said "me" and I don't bother correcting it.

"Yeah. We gotta move now though. He's clearing out, will be gone by tonight so dump your shit and meet me outside."

I hesitate. I can't just leave school.

Can I?

"Give me five minutes," I say.

I dump my books in my locker and walk off campus with two stoners who are sneaking into the woods to smoke. It would come as a surprise to most people, but this will be the first time I've ever skipped class and it's actually crazy easy. I'm kind of aggravated I haven't done it before. The stoners hunker down in the woods along a side street and Milo meets me at the corner. I jump into his battered Crown Vic and we peel off.

"For the record, I'm really digging the scarf," Milo says.

"For the record," I mimic, fiddling with the seat belt only to find it's broken, "I don't do stuff like this. I'm actually a straight-A student."

"I figured as much." Milo makes a right onto the highway, heading for the interstate. "That's how I knew I had something good. You were willing to come to me."

He leans against his armrest, grins at me like he's won something, and I have to bite the inside of my cheek to keep from smiling.

"Shut up and drive, Milo."

"Whatever you say."

"Damn straight."

He laughs and, after a beat, so do I.

We end up in a run-down apartment complex just outside of Atlanta. As it turns out, Milo has done work for this guy before. They're not exactly friends, but Milo's confident he'll answer any questions I have.

"How do you figure?" I ask, rushing to keep up as he strides across the parking lot. "Because you're going to ask nicely?"

"Something like that," Milo says, and uses his fist to knock on apartment 3A's door. Nothing. Milo beats on the door again.

"Maybe he's not home," I say, and Milo gives me an *of course he's home* look.

"Corey," he yells, staring into the peephole. "I gotta talk to you. Now."

I'm about to ask Milo if he has any other genius ideas when the lock scrapes and a moon-pale face wedges between the door and the jamb. Corey, I presume, glares at Milo like he wants to set him on fire.

"Let me in," Milo says. "We have to talk."

The other guy's mouth presses thin, but the door

swings open. Milo motions me to go first while he watches the parking lot behind us. I'm barely across the threshold before Corey makes an angry buffalo snort.

"Who's the chick?"

The chick. Like I'm freaking furniture.

"You remember the Walker job?" Milo asks, shutting the door behind us and turning the lock. It makes Corey shift from foot to foot.

"Yeah."

"She did it."

"Bullshit."

"No shit."

"She's a *girl*," Corey says.

I roll my eyes and neither of them notices. They're too busy glaring at each other.

"Fine. Whatever. Be fast, man," Corey says. "I'm on my way out."

Yeah, no kidding. The small apartment is almost empty. Only things left are an ancient sofa pushed against the wall and drag marks in the floor dust.

"I want to know about the work you did a few days ago," Milo says. "Calling off Barton and Moore's guys."

"It was a job. What else is there to know?"

"Who'd you do it for?"

Corey pales. "I don't have time for this." He picks up a battered duffel bag and jerks it over his shoulder. "I am so gone."

"You won't be if I burn you." Milo says it so pleasantly

that it takes Corey a moment to process the words. He stares at us, slack-jawed.

"You wouldn't."

Milo cocks his head, the ghost of a smile playing at the corners of his mouth.

I search his face, trying to find the lie . . . and I can't. He's serious.

"I'll make it so you'll never work again," Milo says.

"You can't."

"I can."

"This is all I have."

That really gets Milo smiling. "Then tell me what I want to know."

"**I got the** first job through one of the message boards," Corey says. He keeps playing with the strap on his duffel bag, eyes returning again and again to the apartment's sole window. "It was good money, like *really* good money, and after I finished he offered me the Benson and whatever work. It wasn't too hard. They had a flaw in their cell phone messaging system."

Corey readjusts his duffel bag. "Stupid how their guys kept putting off the OS updates for their phones, but good for me, you know, 'cause I was able to get in and text one of the guards. I told him they were both called to HQ."

HQ? Like we're living a spy movie? On the other side of Corey, Milo smirks.

"So I told the guards to report back and they did and

then—" Corey fiddles with his phone for a beat before showing us the screen. Lell Daley smiles up from some newspaper article. I look away, my nose suddenly filled with the scent of mud. "And then *that* happened and I figured that's what he needed to find and I was finished, but I was contacted again."

"Same guy as before?" I ask.

"Yeah." Corey curls into himself, shoulders hunched. "He wanted me to do another job for him."

"What kind of job?"

"Getting into some guy's office at the courthouse, which is, like, totally impossible because that asshole powers down his computer every night."

Milo's expression turns disgusted. "Have some pride, man. You could have found a work-around."

"Like *what*? Breaking into the office? The client's not even sure the pictures he wants are even on this lawyer's computer."

"Pictures of what?" I ask.

Corey wiggles in place, attention focused on Milo. "He didn't say and, before you start, *hell no* I didn't ask him. That's some fucked-up shit that he's in the middle of. You should've seen that BlackBerry he sent me—"

I stiffen. "BlackBerry?"

"Yeah, that was my first job for him, breaking into this BlackBerry. It was shipped to my PO box. Wasn't too difficult to work through the passwords, get inside. Girlie was a piece of work. She was keeping dirt on the guy she was working for. Whatever he wanted wasn't there though."

Girlie? Surely it couldn't be . . . "Do you remember the girl's name?"

"Hell yes, I do." Corey chews the side of his thumb. "It's only in all the papers. Chelsea Martin."

"Any idea what he was hoping you'd find?"

"Yeah, supposedly she had some pictures. If she did, she wasn't keeping them stored on her phone and I told him that and then he asked me to break into the county courthouse."

"Which office?"

"I don't remember." Corey's eyes skitter around the room, landing on everything and nothing. "Some guy named Ed."

"Ed Price?"

"Yeah, that's it. The Chelsea chick had sent the pictures to Ed and my guy wanted them back before Ed found them."

Huh. Ed Price is running against Bay in the election and, if Corey's contact wanted the pictures before Price saw them, could they be something that would damage Bay? "Anything else?"

"I'm not sticking around to find out. Can I go now?"

"Yeah, sure, get lost," Milo says. "We never had this conversation."

Corey pushes past him, muttering something that sounds like "asshole." I speed-dial Carson, and on the third ring, the detective answers. "I was right," I say. "The guards were called off by a guy who got into Barton and Moore's security."

"Good. Bring him to me."

"Can't." The word brings Milo up short. He studies me with raised eyebrows, wondering what I'm saying I can't do. "He's gone."

Milo moves to the door, ready to retrieve Corey, and I snag his sleeve, shake my head hard. I'm not bringing Carson more people he can leverage.

"Can't or *won't*?" the detective spits.

"Can't," I repeat, my eyes on Milo, who's drawing closer, the light scent of his cologne circling him.

Circling me.

"When I said find dirt on Bay—"

"I did. He doesn't know who he was hired by. Everything was anonymous. He did receive Chelsea Martin's BlackBerry. She was compiling information against the Bay family—information she kept in the phone's notes."

"Anything good?"

"Pictures are supposed to be pretty good. Or at least worth breaking into Ed Price's office to get them, so have fun with that."

"Find them for me."

I blink, unable to believe what he's saying. "What good would they do you? Without a warrant, you can't use them in court."

"There are always other uses for information. If this guy wants the pictures, then I want the pictures. Get them for me."

"I don't do break-ins." Then again, I didn't used to drug people either. I shake myself, but Jason's accusatory eyes are still branded on my brain.

"Get them for me," Carson repeats.

"I don't—" Yes, I do, or I will, because, suddenly, the word *leverage* is behind my eyelids and in its glow *damage* steps out of the shadows. If I could get access to Bay's work computers . . . I could make this work for me.

"What if I said I could take down the courthouse's security system for you?" Carson asks.

I hesitate, pretend my heart isn't hammering in my ears. "No way."

"Really? What if I told you that if you do this, I'll let you go?"

It knocks my breath askew. He's lying, but it doesn't matter because I just got an idea. I look at Milo and grin. "It's a deal."

I slip into school between fourth and fifth periods. Considering I've missed almost three hours of class, I'm half expecting Principal Matthews to be waiting, but either I'm lucky or he's busy because I get in without any difficulty.

Tomorrow will be a different story. I'll need an excuse and I spend a few hours in my room, trying to decide on one. I'm known for migraines so that would work. If I play the role of Tragedy Girl, I could claim a panic attack.

A branch taps the window. Griff. I spin my desk chair and . . . he's not there. It's just the wind kicking around. He must not be coming.

I could go to him.

"Bren?" I stick my head into the hallway, listen to my adoptive mom typing on the computer she keeps in her bedroom. There's no way she'll let me go to Griff's place.

She hates the neighborhood so . . . "Could I go to Lauren's for a bit?"

I cross my fingers, praying Bren hasn't heard about Lauren staying home from school to care for her mom. "I need some help with homework."

"Sure, honey. Are you okay to walk? I have to take Lily to ballet in—oh, shoot—twenty minutes. I could drop you off on our way."

"I'll walk. No worries." Bren doesn't respond, but I can feel her objections coming on so I stuff my feet into tennis shoes and hustle out of the house. The schizophrenic winter weather has warmed, making the walk almost pleasant. I know exactly where I'm going. Griff and I lived a street apart for a few years and, even though I've never been there, I know which trailer he shares with his mom.

I'm just not quite sure how to announce myself once I arrive.

It ends up not mattering though because Griff's under the carport, working on his Honda motorcycle. As soon as my sneakers hit the gravel drive, he puts down his wrench, watching me walk out of the dark like he's been waiting.

"Hey."

"Hey." I hesitate. I'm doing that a lot lately with him and I hate it. "I wanted to see you."

Griff gets up, wiping both hands on his black jeans. "I don't know if that's a good thing right now, Wick."

A kick to my stomach and I ignore it. "I wanted to tell

you Carson's given me one last job. If I do it, I'm out. I'm done."

I'm an idiot. I've just laid my words at his feet like the pathetic little girl I am, that I've turned into. *I'm done* is lying there like a gift and I'm standing there like a moron.

Under the orangey carport light, Griff's eyes are electric green. "What's the job?"

"Break into Ed Price's office. I found the hacker that called off Bay's security guards. He was also hired to find some pictures that were sent to Price. They're supposed to be in the guy's office. If I get them, I'm done."

"How are you going to do it?"

"Carson's working out the details, but he's going to have the security system disabled. After that, it's easy. In and out."

Griff nods. "I'll go with you."

"You don't have to."

"No."

"Are you still mad at me about the YouTube thing?"

"I'm still trying to understand you." A door slams inside the trailer, startling both of us. Griff's head dips, shifting the light on his face so his eyes turn into gouged-out holes. "Now really isn't a good time. My mom's . . . not well again. Can I take you home?"

"I could walk."

"Or you could ride." A smile walks slowly across his mouth and I know both of us are remembering the first time he talked me into riding with him.

"Yeah, sure."

Griff cranks the motorcycle and passes me a helmet as I climb on behind him. I love this part: the speed, the touching, the way Griff guns the bike so we shoot out of the neighborhood like we're flying. It's great until it's not because we get to my house too quickly and I have to tell each finger to let him go.

"You really believe Carson?" Griff asks, fastening my helmet to the back of his bike.

"Yes," I say, and I almost leave it at that—almost—because if I'm supposed to be able to tell him everything, I'll start with this: "He'll have to let me go, Griff. I'm going to load a virus onto the judge's computer. It'll upload Carson's digital fingerprints throughout the file system. He said his boss didn't want him anywhere near Bay and I'm going to make it look like he was personally going through the judge's files. Carson tries to touch me again and I'll activate the virus. It's the leverage we've been looking for."

I waver. Did I repeat the word because it is? Or because I'm reminding Griff that leverage was his idea? I wasn't honest with him about the YouTube stuff, about what happened. I didn't give him a chance before, but I can now.

Griff studies me. "And the situation with your mom?"

My mom. The two little words I thought I'd burned and buried. "I don't know."

He nods, spends a moment checking the bike's fuel line. "It bothers me that you don't tell me the truth. You had your mom, Carson, the guys from school . . . all this *stuff* and you didn't tell me any of it. It makes me feel like I don't matter."

"I didn't tell you because you *do* matter."

"You lied."

"I didn't—it wasn't—"

It was. I stare at Griff and the knowledge stains me. "I'm sorry, Griff. I was afraid."

His eyes jerk to mine. "Why? I know what you are in the dark, Wick. I've seen it and you've seen me. I want you for you."

"I didn't . . . think you would." I hiccup and cover my mouth with my sleeve. I'm not going to cry. I'm not going to cry. "I was . . . ashamed and I know how much I have to lose and . . ."

I want you for you.

I hiccup again, smile behind my balled-up hand. "How have we never talked about this?"

"You never *wanted* to talk about it. I was waiting for you to be ready, but you're dealing with all that PTSD shit and you're healing—"

"You think I'm damaged?"

He says nothing and the nothing says everything. "It isn't flattering that you think I'm fragile."

"It's not . . . okay, yeah." He forks one hand through his dark hair, spiking it. "You're not fragile. This shit does . . . *damage* you, Wicked. I can't keep watching that."

"You won't have to anymore." I drop my hand, grin even though tears are still crowding my eyes. "He won't be able to touch me ever again—not if I upload that virus."

Griff rubs one palm against his chest. "You kill me, you know that? I can't breathe when you smile."

He sounds pissed and sad . . . and amazed.

"Can we try again?" I whisper.

"I never stopped." Griff cups my face in his hand. "No matter how this turns out, Wicked, remember I was the lucky one. When it comes to you . . . I am so lucky."

Griff touches his lips to mine and I press into him, realizing that this kiss might be what I really came for. I hook my hands into his shirt, feeling his breathing go uneven and fast. I will fix this.

No matter the cost.

I watch Griff drive off, and once I can no longer hear his bike's exhaust, I head inside. I'm staring at my feet, thinking first about the Bays and then about Carson. I don't even notice how the porch is dark until I'm up the steps, reaching for the door handle.

And that's when I see it.

Someone's nailed a dead rat to my front door.

Move.

I can't.

Move *now*.

I wrench my feet forward and check the front door's locks. They don't look damaged. I check the windows; the inside rooms don't look disturbed.

The porch light is out though. I feel around in the lantern and the bulb still seems to be intact. Someone must have loosened it, using the shadows for better coverage. I give it a twist and the yellow light returns to life. I'm thrilled until I realize I am now up close and personal with the rat. Thanks to the newly restored light, I can see my tiny reflection in its glassy eyes and the splash of blood on the welcome mat. Uck.

What the hell is going on here? If it's a scare tactic, it worked. I'm scared.

I'm also pissed.

I am *so* going to find out who did this.

After I get rid of the evidence. Bren and Lily will be home soon. There's no explanation in the world that will dismiss this, which means . . .

I stare at the rat, shudder. I'm going to have to touch it. Worse, I'm going to have to un-impale it from the door. Using what? Not my bare hands, that's for damn sure.

I unlock the front door and dump my stuff in the hallway. It takes me a minute, but I find some of Bren's Williams-Sonoma oven mitts in a drawer. I stare at them for a bit, trying to decide if I'm really going to do it. I think you go to rich people hell for stuff like this.

Screw it. I put on both gloves and try not to squeal like a three-year-old girl when I pull the rat off the door. Even through the heavy fabric, I can feel its bones and muscles give beneath my fingers. Giving, not breaking free. Shit. The body doesn't want to move. I'm going to have to pull harder.

I fight a dry heave and yank. Hard. The body gives, coming away from the door and into my hands.

"Ohgodohgodohgodohgodohgod!" I whimper, realizing I should've brought a trash bag and now I have nowhere to put the rat. I carry it into Bren's office, dump the body in her wastepaper basket, and pitch the gloves in after it.

If Bren asks about the oven mitts, I'll pretend to know nothing. It won't be much of a stretch. I avoid the kitchen at all costs.

After bundling up the body and burying it in the

outside garbage bin, I clean everything: the porch, the mat, the door. I use enough bleach to kill every brain cell I have. Even after I finish, I still feel dirty.

While I'm washing and rewashing my hands, I let my computer boot up, and once everything is going, I log in to our security camera feed, wrapping one arm around my stomach as I rewind the video, looking and looking until . . . *there*. There he is.

The security cameras got him. It just isn't going to help me.

The guy—dark jeans, long-sleeved dark T-shirt—eases onto the porch. He's looking down. Now he's looking behind him. Now he looks at the camera. He's wearing some sort of a zombie mask. It's the last thing I see before he spins the bulb off the connection and the porch goes dim and the image goes too grainy to see anything more than shadows.

Shit.

I rewind the video, play it again. Still no good.

Honestly? I expected to see Kyle, but this isn't him. In fact, I have no idea who it is . . . wait . . . maybe . . .

I slow the video, playing it frame by frame. The mask totally screws identifying the guy's face. There's something about the way he moves on the balls of his feet though . . . the way his shoulders round under his T-shirt . . . it looks familiar.

The guy reaches for the porch light, his hand and wrist

and *watch* all facing the camera. Recognition punches me in the gut.

It's Jason Baines.

Which means this isn't just a scare tactic or even just retaliation for the roofies. He knows I've been informing and he's reminding me what happens to people who become narcs.

I rub my eyes, feeling the dull thump of an oncoming migraine. Jesus, what have I done? What have I managed to get myself into?

Stop it.

Better to ask: What am I going to do to get out of it?

I don't have an answer for that one.

I close the video file and return to the security system's feed. With Todd and my dad in jail, it's been so long since I've done this, it almost feels like someone else's life and, watching the empty yard and street, I start to think this might be what I do best: watching and waiting.

This isn't the way I wanted things to end up. I have a chance for my very own happily ever after. I can't let details like Jason Baines or Kyle Bay get in the way.

But what do I do about them?

My stomach growls and I press my palm to it. I haven't had anything to eat since this morning so I pad downstairs, keeping the lights off as I pull all the curtains shut. There's still no sign of Carson's watch detail and I don't know what that means. I do know the darkness makes me want to come out of my skin.

Get a grip. Get a grip. Get a grip. I wander into the kitchen to fix a sandwich and avoid the windows. God, it's quiet. I refuse to say "too quiet" even though the description kind of fits. I pick up the television remote and tell myself I'm being a cliché. Too bad it doesn't stop my hands from shaking.

Reality television.

Reality television.

Really stupid sitcom.

Carson?

It's the evening news and they're showing a clip of the detective standing behind a podium, addressing a small group of people. His hair is smoothed back and his clothes look pressed.

"We can't discuss the case details at the moment," he says, both hands gripping the microphone. "We can tell you the body discovered at the Bays' residence is Lell Daley's."

The camera cuts to a picture of Lell and Kyle smiling, mouths slightly apart as if they were a gasp away from a belly laugh. She looks so in love it makes my stomach squeeze.

The picture vanishes, replaced with a close-up of Carson's face. "While I cannot confirm that Miss Daley's death has anything to do with Judge Bay or his family, I can assure you we are taking every precaution possible to protect *all* involved parties in the wake of these terrible tragedies."

Well, protect what's left of them. I watch the interview a little longer before switching it off. I'd rather deal with the silence. The detective's right. It has to be the older son. All of this seems so . . . family-related. Remember me? What if Kyle's trying to tell Bay to remember their dead mother? I know as well as anyone what losing a wife and mom can do to a family. What if Mrs. Bay's death tore them apart? Could work . . . except the Chelsea thing doesn't fit. Or maybe it does—she wasn't a blood relative, but she was there all the time, taking care of Bay; that sort of makes her family. How to explain Lell then?

I blow out a sigh. If not the family thing, there are no other connections between the victims.

Except for me.

Doesn't that prove the rule or whatever? I'm the only person who's outside the killer's scope and that's because I was stupid enough to get caught. Plus, he hasn't gone after me.

Yet.

I take another bite of sandwich and stare at the darkened television screen. Carson's getting better at the whole press junket thing—clothes, hair, manners. He actually said thank you to one of the reporters. I had no idea he knew the words. Maybe it's all part of his whole rising-star career thing. He wants to look more like a hero and less like, well, Carson. I grin, thinking about how he'll probably want an assistant next.

Wait a minute. An assistant. Judge Bay isn't the only connection among the victims.

So is Carson.

At school, Lauren said she saw him talking to Chelsea on several different occasions and she looked miserable during all of them. I'm sure I don't look real thrilled when I get stuck with Carson either. What if Chelsea was like me? What if she was informing? The killings feel like revenge. What if it's because Chelsea betrayed the judge?

I pick off the crusts on my sandwich, suddenly no longer hungry. What if Carson was using Chelsea the same way he's using me? It could mean something.

Or nothing. It could be my hate talking. It's happened before. Look what I thought of him during the Tessa debacle. I thought he was after her. I missed Todd entirely because I was too focused on the people I *wanted* to be evil.

Then again . . . no one hates Bay more than Carson. He's convinced the judge is corrupt.

Enough to frame him for murder?

No, that's stupid. Still . . . if all the victims worked for Carson that would make them valuable assets.

Or loose ends.

Shit. What does that make me?

Carson sets everything up for the next night, which works well for me since Bren is going into Atlanta for a business dinner and Lily's doing her dinosaur diorama at a friend's house. Griff and I are supposed to take the side entrance into the courthouse, the one closest to the employee parking lot. After seven p.m., Carson will take down the security system for a two-hour period, plenty of time to get in, get out.

And get on with my life. The thought makes me smile even though cold sweat rolls down my spine.

"Here." Griff passes me an earbud with an embedded mic so we can communicate even though he's staying near the entrance, watching in case anyone arrives.

"Thanks. You ready?"

Griff nods and we stash his motorcycle in the shadows,

make our way across the deserted courthouse parking lot. My stomach is queasy with excitement . . . and something else I refuse to name, but I know I'm remembering an unlit church parking lot when Griff and I walked into the dark to save my sister.

If we can do this, we can do anything. I squeeze Griff's hand, smile at him.

He doesn't smile back. "Let's make this fast. You know where you're going, right?"

"You asked me that already." I focus on the double doors, check my pocket again. The jump drive is still there, still loaded with the virus. "Second floor, fifth door," I repeat.

But only after I hit the second floor, third door, and upload my virus onto Bay's computer. Ideally, no one will ever know I was there, but it'll look like Carson made himself right at home in the judge's computer.

"Right. Okay." Griff turns the lock and both of us hold our breath as he nudges open the door.

Nothing. No alarm. Griff exhales hard like he really can't believe it. He starts to motion me forward, but I'm already through. I run the length of the hallway without looking back.

Ed Price's office is a total waste. There's nothing.

Less than nothing, actually, unless you count a metric ton of paperwork and a collection of those perpetual motion machines. There must be five or six of them and they wiggle as I mess with Price's CPU.

Corey was right. The computer is off. I hook my laptop into the CPU, bypassing the operating system and turning the attorney's computer into a slave drive. After that, it's just a few more minutes of searching his image files and finding . . .

Nothing. No pictures—unless you count an *awful* lot of Ed Price head shots.

Unease squeezes my lungs and I spend a second glaring at the silver motion machines, thinking. If the pictures aren't on the computer then where are they?

I close the search program, check my phone. I need to get going. I spent my first few minutes loading the virus onto Bay's computer, which wasn't too bad, but I spent longer than I should have going through Bay's files. Pointless really. I wasn't going to find anything on my mom—not after this many years. I couldn't help it though, and, going through his things, I couldn't stop thinking about how many other people he might have used the same way.

I wasted time, and now I'm running behind and still empty-handed. If the pictures weren't emailed then that leaves . . . the in-box?

It's piled pretty high. From the looks of it, Price's secretary has tried to organize everything. Top stuff is faxes. There are some memos mixed in with some UGA alumni stuff. Mail's at the bottom. Nothing good though.

Okay. Moving on. I open the desk drawers, flip through the file names. Case paperwork. I switch to the desk's other side, shutting the top drawer, opening the lower. It's more of the same. File. File. File. Some of them thick as my wrist. Ridiculous. There's no way I'm going to find the pictures. Even if they are here, it would take days to filter through everything.

I shove the file folder into its slot, start to close the drawer, and realize there's a gap behind the folders. I must not have extended the drawer all the way.

Rolling my chair to the side, I pull the drawer forward, lengthening it another foot. The file folders stop and behind them is a clutter of law magazines, the edges of a manila envelope poking out from underneath like it had been forgotten . . . or shoved away hastily as if someone was coming.

I tug out the envelope, peek inside. Something's at the bottom. I stick my hand in, fish around. Huh. Piece of folded paper and something that feels like a jump drive.

I squint at the small white rectangle. Yep, it's a jump drive. Why would you need to hide something like this?

I flip open the paper.

THERE ARE MORE WHERE THESE CAME FROM. I'LL BE IN TOUCH SOON.

Even more interesting. I plug the drive into the USB port of my computer and check the time. Crap. I need to wrap this up. When the file listing appears, I click the first item.

My heart double-thumps.

It's a dead body. Are these crime scene photos?

I scroll through, squinting in the dark. It's a dead woman. Blondish. Youngish. *Lots* of blood.

Why would Chelsea have these? Is it related to a case she was helping Bay with? And why would Corey's client have wanted them?

I copy the files from the jump drive to my laptop. Most of the shots are close-ups of the wounds. Looks like the girl was stabbed to death. I select another photo and pause, enlarge the picture and stare. The girl's face is turned up, eyes and mouth pulled wide.

It's Lell.

"Griff," I murmur, touching two fingers to my earbud. "I think we have a problem."

"Yes, you do."

I jerk to attention. *Milo?* What the hell is he doing on our channel?

"Surprised?" Milo continues in a *come on down and tell her what she's won* tone. "I would suggest you get your ass moving. You have company."

Company? I open my mouth to tell Milo to screw off and hear footsteps. *Oh. God.*

I step away from the desk, listening. The footsteps are heavy, rubber soles thumping against the linoleum. They're not moving quickly, but they are headed this way.

I unhook my laptop and drop it in my bag with the jump drive and envelope. I push the CPU back to where it was and hesitate. Now what? If I run for it, whoever's outside will see me.

"Yep," Milo says, sounding thrilled. "That is definitely an Officer Friendly moving your way, Wick. I would find somewhere to hide. Fast. Looks like he noticed the door you left open."

I cut my eyes to the office door. Shit. Sure enough, I left it cracked. I spin around, looking for a hiding spot. Desk. Two chairs. Bookshelves. Nothing. Double shit.

I rocket around, fling myself behind the door so, if he opens it, I'll be hidden. With any luck, he'll just close the door as he goes by.

Only he doesn't.

He opens it.

The wooden door swings wide, arcing in front of me as I suck suck suck myself in. The officer steps inside, snaps his flashlight on, twirls the beam over the office, and snaps it off.

Almost there. I hold my breath.

He comes inside.

With the door in my face, I can't see where he is, but I can hear him. He's opening drawers, moving things around. Papers flutter.

This isn't a security cop. Can't be.

Holding my bag tight against my chest, I step to my left and peek around the door's edge. The guy's finished with the desk and gone on to the filing cabinets on the other side. He's moving things around with force, not caring about the mess. He straightens and I jerk back. Something slams. A drawer?

Footsteps cross the office, heading for the door. He pulls it shut behind him, and through the space between the jamb and door, I get a glimpse of the guy's profile.

It's Judge Bay.

Milo clears his throat. "Uh, if I were you, I'd get moving right about now."

I'm still pressed against the wall. Moving would be awesome. Too bad my joints have turned to puddles.

"What the fuck are you doing, Milo?" Griff's voice crackles in my ear.

Milo ignores him. "Seriously, Wick. Get going."

"Is Bay gone?" I hiss.

"For the moment."

A wave of nausea rushes over me. Somehow, Milo must have gotten on the security feed. The thought does not make me warm and fuzzy. I force myself forward, peek into the hallway. It's clear.

"He took your exit," Milo continues. "You'll need another way out. Go left."

I can't. If Bay took my exit then he's headed straight for Griff. I can't just leave him. "Not without Griff."

"I'm fine, Wick. Promise." Griff's voice is hushed. Is he hiding? "Go left. The asshole's right. You can get out through the lower wing. I'll meet you by the rear stairwell."

I pivot left, hugging the wall and struggling not to take off running.

And screaming.

My sneakers thud against the linoleum tile and I pray Bay can't hear me coming like I heard him.

"Take the stairs down to the bottom floor," Milo says when I reach the hallway's end. "Use the fire exit."

No way. The fire exits are on a different security system. "Are you crazy?" I'm taking the stairs two at a time now, knowing I'm being loud and not able to stop it. "It'll sound the alarm."

"Not anymore it won't and FYI? You need to run."

I open my mouth to respond when a door on the floor above me scrapes open. Bay. He heard me. He's coming.

I jerk to a stop at the bottom of the stairs, stare at the fire exit doors. Do I believe Milo?

More footsteps. They're coming down, pinning me.

Shit. I tighten my messenger bag's strap, grab the door handles with both hands, and prepare to run like hell.

The doors open with a whoosh, but no alarm, and I take off across the lawn, running hard for a line of trees at the edge of the grass. Have to get into the dark before Bay comes through that door and sees me. If I can get out of the range of the security lights, I can hide. He won't be able to tell which way I went.

Then, from the corner of my eye, I see something move. Griff.

He hooks his hand around mine and we run even harder, tumbling into the shadows.

"Are you okay?" Griff pulls me into him.

I nod. "Look."

The fire exit door opens and Bay lingers under the light, his head slowly turning as he pans the lawns and sidewalks. He can't see us, but Griff still edges in front of me, one arm tucking me so close I can feel his heartbeat: too fast, too hard.

Exactly like mine.

Bay shuts the door and Griff relaxes. I wrap both arms around him, tugging him against me.

"Well, isn't that touching?" Milo appears on our left, walking along the tree line and careful to stay just outside of the security lights' illumination. He adjusts a backpack over one shoulder and stares down at us. "Now tell the truth: How awesome was I? Even for me, I think that was pretty badass."

Griff lunges for him. "The *hell* are you doing here?"

"Saving your girlfriend's ass." Milo inspects Griff's grip on his T-shirt like it's some sort of interesting bug. "No extra charge, by the way."

Griff shakes him. "You had no right barging in like that—"

"Hey, genius, I designed the earbuds." Milo's talking to Griff and staring at me, grinning. "I'll get in whenever I like. Just never felt like it until I realized you were with her. Ballsy move, Wick. All that breaking and entering. I liked it."

Cold curls around me. "How could you see what we were doing?"

Even in the dark, I can see Milo's eyes light up with satisfaction. "Clever girl. Always asking the right questions. I could see what you were doing because your detective friend restarted the security cameras. He was recording everything: you, your little guest, *everything*."

I hold myself very still. "Carson wasn't supposed to be recording anything." The words are coming out sticky, like they refuse to leave my mouth. "That was the deal. If I did this, he said he would make sure the system went down."

"And yet he didn't." Illuminated by the security lights, Milo's smile turns yellow. "Good thing I did."

Griff straightens. "You took down the feed?"

"Neat, huh? Don't you wish you'd thought of it?"

Griff growls, grabbing Milo by the throat.

"Stop it!" I wedge myself between them, willing Griff to look at me. After a moment, he does.

Griff's hands loosen . . . and he strikes Milo squarely in the chest, flinging him back. Milo staggers, and when he looks up, he laughs.

"Give me a minute. I'm going to get the bike." Griff

stalks into the dark and I have to struggle not to follow. A few seconds pass and I realize Milo's still watching me.

"So." Milo shoves both hands into his pockets. "Carson, is it? What's his deal?"

Have to say something. Need a lie. Need a really good lie.

Only I'm too flattened to think of anything. I look at Milo and feel like I'm draining straight through my feet. "Carson knows about my . . . extracurricular activities. He says he'll destroy my family and make sure I go to jail if I don't work for him."

"Shit . . . he's the guy you called after we found Corey?"

"Yeah." I pass one hand over my aching neck, watching him. "You're taking this pretty well."

He shrugs. "I understand better than you know. This is survival. We all do things we aren't proud of."

"Thanks for cutting the feed."

Another slow smile. "You're welcome."

The pause is stretching out into a seriously awkward moment. I should just leave it alone. Let it be awkward. I'm no good at that though. "Why are you doing this?"

"Why shouldn't I?"

"Because it's not your style." I almost said because you're not a good guy. It doesn't matter though. Milo catches my meaning anyway.

"I'm more like you than you think." He jerks his chin toward Griff. "I'm more like you than he'll ever be."

I shake my head. "No, he understands where I came

from. He's been where I've been."

"But does he know where you're destined to go?"

Ugh. It annoys the crap out of me that Milo thinks he does. "I love him."

"More than hacking? More than all of this?" Milo pans one hand to our surroundings. He smiles again, and in that moment, my skin pushes up in goose bumps.

"You should think about that," Milo says, turning away. "I'm sure I'll see you around."

I watch him walk back into the darkness until the shadows have melted him completely. Down the hill, a headlight swings through the lower parking lot. Griff.

I scramble down the hill and I'm barely settled on the bike before Griff pulls away, speeding toward the exit. We make it to the first traffic light before he finally turns to look at me.

"You're never going to get out of this, Wicked."

"I did get out of it. Milo cut the feed. Carson lost."

"For now. What about a week from now? What about a year? Don't you understand? He's never going to let you go. Once you're useful to them . . . it's never finished. You'll never escape."

"Yeah, I will." My bag is wedged between us and it takes me a minute to open it.

"Did you find what Carson wanted?"

"I think so." I hold up my jump drive and Griff gives me a *so?* look. "They're pictures of the dead girl I found—Lell. I don't know how Chelsea got them or why she gave them to

Price, but Bay wants them so there's something good here. I'll make it my ticket out."

"You really think he'll keep his promise?"

He will if he knows what's good for him. I look at Griff and can't smother my giggle. "Yeah, he will. Remember what you told me? Get leverage? Well, I did."

"With the virus?"

"Exactly." I can hurt Carson where it hurts the most now: his career. It's all he has and I'll ruin it. And just thinking about it makes savage satisfaction surge through me. Is this what Carson felt when he blackmailed me? When he looked at everything I had gained and knew it was leverage?

I grin at Griff. "It's done. I'm free."

Carson's house looks bottled up as ever, but after we park, the back door opens and Carson waits for us to come in.

I lean close to Griff as we approach. "Give me a couple minutes to talk to him and then we're out of here."

Griff nods, waiting in the kitchen as I follow Carson into the living room. He drops onto the sofa, pushing paperwork to the side. He looks utterly at ease . . . until I see his hands are shaking.

Rage.

Good. I flick the envelope on top of the pile. "I'm done," I say, and my smile is crazy easy even though I'm sweating under my clothes. "I'm finished."

"Are you now?" Carson slowly opens the envelope, eyes

on me. "We had a deal. How do I know you kept your end?"

"Take a look at what I brought you."

The detective spends a few minutes trying to access the jump drive from his personal computer, and when he finally does, his breath hitches. "These were in Price's office?"

"Yeah, and I found them just before Bay came in. If I had to guess, *that's* what the hacker's client was looking for. Enjoy." I turn to leave and Carson seizes my wrist, twisting it.

"Nah-ah-ah. You're not finished here."

My fingers curve into claws. "I think I am. Deal's a deal. This is your problem now."

"Your problem too if Lell's killer comes looking for you."

"I'll take my chances."

"You said Bay was at the courthouse? You saw him?"

I take a steadying breath. "Yeah, and I quit. We're finished, Carson."

The detective's mouth curls into a knot. "You'll quit when I'm finished with you. That's the way this works, trash. I can make you do whatever I want."

I lean into Carson, smell how his breath is dry as graveyard dirt. "Not anymore. I uploaded a virus onto Bay's computer. One keystroke from me and it will activate, putting your digital fingerprints all over his computer files. Try explaining *that* to your chief of police. You threaten anyone I love again and I will burn you, do you understand?"

Carson's eyes narrow and, again, I can't help my grin. "You're screwed, Detective."

He studies me. "You know you have your father's smile?"

"You know you didn't get anything on me?"

"Maybe so." The detective's eyes flick away from me. He nudges his chin toward Griff. "But I did get him."

"Liar."

Carson shrugs. "Wanna see?"

Before I can answer, he lifts the television remote and clicks on the set, revealing a black-and-white shot of Griff at the side entrance we used. Filmed from only a few feet above him, the image clearly shows his face just before the screen goes black.

"Ta-da!" Carson's smile makes me want to vomit.

Or maybe it's just the image of Griff—time-stamped—on the television screen as Carson plays the silent clip again and again and again.

I flick my eyes away, only that's no good either because now I'm staring at the real Griff, just a dozen steps away in the kitchen, waiting for me to return.

"You know, I think it actually works out better this

way." Carson pauses the video, taps two fingers against his chin. "He has skills. Granted, they're not as good as yours, but he has so much to lose."

He does. SCAD. Art. His whole future.

Carson studies me. "I could make him inform for me— think about how he can be seen around the station. More convenient than using you. Everyone will just think he's visiting his cousin."

"His cousin will never let you do this."

"His cousin's afraid of me. And if Griff doesn't do what I want?" Carson gives me a one-shouldered shrug. "Well, I'll just use that footage to introduce him to the world as a burgeoning criminal and terrorist—breaking and entering, intent to do harm, trespassing charges for starters. It's certainly enough evidence for a search warrant. I wonder what else we'd find if we searched his house? Think he's as careful as you are about hiding your nasty little computer habits?"

No. He's never had to be. Griff's one of the good guys. Always has been.

Carson settles into his couch, remote control in one hand, jump drive in the other. "If I play it right, I can make sure he does a nice bit of jail time as a domestic terrorist."

"I will take you apart if you touch him. So help me I will pull your world down." Strong words for someone whose knees are pushing toward the floor. I need something better here and all I can think of is how Carson has Griff. He's almost eighteen. He'll be tried and convicted as an adult and it'll follow him forever. The future he wants will never happen.

All because of me.

All because he was trying to *protect* me.

"You go after him," I say. "And I'll . . . I'll . . ." Go public? Can't, I would hurt Bren and Lily. "Do not underestimate me, Carson. I will use that virus. You won't be able to explain your way around it. It will destroy you."

The detective's smile evaporates. "I bet it would. Even with me out of the picture, it still wouldn't help him. I turn in that video, you activate that virus. Doesn't matter. Griff'll still be prosecuted. Think that fancy art school will want him with a record?"

"No." The word emerges soft and round and nothing like me. When Griff was picturing his life, it was never like this.

And it's my fault.

Carson's staring at me with the smile usually reserved for newspaper columnists and mothers with babies. "So congrats, Wick, you outsmarted me. You're free. Too bad I'm just going to use him instead."

"Please don't."

"Then offer me something better."

How? If I offer myself, Carson will accept and Griff will go free . . . and then I'll still be working for Carson after I told Griff I was done.

He won't forgive me.

I listen for the shuffle of Griff's sneakers in the kitchen, but there's nothing, and when I sneak a glance, I realize Griff's not moving because he's watching me. His eyes meet mine and he smiles. I have to force myself not to wince.

Can I give myself back to Carson to save him? Without a single doubt.

It would destroy us. I know it would and that's what's so scary because I would still do it. In less than a heartbeat.

I can't decide if that admission makes me cold.

Or maybe I'm just pathetic because, if I lose Griff, I have no idea how I'm supposed to live with that.

"Nothing? No offers?" Carson tucks his arm behind his head, slouching down as he starts running the video over and over again. "Then we're done, trash. You're free. Also? If I find out you told him about the tape before I do, I'll go public with it, understand?"

Another threat. Pointless really. If I tell Griff about the tape, he'll want to steal it and I'll want to help and Carson will be expecting us. Whatever we did would only make things worse.

It almost makes me want to laugh. Carson owns me more now than he did before.

"Don't touch him," I say. "Leave Griff alone and you can have me. I'll work for you, but you have to promise *never* to touch him."

Carson looks up, eyes alight. I've just given him exactly what he wanted. Now he just has to give me what I want.

I swallow. "If I do this . . . how do I know you'll leave him alone?"

"You think he's any use to me?" The detective leans

forward. "You do what I want, I'll stay away from him."

"And the tape?"

"Help me close this case and I'll give it to you."

Or I'll take it. I nod. "It's a deal."

"I'm going to make you a hero, trash—in spite of that bad blood of yours. Think of losing Griff as a growing pain." He cocks his head, studying me with the keen, questioning eyes that belong to addicts or pit bulls. "That boy'll never forgive you for working for me again."

No. He won't.

Carson leans forward, pats my hand. The gesture's so awkward, it feels borrowed. He's slipping into Good Cop again. "Even if Griff doesn't, you were never going to stay together anyway, Wick. I've seen the way he looks at you when we work together."

I stiffen. *Don't say it. Don't say it.*

"It's like he can barely believe what's coming out of your mouth. He can't reconcile his pretty, lost princess with the criminal standing in front of him. This was destined to be messy. It was always going to end badly."

I look away. I hate admitting when Carson's right.

I fake it the whole way home. Everything is fine. The future looks great. We're together.

At first I'm proud I can maintain the lie ... then I realize of course I can. Lying is what I do best, isn't it?

"Do you want to come in?" I ask after we pull into the driveway. Griff nods hard, his smile suddenly too big for his face. I play with my house keys because I don't want to see it, definitely don't want to remember it.

Too late.

We check the house together. Windows, doors, security system, they're all exactly as I left them. Should make me feel safe. Instead, it just feels like a reprieve.

Kyle is still loose. Jason still knows I'm snitching. Carson . . . I still work for Carson. And, for a second, I think I'm going to start crying all over again.

Since Bren and Lily are out, we go to the kitchen. Him telling me about an artists' club he's joined at school. Me counting tiles so I know precisely how far away I have to stay to do this.

"Griff? We need to talk." A cliché, but the best I can do. I don't look at him. "I've decided to keep working for Carson."

There's a long pause, and into it I fit everything I want to say and can't: Carson has a recording of you breaking into the courthouse, I'm doing this to save you, I love you, and I'm sorry.

I'm so sorry.

Griff leans one hip against the counter. "Why?"

Yes. Why? The words I need dissolve in my hands. "Why not?"

"Because you hate it."

I take a shaky breath, wince when his palm snares mine. "No. *You* hate it."

"Yeah . . . I do. I don't understand, Wick. Why'd you change your mind? Does this have something to do with . . ."

I tense. "What?"

"I don't know." Griff scowls. "Is it about Milo's bullshit? How hackers should rule the world or whatever?"

"No."

"Because he likes you. A lot. I can tell."

I close my eyes, open them. I could use Milo to finish this. Griff would never suspect the real reasons.

"I hate how he looks at you," Griff says slowly. I tug at my hand, but he doesn't let go and I need him to. I can't be this close when Griff starts looking at me like . . . like I'm me and not the girl he wanted.

The girl I wanted to be.

"I like him too," I say. "We're . . . the same kind of person, Griff."

Just saying it aloud makes me realize it's true.

Griff's jaw tightens. "You're right. I can't keep up with you two."

Because you're better.

"Every time he looks at you," Griff says, tracing the lines on my palm, "I want to beat his head into the pavement."

I stare. He won't meet my eyes and all I can hear is my breath, rattling past my lips. I don't know what to say.

"I hate that about myself," Griff continues, touching his fingertips to mine. "I never wanted to be that guy, but when I'm with you, I am."

"I'm sorry." It is fast and instant and I mean it. "I'm so sorry, Griff."

"Don't be." His smile is fake, and when he lets me go, my hand goes cold. "It isn't your fault. It's mine. I can't be like this. I think part of me always knew you would never quit. I knew I would have to walk away."

No! Don't! I'll quit! I will do anything you ask! Everything I'm supposed to say and I don't. Can't.

"I'm sorry, Griff."

"Liar." He sounds proud of me though and something buried inside me shatters. "You love this. Tell me you don't."

I . . . can't.

"This work." Griff sighs, shaking his head. "It's consuming you, Wick."

Our eyes meet and I stiffen. He's not thinking of the work. He's thinking of how I fell apart and cried. He's thinking I can't handle it.

He might be right. A pang of anxiety hits me low and spreads through my bones. Is this how he's always seen me? How long has he felt like this? When I imagined this conversation . . . it never occurred to me that I would see another side of myself.

One that was even more loathsome than the person I thought I am.

Griff smiles, and this time it's real. "You're the most honest criminal I know, Wicked."

He takes a cautious step toward me—because he can't trust me? Or because he can't trust himself? He touches my face with the backs of his fingers, runs his thumb over my lips. It drives delighted chills up my spine. My body responds to him like everything is the same.

Like nothing's ruined.

His fingers find the hollow behind my ear, the blunted edge of my jaw. I lean into him and feel how my insides knock loose.

He can bury me alive.

Griff softly touches his lips to mine, a ghost kiss to say

good-bye. It's so damn fitting I want to scream.

"Good-bye, Wicked." He pauses, waiting for me to say it back and I won't. Maybe if I don't, he won't leave.

I can't do this. I have to think of a way around Carson's threat.

But Griff's already walking away and I have to fight not to run after him. Just as well since I don't think I'd make it two steps. His absence is immediate and heavy and I can't breathe around it.

Griff slams the door and my knees hit the floor.

The next day, I play sick. Actually . . . it's not really playing. I don't think I could get out of bed if I tried and the realization makes me want to laugh until I puke. I am truly my mother's daughter now.

Up on the nightstand, my phone vibrates. Another text. Lauren?

Carson.

He wants to meet day after tomorrow and I'll need something good to give him.

I stare at my ceiling, weigh my options. The sniffer is working great if I'm interested in reviewing Bay's work material or discovering what party his now dead assistant wanted him to attend. Other than that, it hasn't been much good. Carson already has the pictures of Lell. So that leaves . . .

Norcut. I'm not super thrilled about pursuing her either. It hits awfully close to home since Bren has been taking Lily and me to the child psychiatrist for almost a year.

Hard to tell what her angle is. Is she trying to help her onetime client? Or is she trying to help cover something up? I could find out. She has less security than Bay, which makes her an easier target.

Except that would mean using Milo, wouldn't it? Finding a way into Norcut's computer files from scratch would take time. Using Milo's in . . . it could be a fast job. But that would require asking a favor from Milo.

Milo, who looks at me in a way that Griff hates.

Then again, that doesn't matter anymore, does it?

It still takes me a few minutes to screw together the courage to call him though. I dial Milo's number and it almost goes to voice mail before he picks up, his voice sleep-sticky. "Aren't you supposed to be in school?"

"Remember when you told me you could get into Norcut's network?"

"Yeah."

"I want to follow up on it."

"Great." There's a rustling from the other end. Milo must be sitting up, throwing off the blankets. "I'll meet you today. We'll talk it through. I didn't make it the easiest system to navigate."

"No." I run one hand over my face and realize my hair is sticking out everywhere. "No need. I already know how I want to work it. I'll get into her office. I just need you to get me a distraction and her passwords so I have time to mess with the computer in her office."

"Fine." Milo sounds deflated. "I'll do something with the security system. I'll call you back tonight with details."

I hang up and flip the phone onto the bed. Now for the rest of the plan.

I go downstairs and find Bren in her office, reviewing a contract as thick as my fist. "Bren?"

She looks up and her face creases into a smile. "Are you feeling better? How's your head?"

"Not that great." I try to arrange my features to look depressed. It's not hard. "I think I need to see Dr. Norcut. Could you get me an appointment?"

Dr. Allison Norcut is one of the East Coast's top child psychiatrists, with a waiting list that's rumored to be three months out. I wouldn't know. Any time Lily and I look sideways, Bren drags us in. And, sure enough, she's able to get me an appointment for the following afternoon.

We pull into Norcut's parking lot precisely ten minutes ahead of time, but because Bren is still on the phone with a client, we spend another five or six minutes sitting around.

Finally, when it looks like the guy on the other end is never going to shut up, Bren covers the cell's mouthpiece with one hand. "Wick, honey, can you go inside without me? I promise I won't be too long."

I nod and get out, take the elevator to Norcut's third-floor office. This late in the afternoon, it's deserted. There's only the office assistant manning the sleek front desk.

"Hi, Wicket," Trina says, pulling off a headset that's probably meant to look more Nicki Minaj than "Do you want fries with that?"

"You can go in," she says. "Dr. Norcut will only be a few more minutes."

"Thanks." I smile, close the office door behind me. The psychiatrist's tastes are a study in grays. Gray chairs. Gray carpet. Gray walls.

I drop onto a gravel-colored sofa pushed against a granite-colored wall and check my phone.

One. Lights go off. Backup generator turns on. I hunch into the cushions, watching the shadows flick back and forth underneath the door. Norcut and Trina are on the move and Norcut sounds pissed.

Two. Norcut asks Trina to get a handle on the situation and Trina say she's trying. She sounds like she's failing.

Three. The alarm system goes off and I launch myself across the room. Norcut's keyboard is shiny clean (God, the woman's predictable) but the keys are worn on the *L*, *M*, and *N*. The number keys to the right are worn on the 1, 5, 6, and 9.

I roll my eyes, unable to stop the grin. God, I love it when people never change their password. I key in Norcut's initials, the password Milo gave me: ALN1965. The home screen populates.

Hot damn. I open her My Documents folder and skim through the file listing, where Norcut's literal brain is a total windfall for me. It's crazy easy to navigate. I click on the file marked Patients and scroll through the list.

BAY, KYLE is near the top.

I double click the folder and skim through the documents inside. Patient histories. Lots of them. Looks like Norcut scans her handwritten notes and saves them as PDFs. I don't know what will be useful so I select the entire group and copy it to my jump drive. After the backup is complete, I scroll down and select the last file she added.

It's dated the eleventh, four days before Kyle and Lell supposedly eloped, and talks all about his rage.

> PATIENT HIGHLY AGITATED AND CONVINCED SOMEONE IS
> FOLLOWING HIM. NO AMOUNT OF REASON CAN SWAY HIM. HE
> IS UNABLE TO ARTICULATE WHY SOMEONE WOULD FOLLOW HIM,
> BUT HE IS INSISTENT THAT IT'S HAPPENING.

Paranoia? That's interesting. Outside, Norcut's voice goes up another octave and I cut a quick look at the door. Not much more time. Kyle's paranoia is definitely interesting. Doesn't make him the killer though.

> BOTH BOYS EXHIBIT DEPRESSION SYMPTOMS. MAY NEED
> TO ADJUST KYLE'S MEDICATION DOSAGE. COMPLAINTS OF
> BLACKOUTS. REAL OR IMAGINARY? MUST SPEAK WITH
> PARENTS TO CONFIRM.

Both boys? I flip to My Documents again and check the file listing for Ian. There's nothing. Was he a patient?

It doesn't look like it. Then again, it's not like I've found everything Norcut has. She could have filed Ian somewhere else. Why keep Kyle here? And how do the parents figure in? Kyle's mom would've been undergoing chemo treatments at this point. Was she supportive?

WILL RECOMMEND AN IN-PATIENT THERAPY PROGRAM FOR LONG TERM. I HAVE SERIOUS CONCERNS ABOUT THE UPCOMING REELECTION. THE PRESSURES IN THE CURRENT ENVIRONMENT COULD PROVE TO BE TOO GREAT. HE COULD RELAPSE. OR WORSE.

SEVERAL FAMILY MEMBERS SUPPORT A LONG-TERM PSYCHIATRIC SOLUTION. THE MOTHER, IN PARTICULAR, FEELS IT'S NECESSARY AND SHE MENTIONED SEVERAL TIMES THAT HER HUSBAND'S ASSISTANT FEELS THE SAME. THEY'RE AFRAID.

Of Kyle. Interesting—even more interesting that Chelsea recommended Kyle be put away and now she's dead. Could the murders be about revenge? What if "remember me" is a question and a command? Remember who you put away. Remember *me*.

Because my head is filled with Kyle, I don't hear the door. It opens with the faintest whoosh against the carpet and I have just enough time to double tap CTRL, ALT, DEL, sending the computer into a full reboot. I spin around, ready to say . . . something.

But it isn't Dr. Norcut standing in the doorway.

It's Bren.

"Get away from the computer," she whispers and, for a second, I think I've misunderstood. This is wrong. Bren should be pissed.

"Get. *Away.*"

Nope, she's pissed. I bounce from the chair, pushing the jump drive deep into my coat pocket as I head for the couch. I sit down and Bren sits next to me. We both listen to Norcut outside, and when the doctor returns, Bren grabs my hand, her palm slick against mine.

"I'm sorry, Mrs. Callaway. We seem to be having computer difficulties. Could we"—Norcut winces, anticipating Bren's response—"reschedule?"

"Yes. Sure. No problem." Bren hauls me to my feet while the psychiatrist stares at us, mouth slightly unhinged. She can't believe her good luck. "I'll call you."

"Please do." Norcut's pale eyes follow us. "I'm always happy to help."

And what a help she was. It's almost enough to make me grin. But even if Norcut helped me with my Bay problem . . . I sneak a sideways look at Bren and my stomach squeezes.

She's breathing light and hard through her mouth, eyes fixed straight ahead. Yeah, I now have a new problem, and Bren won't be easy.

The elevator must have ten people waiting on it so we take the stairs, saying nothing until Bren pushes through the glass double doors and we're out in the parking lot.

Bren spins around on me, her hand reaching for pearls

she isn't wearing. "What were you doing?"

"Nothing."

"What were you *doing*, Wick?"

"Checking my email." I study my Chucks like I'm too embarrassed to meet her eyes, which I'm not of course. I'm *not*.

I am having a hard time looking at her though.

"On someone else's personal computer?"

"Sorry."

"I don't understand," Bren continues. "First the boys at school, now this."

There's a pause. The longer it continues, the more I realize I'm supposed to fill it with some logical explanation: I'm depressed, I'm angry, I'm having flashbacks.

Because all those things are fixable and if I'm not fixable . . .

I slide my hand into my pocket, grip the jump drive in my palm. "I didn't think about it like that."

Another pause. "Why don't I believe you?"

Is that a rhetorical question? Now I do glance up, try to gauge her mood and realize I can't.

This isn't a Bren I've seen before. She isn't staring at me like I'm broken. She's watching me like I'm dangerous.

As promised, I turn in everything I found to Carson and I'm surprised to realize it's kind of weird for me to operate like this. When I ran my own investigations, I put together an entire profile for customers: finances, job histories, online interests. By the time I was done, I knew my target inside and out.

Working like this is totally different. I give pieces of the person to Carson and he does . . . what? I probably don't want to know. It gets him off my case though. Carson hasn't bothered me for almost a week, letting me pretend he doesn't exist and my life is back to normal.

Lab project? Done.

Homework? Done.

Sleeping? Sort of.

My life is normal, or as normal as it can be now that Griff's no longer in it.

Now that I have the Mini again, I roll into school as late as possible, careful to avoid him in the halls. This is easier than expected since I never see him anymore. Well, that's not entirely true. I see glimpses. His dark head moving through the crowded hallways, his bottle-green eyes slashing away, his smile cutting through the afternoon dark.

God, Griff's smile.

My smile.

Only it isn't mine anymore.

It's easier to smother those thoughts when I stay busy though so I end up riding around with Lauren a lot over the next few days. After being gone for almost two weeks, she's back and wound tighter than ever. We haven't talked about her mom—she doesn't want to—but I'm helping her catch up on homework, waiting for her to finish cheer practice and gym classes. I get home later, but I don't mind.

Actually, considering the way Bren's watching me, it's kind of a relief.

"Wick!" Lauren bounces up behind me and locks one arm around my neck, dragging me toward the parking lot.

"Jesus!" I laugh and press my shirt against my nose and mouth. "You reek! What did you do in there?"

"Kickboxing." Lauren does a one-two punch into the air and spins into a roundhouse kick narrowly missing someone's Jeep.

"I thought you were doing spin classes."

"Nope, I like this stuff better." She shakes her sodden dark hair out of its ponytail. "Turns out, I really enjoy kicking things. You should try it sometime."

"I probably should."

Lauren's gaze hitches on my face. "Everything okay?"

No. "Yeah . . . no."

Lauren studies her car keys as we walk. "I talked to Griff this morning."

My chest seizes up. "Oh yeah?"

"Yeah, he said you guys broke up because you were working again."

I spend a few seconds picking at my nails. Interesting that he said it was my work, not that there was another boy. I wish Griff hadn't told Lauren about Carson. . . . Then again, it's almost easier now that he has. Almost.

"Yeah, Carson offered me another job." And after I gave him Norcut's files on Kyle, he disappeared. "It's not just the work. I found some information on my mom too."

"Like what?"

I quickly sketch out the details: the DVDs, how my mom was an informant, *see what they did to her*, Lily's reaction, Griff's reaction—I even add how I want to give it up and how I don't feel like I can. Lauren doesn't say a word. We reach her car and she leans one hip against it, listening until there's nothing left for me to say.

"People don't understand what it's like to have parents like ours." For the first time, Lauren's gaze breaks with mine. She stares into the gym parking lot's shadows. "Parents like ours are so broken and it doesn't mean we love them any less. Maybe it makes us love them more."

"Not for me. Not at the time. I was so angry with her for not leaving him and then . . . for jumping and leaving us."

"And now?"

"Now I don't know what to think."

Lauren shakes her head. "I don't like it. You're surrounded by all this . . . evil, Wick. How long before it pollutes you too?"

Maybe it already has. "It won't."

"How do you know?"

I tug both hands through my hair, rubbing my suddenly thumping temples. I should be pissed and yet there's something so sad and earnest about her tone that I can't be mad.

Maybe it's because I worry about the same thing.

We're surrounded by darkness. Sometimes it's everyday evil. Maybe it's the guy who beats his wife or cheats on his taxes or belittles his kids, but he still considers himself a good person. It's a talent most of us have, telling ourselves we're good when we're not.

Then you have evil like Todd or Kyle, evil that shows us just how breakable we all are, and how much our safety depends on everyone playing along.

Until someone doesn't.

I climb into Lauren's front passenger seat and wait for her to finish adjusting the radio before we pull out. When did I learn about the biggest fairy tale of all? Was it from my dad? Carson? When did I realize that, deep down, we're all nothing, just sacks of organs and blood, and someone can flick us off like a light?

I don't want Lauren to know that.

"So Jenna Maxwell was asking me about Griff. She wanted to know what the deal was."

My breath dries up. "What'd you tell her?"

"That you guys are forever." Lauren's eyes crinkle in amusement. "He'll come around, Wick. It'll be okay."

"Yeah." But I know it's never going to be okay. There are some things that once broken, stay broken. I smile like Lauren's right though, fake like I believe her.

Feels so good I almost believe it too.

Then I get home and find another DVD waiting for me.

That night, we eat Chinese takeout and watch some movie I don't remember because Bren and Lily talk straight through it. Every once in a while, they pause, looking to me to add something. I never can. The new DVD is looping through my head. And when I finally go up to my room, I lie in bed with every light on, still too afraid to close my eyes.

I need to sleep and I can't. "Remember Me" twirls through my head in gory colors, a whisper stuck on repeat. Maybe that's why I watch the last of the interviews. I haven't had my fill of monsters.

"He isn't home much anymore," my mom repeats, not even bothering to wipe away her tears. "He's always gone and he gets mad if I ask him about it."

I bite down hard on my thumbnail, tasting blood. I remember those arguments. I can smooth the crushed edges of probably ten different memories where she would ask him questions and he would answer with a slap. Or a punch.

How could I have not realized what was going on?

"Anyway, I need to go." She bends down, drags her purse from the floor. "I need to pick up my girls. It's hard to find someone to watch them."

"I don't care as long as you never bring them here." There's a pause as she stares at him, waiting to be dismissed.

"Who has them?" he asks.

"Samantha."

My breath goes light and fast. I haven't heard that name in years, but it leaps from my mother's mouth like it was waiting for me. Sam and my mom were good friends—actually Sam might have been my mom's *only* friend.

"She know where you go?"

"No." The answer is too quick and my mom knows it. Her eyes dart side to side, never landing. "Maybe," she amends.

"Which is it?"

"Yes."

I sit up straighter, chest suddenly tight. Sam knew about this? At first I'm shocked, then something else lies on top of the shock, smothers it: If she knew, maybe she could tell me more.

"You think that's wise?" the interviewer asks.

"Is any of this 'wise'?" It sounds defiant even if my

mother's shoulders round in a cringe. From him?

From everything, I realize. She was never a tall woman and under the fluorescent lights she looks tiny . . . breakable.

"Get us better information and it'll be done."

The screen freezes, leaving my mom's mouth twisted in a frown. I want to trace it with my fingertips, so I sit on my hands, watch the image dissolve into black.

What Are You Going To Do?

My skin crawls and I have an overwhelming urge to look behind me. There's nothing I can do. It's done. She's gone . . . so why can't I stop thinking about her best friend, Sam?

When my mom was alive, Samantha was a mostly functioning alcoholic. After my mom died, Samantha . . . was no longer functioning. Last I heard she was living on the streets in Atlanta. It would be next to impossible to find her. I don't have the contacts. I don't have any way of searching for her.

Unless I knew who to ask.

Milo might know. His dad is in a similar situation. Maybe he would know someone. I pick up my phone . . . and my fingers stick. We haven't spoken since the Norcut thing and I don't need Milo more involved with me than he already is. Plus, running after Sam would be stupid. I won't find anything. She won't remember.

But I have to try.

I run my fingers over the keypad, feeling sick. I should be reaching for Griff. This wasn't how it was supposed to be.

I stab the send button and he answers on the first ring. "Yeah?"

"Milo . . . I need your help."

Milo calls me back late Sunday night and says he thinks he knows where she might be. One of his contacts at the shelter saw Samantha two days ago.

"Great." I stand up, look for something to write with. "Tell me."

"No, I want to go with you."

"*Why?*" I rub the skin between my eyes. That was not the right response. "*No.* This has nothing to do with you."

"True."

I stare at the ceiling, waiting. "So you're going to tell me where she is?"

"No." Milo laughs. "Seriously, why would you *not* want me to come? Is there some prereq to hanging out with you? I have to be a skinny emo kid?"

"Griff's not—"

"Whatever." The laugh curls up. "You want your Samantha? I get to come along. I've earned the outing. You wouldn't have gotten into Norcut's files without me."

"Um, you do remember who you're talking to, right?"

"Okay, fine, you wouldn't have gotten into Norcut's files *as fast* without me. Let's go tonight."

I study my closed bedroom door, listen to the house settle. It's almost midnight and Bren and Lily have been asleep for hours, but they could wake up any minute.

Or they could stay asleep and I could sneak out and be back before anyone even knew I was gone.

I glance at the security camera feed running across my second computer monitor. Yard and street are empty. Either Kyle hasn't found me or he's biding his time.

I could use this opportunity, but . . . "Don't you have anything better to do?"

"At the moment? No."

I am *so* not playing these games. I let the silence stretch between us as I debate how long it would take me to track Samantha down myself. I could try calling some of the shelters, pretend I'm a concerned relative.

"Why do you want to come?" I ask.

Milo's sigh barrels down the line. "Morbid curiosity."

It's faster this way. Just do it and be done. "Meet me at the Waffle House at the airport exit." I snatch my keys off my desk. "Be there in thirty or it's off and I'll do it without you."

"I'm already on my way. I'll see you in fifteen."

By the time we reach Five Points, it's raining again and the streets are starting to flood. Milo finds a parking spot along a side street and we spend a moment staring through the windshield, saying nothing.

"For the record, this is why I needed to come along." Milo gestures at our surroundings. "See? Scary, isn't it? If the need to hold on to me overwhelms you, please feel free."

"Somehow I'll find a way restrain myself."

"Well, you can try." Milo cracks his knuckles, watches how the rain spreads like fingers against the glass. "You know this is stupid, right?"

"Yeah."

"You know you won't find anything?"

"Yeah." Slowly, I turn my head to stare at Milo. He meets my eyes and whatever he sees makes him blow out a long-suffering sigh.

"Jesus, fine. Let's get this over with. She should be this way." He points to our right, down a narrow alley that runs parallel to the subway stop.

"Ready?" he asks.

I tuck a bottle of Bren's wine, still cold from the refrigerator, under my jacket and nod. We slog down the flooded sidewalk and turn in to the alley, pulling up under a tattered awning.

"I can't see a damn thing." I pull my hood tight, hunching against the rain blowing in. "How're we going to find her in this?"

Milo shrugs. "We actually have a *better* chance of finding her—only so many dry places she can be. Plus, she might not feel like running away if it means getting soaked."

He has a point.

"Little farther in?"

I nod. If this were a movie, this would be the part where we find her. Except we don't. We look through lean-to tents and under shop awnings for almost an hour and never see her.

"Wick."

It's Milo. I turn away from a homeless woman whose eyes remind me of my mom's and wait for him to catch up with me.

"I'm sorry." Milo wipes rain out of his eyes. "But I told you it was stupid. I told you—"

Behind him, an unsteady figure moves out of an alley. It only takes a few seconds for me to recognize her. I point and, slowly, Milo turns. We both stare at Sam.

Sam's eyes are cloudy and faded. They widen as we near and I know this is a mistake. I recognize her. She doesn't recognize me. "Who's there?"

Milo motions me forward with one hand and an eye roll. I bump my chin into the air and brush past him, making sure my shoulder catches his arm.

"Samantha Stewart?"

Sam's mouth twitches like her name has a taste.

"I wanted to ask you a few questions."

"Wiiiccckkkeettt Taatte." She draws my name out. "The drug dealer's daughter . . . Sia Tate's daughter."

I stop. I don't like the way she says my mom's name. "Yes, that's right. I wanted to ask you a few questions about my mom."

I wait and Sam doesn't say anything. I can't tell if that's a *Yes, go on* or a *Hell no* so I plunge ahead.

"I know that my mom was an informant. I know she was scared."

"Your mama was scared of a lotta things."

"Like what?" The rain starts to come down harder, leaking under my jacket.

"Your daddy . . . your daddy's friends . . . how you would look at her." Sam's smile is slow and secret and I can't tell if it's for me or the bottle she sees in my hand. "She *hated* how you would look at her."

"I hated how she looked sometimes." I sound defensive. I *am* defensive. Gritting my teeth, I put myself between

Sam and Milo and tell myself it's so he can't see her nasty smile.

I know it's because there are tears in my eyes.

"She loved you." Sam's attention drifts up and away, following something no one else can see. "She didn't understand you, but she loved you. She was in awe."

I don't want to hear it. It doesn't matter.

"What—" My voice cracks and I clear my throat. "What do you mean my mom was afraid of my dad's friends?"

"They were a problem. He was a problem. Always following her, pressing up on her."

Something cold coils in my stomach. "Which friend?"

"The big one. She was so afraid of the big one."

I wince—can't help it—and I have to force myself to ask even though I know the answer. "Do you remember the big one's name?"

"Joe. His name was Joe."

"He scared her enough to commit suicide?"

Sam shakes her head hard. "Not suicide."

"She jumped off a building, Sam. That's called suicide."

"You seen the tape?" Her eyes fix on the bottle and I draw it away, watching how she watches it.

"What tape?"

"The security tape. I haven't seen it either, but I was told all about it. Those policemen never figured out who else was up there, but she wasn't alone." Sam runs her tongue over her cracked lips. "Sia didn't jump. She was pushed."

Pushed? Dimly, I'm aware of Milo coming closer and I pray he won't touch me. I feel like I'm breathing through a straw, like my skin may split. *Pushed!*

"Who told you about the tape?" I manage.

Samantha shakes her head, eyes still fixed on the bottle in my hand. I want to throw it at her.

"Do you remember anything else?" I ask.

"Maybe if you come again later, I'll remember more."

I bet. And if I bring more booze, I bet you'll remember a ton more.

Whether or not any of this is true is the real question.

"Thanks for your help, Sam." I put the bottle on the ground between us and leave, making my way back to the car with Milo trailing behind me. He pops the locks on the ancient Ford and we pile in.

Pushed.

"It doesn't make any sense." I paw wet hair out of my eyes, tuck it behind my ears. "If you're going to kill someone, you don't drag them up flight after flight of stairs and throw them out a window."

"You do if you need it to look like a suicide."

I cut my eyes to Milo. I don't get it. He's not being an ass. He sounds . . . thoughtful.

I yank my gaze forward. "If you're going to kill someone, you make sure it takes. Gun. Knife. Strangling. You don't want witnesses. You don't want any chance that the person survives."

"True. Ideally, that's exactly what you do." Milo stretches out his legs, settling into the driver's seat like he's settling into the idea. "What if you need to eliminate someone without risking repercussions?"

"Like with the cops?" I ask. *Like with my dad?*

Milo turns, realizes I'm staring at him. We both wrench our eyes away.

"Yeah, like the cops." This time, his tone has shifted. Milo agrees so easily I know he doesn't agree at all. He's thinking of my dad too. Or someone like him.

Amazing how I remember so much about my dad and I don't remember her loving me. . . . I want to. Desperately. What kind of sick joke is it that I can remember the things I want to forget, but *this*? This memory that Sam has and I don't? It's a memory I want to keep and I've lost it.

"Let's get out of here," I say.

Milo nods and turns the ignition. As we pull away from the curb, I stare through the rain-spattered windshield, trying to decide if I believe any of what Sam said.

I'm scared to admit it . . . I do.

Milo makes a hard right and plows the Crown Vic through an enormous puddle. "So, all flirting aside, why'd you call me for this?"

"Figured you would have better contacts with this stuff."

"What's that mean? I know crazy better than you do?"

I drum my fingers against my leg, debating my answer. I recognize the pissed-off simmering under the joke. I use it too frequently myself and it's another unpleasant reminder of how similar we are. "Sorry, yeah, because of your dad and all."

Milo nods. "And your artist sidekick?"

My insides clench. "We broke up."

"I don't believe you."

"Believe it. I got some bullies expelled. He was . . . upset."

Milo settles deeper into his seat as we switch lanes. "Getting bullies expelled sounds like a good thing."

"Griff had a problem with the way I did it."

"Do tell."

"I got ahold of one of the guys' cell phone. It had video of them smoking up and drinking at a lacrosse game so I, uh, posted it to the school's YouTube account and then locked the account."

"Nicely done."

I glance at Milo, search his face to see if he's lying. He's not and a flicker of pride licks the inside of my rib cage. "Griff was pissed. He thinks I stooped to their level."

Milo shrugs. "You believe in true love? Like love at first sight or whatever?"

I have no idea where he's going with this, but I know my answer. "No."

"Me either. I think it presupposes that love is perfect—that people are perfect or they can be. I think you're supposed to fall in love with someone who's perfect for you. Someone whose failings are arranged in a way that they hinge with yours."

"Wow, that sounds like something out of a fortune cookie. A really big, long-winded fortune cookie."

"I'm being serious. Love is supposed to make you a better version of who you really are—not who the other person wants you to be."

"I'm not sure I want to be the person I am."

Milo cuts me a quick glance, his face half illuminated from the dash. "Is that him talking? Or you?"

I look out the window so I don't have to answer. "You think Sam was lying?"

"No."

"Me either."

"How'd you know to go looking for her?" Milo asks. "What made you decide after all this time?"

Because I got some gifts in the mail. Sounds incredibly

stupid though and would be even worse if I said it out loud. Griff may have been right about this being convenient. Considering the messages attached to the end of the interviews, he might have even more than just a point.

But I'm not walking away.

"Oh, you know how it goes," I say at last. "I've been thinking about her for a few years now. Went ahead and decided to follow up."

"Riiiigggghhhhtttt. You going to get that security footage?"

Finally. Something I can be honest about. I look at Milo, smile. "Without a doubt."

I am now going on less than four hours of sleep and I look like it. Bags under my eyes? Check. Pasty? Check. Bloodshot eyes? Oh my God, yes.

I have a history test this morning and all I can think about is Kyle Bay and that security video.

I need it . . . I'm just not sure how I'm going to get my hands on it.

I zip my messenger bag closed and check my phone. Twenty minutes until Bren has to drop Lily off at school and our adoptive mom is still running around in bare feet. Looks like I'm not the only one who's had a bad night. Bren streaks past me, muttering about her keys.

"Do you want help?" I ask.

"No, no, I'm fine. Just do some deep breathing or something so you're calm before your history test. We want you to do well."

The only way I'm going to do well on my test is through divine intervention, but whatever. Bren gallops past again and I watch her go.

So how am I going to get that video?

The building my mom jumped from has changed property managers twice in the past four years, so odds are pretty good that the recording has been off-sited into storage. And, unfortunately, neither company has any sort of employee portal that I could manipulate, and that would only work if—*if*—the companies actually kept that sort of material online.

Which I highly doubt they do.

There might be a copy of the security footage at the police department, but that would involve asking Carson for a favor and I'd rather dig my eyes out with spoons.

"Wick, honey, are you getting sick?" Bren slides to a stop in front of me, feeling my forehead with one hand, juggling her car keys and purse with the other. "You don't look like you feel well."

Nothing that the contraband energy drink in my bag can't fix. Bren thinks caffeine will stunt my growth so I have to sneak it.

"Just tired," I say, and give her a smile.

Still surprises me when she smiles back. Suddenly, we're one big happy family. I'm pretending and she believes. I've made her feel better and I should feel really good about that. I don't.

"Okay. I'll be ready to go in just a few. I just need"—Bren

gropes around in her bag—"my planner. Where's my planner?"

She dashes into the kitchen and the home phone rings. Bren picks it up and for a couple minutes there's nothing, just low-voiced mumblings, giving me more time to obsess about the footage and still come up with nothing.

"Wick? That was Manda Ellery."

The way Bren says our neighbor's name makes me stiffen.

"She said she saw you coming in after four in the morning last night." Bren appears in the doorway, head tilted in confusion. "What were you doing? Did you . . . sneak out?"

Oh. Shit. I need a lie. I need a really good lie.

"Did you need something?" Bren asks.

Milk? Stupid. There's no way she's going to believe that. I chew the inside of my cheek, unable to believe that even after all my care—putting away the Mini in total darkness, taking off my shoes before slipping inside the kitchen—I end up getting busted by our nosy insomniac neighbor.

I guess I should be glad Manda didn't pay any attention when rats were getting nailed to our front door.

"Well?" Bren demands, twin spots of color blooming on her cheeks.

"What's going on?" Lily jumps down the last stair, hair and clothes immaculate, book bag strapped on. "What's wrong?"

Better to just confess, right? "Sorry, Bren. I had something I had to do last night."

"Something to do?" she echoes. "You sneaked out! How could you do that?"

"*Wick*," Lily says, and suddenly, Bren and my sister look so much alike I nearly laugh.

Thank God I don't though because Bren looks ready to kill me on the spot. She holds up one finger, pointing it at the ceiling. "What exactly did you have to do that would necessitate *sneaking* out of the house that late?"

I was wrong. I need the really good lie right now, not earlier. "I was restless. I needed some air. I'm sorry."

I'm also lame as hell. I should have a better excuse.

Bren's nose wrinkles. "You were restless? Were you partying or something? Did you go see Griff?"

I wince at his name and Bren sees it. She opens her mouth and I cut her off. "Yeah, I went to see Griff. It was . . . unexpected. I should have asked you. I'm sorry."

"You're right. You should have asked." Bren's nodding hard now, strands of hair popping loose from her chignon. "You don't get to just wander around whenever you feel like it, Wick. It's dangerous out there—especially with what's going on with your dad's case."

Again, it's the inflection that tells me whatever is about to happen, I'm not going to like it. I watch Bren warily.

"You're grounded," she says. "Total lockdown until further notice. You go to school. You come home. That's it."

"You can't do that. I have—"

"You don't have anything. Not anymore."

This is ridiculous. I brought down a child rapist by infecting his computer with a virus I created. I used to catch cheaters for pay. I worked for my dad, an epic douche canoe, for *years* as his personal hacker.

And I'm grounded for sneaking out of the house.

I should probably find it funny.

I've caught up on my history work, finished all my midterm projects, and rechecked the security system in case any unwelcome guests should decide to show up. Considering my luck right now, an appearance from Kyle or Jason would be pretty much on point.

Being pissed keeps me from being scared.

Well, *that* and working for Carson again. He wants something, anything that will give him an opening to Bay. The entire city is treating the judge with kid gloves and

Carson wants to choke the life out of him.

And as much as I hate to admit it, I can't blame the detective. We hate the judge for different reasons, but it's still hate living underneath both our skins. Bay has gone to the papers, telling everyone who will listen how horrible this has been for him, how his family is gone, destroyed.

It sent the newspaper blog into a frenzy of pity. Funny. I don't remember anyone being upset when Bay didn't protect my family from my dad. No one mourned when my mother's life ended.

But I do remember how these same people wanted Lily and me sent away after she died.

Since the sniffer is still only giving me work info on Bay, I dig into the pictures I stole from Ed Price's office. Everything is copied to my laptop, so I can access the images' Exif files.

It's useful stuff, since it captures all of the camera settings and information for each photo, things like the shutter speed, focal length, and date/time stamps. Looks like all of the photographs were taken with the Nikon D90 SLR camera registered to an IBay. No mystery there. That must be Ian. Considering they were all living together at the time, Kyle probably borrowed the camera and, later, dumped the images onto a computer hard drive or jump drive. So that leaves . . . what else?

Ugh. The pictures themselves. Whoever took them enjoyed the process. The shots are all from different angles. In one, you can see Lell's entire mutilated body. In another, there's only her bloodied chest. There are a few close-ups that are more awkwardly placed. The camera angle is cocked and you can see another person's hand and forearm in the shot, posing Lell's head so it better faces the camera. There's a small splatter of blood on the guy's forearm. Or is it a birthmark? It kind of looks like one of the amoebas we studied in biology: lumpy-edged and tiny, which makes me believe it might be a birthmark.

It's, quite literally, very little to go on. After another hour of staring at the pictures, all I have to give Carson is the "blood splatter that looks like a birthmark" theory and the fact that both the victims were stabbed to death. I'm sure a forensic specialist would be able to get more from the photos. All I'm getting is nauseated.

No matter how many times I scroll through the pictures I don't get over being disgusted. They're horrifying. No one deserves to die like that.

It's only because I've pulled back from the screen that I notice the movement on my second monitor screen. A man steps out of the shadows down on the street. He's looking at our neighbors, our yard, the setup of our house.

He's too far away to get an ID, but I don't really need one. I recognize the walk, the agitation. He paces the same way now as he did in the woods when he chased me.

Kyle Bay.

He's found me.

Kyle leaves around two, but I can't manage any real sleep after that. I keep getting up to check the security feed, and when I finally put my head on my desk and doze off, I dream about being buried alive.

The alarm goes off at seven. I stumble downstairs, late, and Bren tells me I can drive myself to school. Gotta think this is a good sign. Either she's getting tired of taking me to school or I'm on the verge of being ungrounded.

Because I'm running behind, I get stuck parking at the very back of the lot and have to hoof it to my locker before the homeroom bell rings. I don't even have the lock open before I hear someone's throat clear.

"I never see you anymore."

I turn around slowly, stifling a sigh. Ian Bay is leaning against the lockers, both hands fisted around his book bag straps, a new travel magazine stuffed in the bag's side pocket.

"I've been busy," I say. "I'm still finishing up midterm projects."

Which is mostly true. I'm just omitting the part where I've been kinda sorta avoiding him ever since I turned in our computer science report. I've had things to do for Carson and I've been looking into my mom. The way those two things are seeping into each other bothers me. A lot.

Then again, now that I'm face-to-face with Ian I feel worse. I'm not the only person who's lost people—and he stands to lose even more if Carson doesn't catch his brother.

"Maybe we could do something after you're done?" Ian asks.

"Yeah, maybe."

I take my history book out of my bag, open my locker, and scowl.

There's another DVD on top of my books. Must be more interviews. This is starting to move past creepy and slide straight into annoying.

I turn the DVD over, check the inside of the case. No labels.

"What is it?" Ian asks.

"Nothing." And it is nothing. I'm half tempted to leave it there and slam the door. What's the point of watching anymore? What's the point of any of it?

There isn't.

But I still end up pocketing it.

I wish I hadn't.

I wish I'd thrown the DVD away, buried it, *burned* it.

God, I'm such a liar. I wanted the security footage. You'd think I would have been thrilled, done some sort of happy dance rather than vomit in the toilet.

Yeah, you'd think.

I tell Bren I have a migraine and I go to my room as soon as I get home from school. First off, I check the security cameras for our house and, to my relief, there's no sign of Kyle or Jason. The front yard stayed empty except for the neighbor's dog coming by to use Bren's bushes as his personal potty. Feeling better already, I pop the new DVD into my computer and wait for the virus check to finish while I change.

It's only when I look at the screen that I realize something's wrong—well, not wrong, *different*. There's just one file and usually the interview DVDs include around twenty different video clips.

I sit down, hit play. The video is short, less than four minutes, and it's at a distance, shot from a telephone pole near the parking lot . . . you can see my mom step onto the ledge, you can see her hesitate, and then jump.

Watching it the first time made me hurl. The second time, I nearly cried. The third? I realize she hesitates because she's talking and my heart rams into my throat.

I sit up straight. Is there someone else there? I rewind the video. She talks. She jumps.

I do it again. She talks. She jumps.

I close the video, pop a CD into the other drive, and install an editing software package I downloaded last year from a Russian site. Running the security video back through the program, I can pause on the frame where my mom looks like she's talking. Then I enlarge it, lighten the shadows, tweak the coloring. . . .

And realize there's not just one person standing behind my mom. There are two.

The one on the right is slim, tall, and could be anyone. The second is bulky, tall, and has to be Joe. Has to be.

What's he doing there?

I rerun the enhanced video, watch how the figures move, sweat breaking out between my shoulders. I can't tell what they're doing. There's light from the streetlamps below—enough for them to see, nowhere near enough for me. After another minute, I turn it off, sit on my hands to make them stop shaking. It's been four years. This shouldn't be so hard.

So why's my face wet with tears?

Get it together. Get it together.

Think it through. Why did I get the DVD in the first place? Is this linked to the other interviews I've been receiving?

Possibly, but there's no label, no message at the end of the video, no handwriting like before, so either the person who's been giving them to me has changed it up . . . or someone else gave me the security video.

So who would that be?

What a joke. Like I care. Now that I'm past crying all I can think about is Joe. I know it's him in the background. I *know* it. It's in the line of the shoulders, the way the figure swings to the left after she jumps. It's him and it makes me think of his nasty smiles. Except they weren't just nasty, were they? They were . . . knowing. Smug. Dangerous.

In the months after my mom's death, he used to watch me. It felt like every time I looked up, he was staring. I thought it was because he had forgotten how to grieve. Really it was because he enjoyed watching my pain.

Or because he was trying to figure out if I knew.

If I guessed.

My temples really are thumping now, my pretend migraine coming to life. I scrub them hard with both hands before hitting the eject button. The DVD slides out and, for a second, I just stare at it.

Is that . . . ink?

Picking it up by the edges, I examine the DVD's inner ring and think—*think*—there's a smear of green ink on the inside. Like someone's thumb was stained, smudging ink onto the plastic as the DVD was put into the case.

Griff draws in green and blue ink, but he would never have given me this footage. He doesn't think I should be pursuing this. He doesn't—

Oh, shit, now I'm crying all over again.

It takes more courage than I would have thought to walk up to Griff the next morning at school. I wait for him in the hallway, feeling a bit like a spider hiding in a corner, until he stops by his locker on the way to homeroom.

"Griff?" I put my hand on his arm and he recoils.

"What is it, Wick?"

Heat rolls up my neck. "Did you give me the DVD? Of my mom on that building?" I can't bring myself to say "suicide" anymore because it's not accurate. I can't bring myself to say "murder" either.

"No idea what you're talking about," Griff says.

He does though. Griff's barely breathing. His body's strung so tight and I don't understand. We're not together. He gave me something he knew I would want even though he didn't approve, didn't think I should have it.

He helped me even though I'm the last person he should ever want to help.

How did he even know?

"Thank you," I whisper, rolling my hands into fists so I don't touch him.

"Don't read anything into it."

How can I not? I need to say something here and I don't know what it is. I want him to look at me, but he won't.

Griff shuts his locker hard. "Milo told me you wanted it."

I blink. Milo had no business telling Griff anything. "I . . ."

"What kind of person would give you something like that?"

I bristle. "Someone who wanted me to know the truth."

"You really believe that's what this is about?"

"That's *exactly* what it's about."

Griff yanks his book bag onto his shoulder. "I asked my cousin about your mom and he got the recording from her file. I wanted you to get it from me, not Milo, from someone who cares about you, not someone who's egging you on."

The pain is brief and brilliant and all I can hear is my mom saying how you will hurt the ones you love even if you shouldn't. This hurts. Once upon a time, Griff would never have hurt me. Maybe that's the difference. He no longer loves me like I still love him.

I shake myself. "He's not egging me on. He's—"

"If you want to concentrate on the truth, remember that there was nothing to see. She jumped. She was alone."

She wasn't, and if she was murdered, if she jumped to

save us, if I spent all this time hating her . . . but Griff walks away before I can say a word. He doesn't even look back, which is just as well probably because now I'm slumped against the lockers, arms folded across my stomach.

It wasn't supposed to be this way.

Then again, maybe it was.

I love him, and it's ruined me. He's ruined me. He walked into my life like any other person, but there was something about the way he talked to me and then something about the way he treated me and then . . . there I was, hostage for another smile. My life was not my own anymore.

I sacrificed Griff to protect him and Lily and Bren from Carson and from the futures they deserve and he could destroy.

What does that leave for me?

In my bag, my phone buzzes and I ignore it. I can't take my eyes off what's left of Griff. I can see glimpses of his head, his shoulders as he moves through the crowd. I watch until he's gone.

My phone stops buzzing.

Starts again.

I stick my hand in, fish around a bit before finding my cell. Milo. I'm not sure I want to answer. Yeah, I'm glad (is that the right word? I'm not sure) I got the security video of my mom. I'm also pissed at him for going behind my back.

As I try to decide, the call rolls to voice mail, starts ringing again.

I press the answer key. "Milo?"

"Wick . . . I need . . . please."

He sounds rough—*hurt*—and my throat twists shut. "Are you okay?"

"Please come. Please?"

I can't. I'm at school. I'm grounded. I'm—the phone clicks. The line's dead. I hit redial as I head for the parking lot. There's no answer.

No matter how many times I call.

The restaurant looks as abandoned as ever when I pull in almost thirty minutes later. I beat on the door, but no one answers. I try Milo's cell again. Still no answer.

Pressing one hand against the front window, I peer through the hazy glass. Someone might be in there. Lights are on and I think—*think*—I can hear a television playing.

So where the hell is Milo? I start to pound on the door again and pause. There's a small half-moon carved into the wood next to the doorjamb, a Cheshire cat smile. It's the same mark Milo left on my CPU's case and reminds me of his smile.

Which I'm going to wreck if this turns out to be some stupid joke.

I grab the door handle and it turns in my hand. "Milo?" No answer.

I pick my way around the dust-covered tables, heading for the kitchen door. Is it possible he's in the computer room? I brush the door with my fingertips, hesitating, and

264

then push my way in. The empty kitchen stretches out on either side of me.

"Milo?"

"Wick." It's so soft I almost miss it. I turn, spotting Milo on the kitchen floor. He's splay-legged with a bottle of Jameson held loosely in one hand. He looks like he's been airlifted in from some epic party and I'm instantly pissed.

Then he lifts the bottle, revealing a smear of red along his torso.

"Milo, you're hurt!"

"Just a flesh wound." He laughs, winces, and settles with giving me a weak smile and swallowing more Jameson. The smile turns into a grimace.

I drop to my knees, using one hand to peel the sodden T-shirt away from his rib cage. "Jesus, we gotta get you out of here."

Milo doesn't respond so I wedge one shoulder under him, boost him to his feet. "How did it happen?"

He winces and stares into space, teeth gritted.

"Milo," I prompt, but he still won't look at me. "It was your dad, wasn't it?"

"He's . . . not well. I upset him."

I angle us through the door and Milo puts out one hand to steady himself, gasping as he does.

"He wasn't always like this. Tomorrow he might be totally different." Milo pauses, his face going pale as he fights through a wave of pain. "I think crazy is like a bug in your brain, scuttling under your skull, wrenching loose all your wires."

"Milo, this is way worse than some bug."

"It's fine. Really. He's actually perfectly normal . . . except when he's not." He draws in a wobbly breath. "There are monsters living inside us and, sometimes, they win."

God help me if he's going to get all philosophical again. "We should get you checked out by a hospital."

"No hospitals."

"Look how much blood you've lost. You could be cooking up an infection." I stagger a little as I reposition him against me. "You sound freaking delirious."

"No hospitals," Milo repeats. "They'll ask questions about him."

He pulls his face close to mine, and for a moment, I'm not staring at Milo the computer builder. I'm staring at Milo the little boy and, somehow, I recognize this Milo even more than the first.

It's the fear. Both of us understand what it's like to hide our wounds.

"Just . . . get me through to my room," Milo grates. "It's no big deal. Perfectly normal. I've got first aid stuff there."

I roll my eyes. *It's perfectly normal to keep first aid kits in your bedroom? Whatever.*

Milo sidesteps to avoid an overstuffed arm chair and his legs buckle. "Shit," he whispers, arms tightening around me.

"Milo, you're too heavy. Milo—"

He slumps toward his bed, dragging me with him, and I roll, pushing him backward. It turns me onto my hands and knees. On top of him. I start to scramble off and Milo grabs my sides, pinning my hips to his.

"I think you're good for me, Wicked."

"Don't call me that."

A shadow falls behind his eyes. Regret? I can't tell and I don't think I want to know.

"I think you're good for me, *Wick*."

"Why's that?"

"Because I'm broken."

I almost laugh. "Then I'm no good to you at all. I don't do broken. I'm not the healing type."

"That's why you're perfect."

I go still.

"I can't ruin you because you're already ruined." Milo eases one hand behind my neck, cradling the base of my skull like I'm fragile. "I can't corrupt you because you're already corrupted. It makes you incorruptible."

He laughs like the word is hilarious . . . or amazing.

And then he kisses me.

Milo's hands are hot against my skin. He holds me carefully, easing me closer like he's afraid. The kiss is soft . . . sweet. It might even be kind of perfect. If my lips didn't still expect Griff. If my skin didn't still burn for him.

He isn't there, but my body hunts for him like he's everywhere.

Milo kisses my upper lip, the corner of my mouth, the tip of my nose. I'm completely still. He probably thinks it's because I want him—maybe part of me does. Most of me though is trying not to cry, and when I open my eyes, he's studying me.

"I would do anything to make you want me," Milo whispers.

I shake my head hard like I'm sure he couldn't . . . then again maybe he could. Maybe if things were different and I didn't want a guy who doesn't want me.

Milo curves me against him, fitting his mouth to mine. His hands are everywhere, telling stories on my skin.

About how we could be together.

About how all things can be fixed.

Forgiven.

I break away and Milo cradles my cheek with his palm, his thumb rubbing my lower lip. "He doesn't understand you. He doesn't understand what you could be."

I try to laugh and it comes out strangled. "But somehow you get it?"

"Yeah, I do."

Now is the time to really laugh . . . and realize I can't. Because he does get me. Milo's the first person who hasn't made me feel ashamed for what I am.

I have no idea if that's a good thing.

"Why did you ask Griff for the security video?"

A shadow slides behind Milo's eyes. "I wanted to give you something no one else could."

And be my hero? Of all people, I would have thought Milo would realize we're the bad guys. "I saw it. Thanks."

"Bastard gave it to you? Should have known he'd cock-block me."

"It's not—" I pull back and Milo sags into the pillows, wincing. "Jesus, you look bad. Where's the first aid kit?"

He nudges his chin toward the bedside table and I spend a minute rummaging under computer part magazines before finding a white box filled with bandages and antiseptic.

"I'm going to warn you now," I say, dousing a gauze pad

with rubbing alcohol. "I paid absolutely no attention in health class."

"Lucky me." Teeth gritted, Milo tugs off his T-shirt, revealing a hardened chest marred with blood. He leans one tattooed forearm against his eyes. "Just do it."

I press the pad to his side, hold tight even though Milo flinches. "I'm sorry."

He doesn't respond so I work faster, cleaning the wound until I can cover it with another thick gauze pad and tape it in place. There's a light sheen of sweat across his skin now, but he doesn't complain—just takes swallow after swallow of Jameson.

"There. You should be good now." I tug the bottle out of his hand and set it on the nightstand—just out of reach.

Milo smiles bitterly. "See, Wick? You're good for me."

"You're drunk. Go to sleep." I push up, ditching him on the bed. Once Griff thought I was good for him too. I'm tired of being good for other people.

I want to be good for me.

I head for the door, stepping around mounds of discarded laundry and making it only a few feet before I turn around. Should I leave him like this? I chew my thumbnail. Unconscious, Milo looks younger and smaller than he usually does. What if he wakes and needs something? What if he wakes and his dad's returned?

Oh, screw it. It's not like I'm going to go back to school. I push a balled-up sweatshirt off a nearby armchair and curl my legs under me, watching him. I don't feel myself fall asleep. I must have though, because when I open my eyes, Milo is watching me.

"Do you always sleep like that?" His voice is frayed like he's barely holding himself together.

"Like what?"

"All tucked up into yourself, like you're an animal used to sleeping underground."

I roll to my other hip, draw my legs tight underneath me. Too many nights of no sleep and too much stress and too much, well, *everything* have gotten to me. My entire body feels weighed down by rocks. "Go to sleep, Milo, or I'll call 911."

His laugh is low and dark. It's the last thing I remember before I slip under.

I wake up again two hours later and Milo is still sleeping hard. I spend a couple minutes staring at him, trying to decide how I feel about him getting Griff to give me the security feed, and because I *can't* decide, I concentrate instead on whether Milo's dying.

And whether I *should* call 911.

But his coloring is almost dark cinnamon again, which is closer to normal for him, he seems to be comfortable, and, honestly, I have zero way of explaining any of this to the EMTs, so I leave him alone.

I pad across the room, heading for my sweatshirt, and something soft catches my foot. I look down, roll my eyes. That's a bra. Who would leave her bra behind?

A girl who wanted an excuse to come back.

I pull on my sweatshirt and check the time on my phone. Huh, right now I would be in Spanish class, which means I have almost four hours before I need to be home. So what am I going to do with myself?

In response, my stomach pinches. I need to eat. Considering this is Milo's place, though, I have an equal chance of finding food or blowing myself sky-high. I study the door to his pantry, weighing my options. What if he's booby-trapped it?

I take a deep breath, tell myself I'm being an idiot, and yank the door open. No explosion. Not really any food either. Most of the pantry is devoted to spare computer parts. What does Milo do for meals around here? Ethernet cables and soldering equipment?

Eventually, I find club crackers and ginger ale sitting on a crate of motherboards and I take a sleeve of crackers and a soda for me, leaving the rest on Milo's bedside table.

Four hours to kill is a seriously nice windfall. What should I do with it?

My computer's at home, but I don't really have much to work on anyway since I already turned in my limited findings to Carson.

That leaves my mom. I could drive around Five Points, see if I could find Sam again. Stupid idea . . . that lingers.

What if I told her I saw the video? I could say I know my mom jumped. She wasn't pushed.

I don't know why I need to make that distinction.

Maybe because I'm hoping she'll remember something else. Maybe because I'm pissed.

Either way, I take the keys off Milo's worktable, lock the door in case his dad returns before I do, and head for Five Points. Milo's contact had said Sam sticks to the same general area, so I head for the alley we found her in and waste fifteen minutes looking for her. There's no sign of Sam anywhere, but as I pass by the same pile of trash again, I recognize the bottle I stole from Bren's wine fridge.

It's empty, of course. And what I assumed was trash isn't actually trash. I think it's Sam's stuff. I toe through mismatched tennis shoes, a box of lighters, a one-eared stuffed bunny. Impossible to tell if any of it's hers. I think it might be though.

Which means she'll be back soon, right?

Behind me, a bottle tips over and rolls past my feet. I turn, hope screwing tight around my chest.

But it isn't Sam.

It's Jason Baines.

"Heard you were looking for me," he says.

"Somehow I doubt that." I ease to my feet, eyes already hunting for the exit. No good though. Only way out is the way I came in and Jason's grinning like he knows he's blocking it.

"Let me clarify." Jason runs one hand through his short, dark hair, and the oh-so-casual move reveals the nine millimeter tucked in the waistband of his jeans. "Sam told me you were looking for some security footage."

I start to say I've already seen it and something keeps me quiet. Someone told Sam "all about" the footage and if that someone is Jason . . . I bump up my chin. "And? Sam's the one who told me about it."

"I think you should leave this alone."

I swallow hard. "That's . . . not going to happen."

Jason nods slowly before looking behind us, up the alley where no one's around. "You know, Wick, Joe Bender taught me everything I know about this business."

"I remember."

"You see that tape . . . you goin' to tell your dad what you see on it?"

Chills skitter across my skin. "Why would I tell him anything?"

"Maybe because it would be beneficial to both of us."

"Go on."

Jason's tongue touches his lower lip. "We knew your mom was snitching on us. Joe found out first and told me. He said we had to do something."

The dealer smiles. "That something ended up being the two of us taking your mom up to that building at three in the morning. Joe told her all about how he knew. She denied it . . . for a while."

The truth is supposed to be bright and I feel like I'm buried. "Did he hurt her?"

Jason stares at me, saying nothing.

"Do you have to think about it? It's a yes-or-no question."

"I'm just surprised you have to ask." Jason takes a pack of cigarettes from his jacket pocket and lights one. "Of course he hurt her."

I nod. Of course he hurt her. Of course. The whole thing makes more sense than I want it to. I believe Joe would hurt her—I do—but it doesn't match with the body language from the tape. She wasn't running away. The movements were so deliberate.

I force my chin up and hope my voice won't break. "What happened? Why did she jump?"

"Joe said he would kill you and Lily if she didn't."

What? Briefly, I'm spinning far above my head; then, just as suddenly, I'm concreted to the ground.

Jason's searching my face now, interested in what he sees, and because I'm afraid of what that might be, I turn it around, go on the attack. "And you did *nothing*?"

He flicks ash from his cigarette. "You wanted the truth. I gave it to you—free of charge. Here's another truth: You ain't as safe as you think you are."

"Yeah, good luck with that." I roll my eyes. "My foster mom gets one look at you lurking around and she'll call the cops. They actually listen to people like her. It's kinda amazing."

"Not what I meant. Thanks for the tip though. I'll keep it in mind." Jason takes another drag on his cigarette. "What I'm more interested in is why that detective's always talking to you."

"Yeah, I got your present. Appreciate the thought. You're way off though. He's trying to press more charges against my dad. He thinks I'm an inroad."

"He thinks? Or he *knows*?" Another drag. This time, Jason takes a few seconds before blowing out the smoke. "I don't remember what happened at that party, but I'm pretty sure something did and you were behind it."

"I heard you couldn't hold your booze."

"That's the rumor. Since you were so kind to give me a tip, I'll give you one too: Nothing folks around here hate more than snitches. Maybe if you did me a favor, no one would have to know."

We stare at each other, the silence between us stretching thin as a string of taffy.

"Tell your dad." Jason's eyes go light. "Tell him what Joe did—just remember to leave me out of it."

I need space to unpack this information and I'm already turning away when—wait. *Wait.* "Why does my dad need to know now? What's changed?"

Jason stares at me like I'm a moron. "You think I want to be a secondhand man forever? I need Joe dead. I already have his people, his contacts, his position. They answer to me now. I want to keep it that way."

"That so?"

"Yeah, that's so. How'd you think I found you? I have eyes everywhere now. I'm just a phone call away. I still need him gone though. Clean break, you know?"

I nod like I do.

Jason picks a piece of tobacco from his tongue and flicks it away. "If you tell your daddy, he'll kill him."

It takes me forever to get back to my car, and once I do, I manage to drive off like everything's fine.

Too bad I don't even make it to the interstate before I have to pull over. I stop the car on the road's shoulder and try to take deep breaths. It doesn't help.

I press one chilled hand to my forehead. My mother was murdered—*murdered*—and, somehow, it makes . . . sense?

No. That's definitely not the word. I don't know what else to call it though. All that's left of me is broken puzzle pieces. I can jam them together, but there are still empty spaces, chipped-edge continents I didn't know existed—and that's where my mother lives, in the space between.

There's a twinge in my arm, the nerves are starting to burn, and when I shut my eyes against it, all I see is my father grinning. He wouldn't kill someone. He wouldn't.

Yes, he would.

This is Michael. *Michael.* The man who almost killed me when I was growing up, the man who beat my mother, terrorized my sister. And we were his *family*.

The men who work for him have even worse stories. Everyone knows you don't take anything Michael doesn't give you and, once you work for him, he owns you forever.

My mother belonged to Michael. Joe still belongs to Michael. What would my father say if I told him Joe murdered his wife?

Two cars pass me and I stiffen, checking my rearview mirror for cops. The last thing I need is one stopping for a game of "Are you lost, little girl?"

I still can't put the car in drive though. Obviously, Jason has his own agenda. He isn't confirming my suspicions to be helpful. If I told my dad, Jason would benefit and I'd know.

Then again, if I told him, I could promise myself I did it for Lily. I did it for my mom. . . . Deep down though I'd know that I did it for me. Joe murdered my mother. He threatened to murder my sister and me. It's fitting and yet . . . and yet . . .

I grab my phone and dial Stringer.

"My my," he says upon picking up. "You need another batch of roofies, girlie? I didn't think you were the type."

"I need information."

"That costs money too."

"I'm good for it." I take an unsteady breath, grip the phone a little harder. "I want to know what's up with Jason Baines. Is he really taking Joe's territories?"

There's a soft squeaking noise from Stringer's end. The dealer's chewing something, thinking about my question.

"Who wants to know?" he asks finally.

"My dad."

The chewing stops and I almost smile. In certain circles, Michael's name is like a spell. It's the Open Sesame command no one can resist.

"I pay your daddy like I'm supposed to," Stringer says. "I don't want no trouble."

"Then tell me what I want to know."

"Everybody from Tate's crew reports to Jason now. Everybody. The boy wants a promotion."

By having Joe killed. "One more thing, Stringer." I hesitate because I haven't decided what I'm going to do so I shouldn't even ask . . . "Do you think you could get a cell to my dad? I may have something I need him to see."

"All things can be accomplished with money."

My laugh is a silent puff. "Thanks. I'll make sure to send something your way for your time."

"You better." He hangs up and I spend a moment fiddling with my phone.

Michael would kill someone. True. But he wouldn't kill someone for me or for her . . . would he?

I wrap my fingers around the steering wheel, grip until the veins look like worms beneath the skin. If Michael would kill Joe, I can't tell him. It would be wrong, unforgivable. It makes me into someone Jason used. I'd be an accomplice.

Or I could think of it as being a weapon.

My breath hitches. If I did tell Michael, I would avenge my mother.

I walk in the door at three forty-five exactly and Bren is waiting for me in the front hall. For a second I panic. At first I think she knows I've been skipping. Then I see the suitcase at her feet.

"Oh good, Wick, you're home." Bren hops from foot to foot as she wiggles into a pair of heels. "I wanted to talk to you. I had an emergency meeting come up. I have to fly to Dallas for a few days."

"Okay."

Bren chews her lower lip, studying me. "You're still grounded. So that means Manda's going to check in on you."

Lucky me. "Okay."

"She'll call every day to make sure you're home and to see if you need anything. I've done some extra shopping so you should be good for food and there's always that emergency credit card I gave you—" Bren cuts off, her face screwing tight as she remembers something else she's supposed to be doing instead of lecturing me. I feel kind of sorry for her. She's stretched so thin these days.

"It'll be fine, Bren. Don't worry."

She gives me a suspicious look. "Lily's staying with the Harrisons. She's gotten really close to their daughter and it'll work out better for her to get to school since she can ride in with them. I hope you don't mind being alone for a bit."

I shrug. Lily hasn't spoken to me in days—since the morning I got grounded—so even when I haven't been alone around here, it feels like I am. "No, I'll be fine. I'm glad she's making friends."

Bren nods, starts to say something, stops. We're in that place again, where things are awkward.

"When does your flight leave?" I ask.

She grimaces, checks her phone. "Next few hours. I need to go. Are you sure you'll be okay?"

What would she do if I said I wouldn't be? Take me with her? It's so stupid it's funny until I realize Bren would probably love that. It would make her feel needed and that's not something I can offer.

"I'll be fine, Bren. Promise. I'll call you if I need any-thing."

She brightens so much at that I make a mental note to actually call her. Maybe I can ask Bren's advice on some-thing . . . like how to heat up noodles or whatever, because

I'm pretty sure her head would twist off if I told her about how I'm going to use her time away to talk to my father.

In my bag, my cell buzzes with another text and, while Bren's back is turned, I check the screen. Milo.

thanks

It makes me smile, but before I can respond, Bren's hauling all her stuff out to the car. I walk with her, promise twice to behave, and watch her pull out of the driveway. Then I call forward the home phone number to my cell phone. Now, whenever Mrs. Ellery calls I'll be home.

Even when I'm not.

Next step? Confronting Joe. I make the necessary phone calls from Bren's front office—not because I need the desk or the computer but because I can watch Mrs. Ellery adjust her front yard's garden gnomes. There are two of the grinning little suckers. I wonder if I could sneak over there tonight and put them in a compromising position.

Then again, she might just think they're playing leapfrog.

I turn back to my phone, using the browser to search for the county jail's phone number. The trick will be getting Joe to see me. This takes a little preparation on my part. I have to call the day before to schedule an appointment and then I have to call again to see if he accepted it. Sitting on the phone with the receptionist, I consider using one of the fake identities Joe's given me over the years. In the end, I decide against it. With my luck, Carson will have friends at the Fayette County Jail and giving him identity theft as ammo would be the end of me.

Talking murder with Joe is condemning enough and I'm banking on budget cutbacks to cover my tracks. They used to video record all prisoners' personal visits. Considering the county can't afford new locks on the cells though, I highly doubt there will be decent recording equipment.

I call the jail during lunch the next day and my stomach does an uneasy flip when the receptionist confirms Joe agreed to the meeting. I don't back down though and I show up, ten minutes ahead of time, to let a security guard sign me in and motion me through the metal detector.

I follow him down a rainbow-painted hallway where squat metal stools and black telephones sit in front of Plexiglas windows. It's like a Very Special Episode of *Teletubbies*.

"Go to the last station and I'll send him to you."

I walk to the end, checking cameras as I go, and it's hard not to grin like an idiot. Sure enough, the hallway is being monitored, but the cameras positioned above the visitor stools aren't even on. Sure they're plugged in. The little green lights that indicate activity though? They're dark.

I only wait a minute or so before an interior door cranks open. I hear Joe's shuffling before I see him and, briefly, my chest cranks tight. This might be a mistake.

Too late.

Joe doesn't sit. He collapses. And for a moment, we stare at each other until he picks up the black telephone.

"I didn't believe them when they said who it was."

"Yeah, I bet you didn't."

Joe angles himself forward, propping both elbows onto the counter. "So what is this? You miss me?"

"Oh, yeah, totally. Seeing you in that orange jumpsuit is a thrill I didn't know I was missing. I might have to do this more often."

Joe's eyes shutter. "What do you want?"

I want you to pay. The thought makes my heart surge against my rib cage. It bubbles up so clearly I realize I've wanted this all along. I just didn't know it. "I want . . . you to know I know what you did to my mother."

Joe doesn't move.

"I saw the video. I recognized you."

"No idea what you're talking about."

"Do you think my dad will?"

Joe's eyes flicker with uncertainty.

Fear.

I lean in a little. "They separated you two, didn't they? 'Cause they were worried about what you'd do together? Thing is . . . cops don't realize you're never really away from my dad, are you? Remember how you told me he always has friends?"

Another flicker in Joe's eyes, and under the fluorescent lights, sweat breaks out along his upper lip. "Friends that belong to me too."

Friends that belong to Jason now. "Maybe," I say with a smile.

"Why would your daddy even care?" Joe shifts against the chair and casts a casual look behind him, scoping out the guards. "Your mother jumped. No one's fault but hers. Your daddy always said she wasn't right."

"Getting used like a punching bag has a way of doing that to people."

Joe's laugh is belly deep. It shakes all the loosened skin on his face. "Fair enough. So what's this supposed to be then? You trying to make me feel guilty?"

He leans in close, touches the glass with two fingers like he's tracing my face.

"Get back!" On Joe's side, a guard notices our exchange and steps toward him. "Keep your hands off the glass!"

Joe turns, gives the guy an easy smile. "Sure thing, boss." The easy smile is still there when he turns to me, looks me over. "You can't touch me, Wick. Couldn't before. Still can't now. People like you—like your mom—were meant to take what people like me dish out. You were born to be used."

He waits for me to respond and I can't squeeze anything past my rage.

Joe chuckles. "Maybe you're the one who should be worried, Wick. What if one of my friends came by to visit you? Teach you a thing or two about manners? Remember how that goes?"

My mouth goes dry. Of course I remember, and judging from Joe's smirk, we're both thinking about the time he left me coughing blood on the carpet.

Remember Jason. Remember. I smile.

And it makes Joe's smile falter.

"I'll take my chances," I say, standing up. It makes me just a bit taller than Joe, who sits with his body slumped in half like an old pillow. "Because I do remember. Everything. Maybe I should start answering all those questions the detectives have. I bet I could tell them even more."

Now Joe's standing. He bares his teeth at me, and when he speaks, spit hits the glass. "That a threat? You'll pay for it."

I turn around. "No, I won't."

Thing is . . . if I were really a badass I probably wouldn't have sat in the women's restroom for ten minutes trying to collect myself. Not going to lie, standing up to Joe felt awesome.

I just wish my legs would stop shaking.

They only get worse when I spot Carson leaning against my car as I'm leaving the jail. I push my feet, one in front of the other, until my Chucks are almost touching his slouched shadow.

"Aren't you supposed to be in school, Wicket?"

"Aren't you supposed to be at work, Carson?" The detective's mouth flattens and a muscle in his jaw ticks once. "What? I thought we were playing State the Obvious."

Behind the Mini, the detective's sedan is parked and

running, an officer I don't recognize sitting shotgun. It's creepy the way he's staring at me—like I'm the one that got away.

Which I guess I am.

"What were you doing visiting Joe Bender?"

I shrug. "My good deed for the day. I thought he might be lonely."

"You're up to something, trash."

Interesting how the insult seems . . . chipped . . . like it belongs to someone else. My visiting Joe has made Carson anxious.

"What would you two have to say to each other?" the detective asks.

I'm not sure yet. I'm not entirely convinced I should tell my dad what happened. It's not that Joe doesn't deserve punishment. I'm just not sure I want to be the one responsible for his death.

"Considering Joe's going to be in jail for the next bazillion years, I doubt you have anything to worry about."

"A bazillion years, huh?" The detective snorts. "Not likely. Joe Bender's the Feds' new favorite boy. At the rate he's going, he'll be out by next year, so whatever you're playing at, trash, you should watch your back."

I study Carson, looking for the lie. "What are you talking about?"

"Bender's testifying against two other prisoners in return for a reduced sentence. He'll be out soon." A lopsided smile kicks up one corner of the detective's mouth. "Judge Bay helped set it up. Be sure to remember to thank him for both of us."

"What kind of case?"

"What do you think? More internet bullshit." Carson shrugs, studying something in the distance. "This is his first conviction and, considering how useful he's making himself, he'll be out soon."

Shit.

"Doesn't matter to me," I lie, sounding calm even though my brain is screeching. Aside from the whole *do I tell my dad or not?* thing, Joe getting out could be a real issue. When he was free, I was expected to work for him. If I had refused, he would have hurt everyone I loved.

And I just royally pissed him off.

Joe promised he could get back at me. Looks like he wasn't lying after all. Means next time will be brutal.

Which also means there can't be a next time.

I look past Carson's shoulder and notice the officer still eyeing us with interest. "You really think it's a good idea for your clown to see us? Aren't you a little worried about people finding out how you get your information?"

Carson lifts one shoulder. "I pick my team carefully. I know they'll stay loyal."

The same way I do? Through blackmail?

"What did you do, Wick?"

Funny. I'd rather he call me trash than use my name. "Nothing."

Yet.

I lift my chin. "Are we done?"

"No." Carson's attention is pinned to the building behind me. "We've been doing a bit of digging in Bay's woods. Guess what we found?" His eyes flick to me. "More bodies."

"Whose?"

Carson shrugs. "Not sure. Looks like there are animal and human remains. Whoever did this has been busy for years."

Eww. "When will you get an ID on the bodies?"

"Not fast enough. There are multiple graves, multiple skeletons. It's a lab nightmare."

"Maybe you could narrow the focus? Girls disappear from our neighborhood sometimes. Maybe Lell wasn't a victim because she was Kyle's girlfriend. Maybe she was a victim because that's where he . . . hunted." It's hard to say the word knowing it might apply to me right now. I take a ragged breath. "You could compare teeth or something to missing girls' dental records."

"I'm working on it."

"You should also think about who would benefit from pretending Kyle's still alive."

"No shit."

Anger flares through me. "Well, if you've got it all figured out, why're you bothering me?"

"Why indeed."

"You owe me protection. That was the *deal*, Carson." I

hate how my voice is sliding into a whine and I can't seem to stop it. "You haven't sent any more officers to watch our house."

"Well, you know how these things go. It's hard to maintain personal projects in this economic climate. Shame really." Carson turns to leave and stops. "Remember to stay useful, Wick. Otherwise, what's the point in keeping you?"

I leave Carson and drive straight to school, swinging my car into the parking lot as everyone else is leaving. I'd rather not be here at all, but I have a history paper due at the end of the week, and if my grades drop, Bren will come snooping.

If sneaking out of the house equals grounding, I can't imagine what skipping school would require . . . an electronic tracking anklet?

Best not to think about it.

I head for my locker, being careful to avoid any of the teachers whose classes I missed. It's not terribly difficult. The hallway is still pretty crowded—so crowded I don't see him until I'm too close to turn around.

Milo.

He grins, looking like something out of a Ralph Lauren ad. The only thing the boy is missing is a wind machine and some half-naked model hanging on him.

"How do you keep getting past security?" I ask.

"It's public school. They can't even spell *security*."

"You're feeling better."

"I'll heal. I wanted to see you, say thanks."

"No need." I concentrate on my locker combination—maybe a little more than necessary—because when he's this close I swear I can feel the heat from his skin.

The way his lips felt on mine.

"Thought I would repay the favor," he adds.

"I'm good."

"Really? Even if it takes care of your Carson problem?"

I jerk my head side to side to see if anyone's listening. "Could you be a little quieter?"

Milo chokes on his laugh. "Someday you're going to have to explain to me why you care what anyone here thinks of you."

"It's not about what people think of me, it's about staying out of jail. No one knows about my hobbies, much less about Carson's and my . . . *arrangement*."

"Like when he promised he would turn off the security cameras and didn't?"

"Seriously? Shut. Up." I glare at him and it only makes Milo's smile slide wider. "Not here."

"Again, who cares? You can't tell me you don't want to know all about your detective's storage unit and all the new compounds I put in there."

My hands slacken. "Compounds?"

"Yep, specifically, the kind the ATF gets really, really excited about. Lucky for him, I had extra lying around the restaurant. Just wait. *Someone* will call in a bomb threat. It'll be epic."

I gape and Milo grins like he enjoys it.

"Still think I don't understand you, Wick?" He edges closer, and this time, I don't move away. "We could be great together if you would just realize the past is dead, but the future is yours for the taking. *We* can take it together."

"Why me?"

"What?"

"Why *me*, Milo?"

"Because when I'm around you . . ." His dark gaze climbs across my face, stroking something nameless inside me. "Around you, I feel like I've been smacked awake. You're everything I could never be."

"And that is?"

"Powerful. Hackers are meant to rule the world. You could take it all and I want to watch you do it. I like you—for what you are and what you could be."

I like you too. It blooms under my tongue, but Milo's attention shifts, tracking something beyond my shoulder.

"Gotta go," he says, peeling himself off the lockers. "When Carson's shit hits the fan, call me. I'll want all the details on how impressed you are with what I can do."

Milo slips into a crowd of band geeks heading for the exit, and when I turn around, I see why: Griff and Mrs. Lowe, the computer lab teacher, are heading my way.

"Is everything okay, Wicket?" Mrs. Lowe asks, drawing down on me with narrowed eyes.

Unable to breathe, I nod.

"Was that a new student? I don't recognize him."

"I think so. I didn't really ask. He just wanted to know where the gym was."

Mrs. Lowe nods like this is totally understandable since only a new student would ask *me* where the gym is located. I sneak a glance at Griff and catch him staring at me. We both look away.

All it would take is one word from him and Griff's staying quiet.

"Okay then," Mrs. Lowe says, shifting her purse higher on her shoulder. "You two have a nice evening."

"You too," I say, and wait, staring at the floor, for Griff to leave too.

"So. You and Milo, huh?"

I look up. "It's not what you think."

Except it is, isn't it? Plus, unlike Griff, Milo isn't ashamed of me. I'm ashamed of me though. I'm ashamed of how tied up I am with Carson, how I've disappointed Bren . . . how I can't get over the boy who's over me.

"If it's not what I think, then what is it?" Griff asks.

I work my mouth around. What Griff thinks he saw is bad. What actually happened is worse.

Much worse.

I mean, I was going to frame Carson too, but the plan jumped off something the detective was already doing—digging into Bay—this . . . this is accusing him of something that won't just ruin his career. It could get him jail time.

I should do something . . . but I'm not going to. I'm not

sure what that says about me. I'm definitely sure I don't want to know.

In the meantime though I've taken too long to respond so Griff thinks he already has my answer.

"That's what I thought," he says, and I watch him walk away. Again.

I should follow Griff, tell him it was all a mistake, feed him lies . . . so why am I not running after him?

Because this feels too familiar to ignore and, suddenly, I'm not in my high school's hallway, I'm standing in my parents' house, watching my mom run after my dad, pouring words of love from bloodied lips.

Griff would never hit me, but he doesn't get me either and I'm embarrassed of what he sees.

Of what it makes me see.

So I turn to my locker, taking extra time to make sure he's long gone before I leave the school. This is my fault. I gave Griff a piece of me. He didn't ask me for it. Hell, maybe he did, he wanted me—at least the idea of me—for a time. And here I am now: eaten from the inside out, craving someone I didn't know I would ever crave and, if I'd been told, I would never have believed it.

I should never have allowed myself to want him. The least I can do now is protect him and I'm doing that. It should be enough.

But it's not.

So I think about my Joe problem instead and it's amazing how quickly my hands curve into claws. What am I going to do about that?

I have no idea. In fact, I could really use a bit of inspiration, but when I turn in to my driveway all I get is Jason Baines sitting on my front porch, waiting for me.

I glare at him as I park. Jason doesn't seem to mind. He walks straight to my car door and waits for me to get out.

"You know this is creepy, right?" I ask, nearly bumping him with the door as I open it. "We're not living in a sitcom. Waiting for me to come home is not cute. It's stalkerish."

"We really going to do this out here? Where your neighbors can see us?"

I'd tell him to shove it if he didn't have a point. Mrs. Ellery is standing by her mailbox, watching us. Wonderful. That's all I need right now.

"Five minutes," I say, and motion for him to follow me to the side door.

Which is still no good because Mrs. Ellery just walks farther into the road so she can glare at us.

"Kitchen," I mutter, and unlock the door, watching Jason from the corner of my vision as I key the security code into our system. He ignores it. "Talk," I say.

"I want to know your decision."

"I haven't made one."

"When will you?"

"I haven't decided."

"Fair enough." Jason wanders to the kitchen doorway and stares down the hallway, head cocked like he's considering our color palette. "Nice house."

I stiffen. "Even nicer security system."

Jason grins. "You like living with that lady?"

"Bren? Of course. She's awesome." *When she isn't overreacting.* "You don't have anything better to do than ask me personal questions?"

Jason swings around, one hand rubbing the back of his neck like it aches. The movement makes the sleeve of his shirt droop, revealing the pale skin of his forearm, and my heart trips.

There's a curl of faded ink along his forearm, the edge of a tattoo.

It's . . . lumpy. Like a birthmark. Numbness crawls up my legs. In the picture, I wasn't looking at a birthmark. I was looking at the edge of a *tattoo.*

Jason smiles. "Everything okay?"

I swallow. "'Course. Why wouldn't it be?"

He shrugs, searching my face for a beat.

All I can think about is that faded tattoo. It means Jason's holding up Lell's head in the picture and, based on the angle of the shot, that also means he was holding the camera.

Which suggests he was alone.

Kind of like I am now.

Cold creeps across my skin. I have no idea what to do here. Call Carson? How? It's a little obvious if I announce I need to take a personal call. Furthermore, what can Carson even do? I don't even know if he can arrest Jason. The incriminating pictures were obtained illegally. They won't stand up in any court of law. So that leaves . . . I have no idea.

My cell rings. Keeping one eye on Jason, I check the screen. Shit. It's Manda Ellery.

I mash the green answer button. "Hello?"

"Wicket? Wicket Tate?"

I roll my eyes. *Are there any other Wickets running around?* "Yes, it's me, Mrs. Ellery. Is everything okay?"

"Of course everything's not okay. You know you're still grounded."

Was that a question? I agree anyway. Jason is on the move again, and while Mrs. Ellery reams me a new one for having a boy at the house, I study him. He's the right height for the guy I saw in the woods and I guess the walk is similar. Really though, aside from a limp or something, how distinctive is a walk?

It makes sense and it doesn't. Or maybe it's just me. I can't wrap my head around the idea, and as Jason passes me to look in Todd's old office, I press my back to the cabinets, making yes or no noises into the phone.

"It's just a guy from school, Mrs. Ellery," I say, interrupting her tirade. "He's just here to pick up a homework assignment. He'll be gone in a few minutes."

Jason pops into the kitchen again and leans against the oven to listen. Then he checks his phone . . . and starts to whistle, and my heart crams into my throat. He looks at me and I straighten, gripping the phone. Still whistling that long, low tune that makes me remember the taste of blood and mud, Jason begins to pace again, circling the kitchen—circling *me*.

He's not just looking around. He knows.

"Wicket, are you listening to me?" Mrs. Ellery is getting screechy.

"Oh, I'm listening." Golden afternoon light slants across the kitchen, catching on the cereal bowl I left in the sink.

The paring knife Bren left there to dry.

As Jason watches, I switch the cell to my other ear, pretend I'm fiddling with a strand of hair. Then I slide my hand into the sink, curling my fingers around the knife's plastic handle.

Just having it makes me feel better, but now what do I do? Wave it around? Not likely.

I feed the handle up my sweatshirt sleeve, leaving the tip of the knife pointing toward my fingertips. If he jumps at me, I can stiffen my arm and the knife will drop into my hand.

In theory.

In practice, I might cut off my fingers. Well . . . it's better than nothing.

"Homework or not," Mrs. Ellery continues, "I don't think your mother wanted you to have guests while she was gone."

"You're right." I have to force the words through gritted teeth. "Maybe you should come over. You can wait with me until he's gone."

Jason's eyes narrow.

"I'm already here," Mrs. Ellery snaps, and starts pounding on the front door. Still watching Jason, I slide past him and hustle down the hallway. I barely have the door open before Mrs. Ellery shoves her way inside.

"Honestly, Wicket, I don't understand why you have to be such an obstinate girl," she says, glaring at me. "My children weren't half the trouble you and your sister are to poor Brenda."

I retreat a step to give Mrs. Ellery room, but she's already swishing toward the kitchen, head swiveling from side to side as she checks the rooms to the left and right of the hall.

"Where is he?" she demands.

"He's—" We both push into the kitchen, look around.

No one's there. Jason's gone.

Mrs. Ellery searches the house, paying extra-special attention to the bedrooms. In the interest of trying to look like a Good Girl, I follow her, trying not to laugh when she bends down to check under the beds. Repeatedly. Someone's been watching Dr. Phil talk about teenage sex parties again.

I'm tempted to tell her that, when engaging in wild orgies, we hide our partners in closets, but Jason actually could be, so I help Mrs. Ellery look. Once we're both satisfied the house is empty, Mrs. Ellery makes me call Bren while she stands and watches. Unsurprisingly, I get voice mail. I wait for the beep and leave a message, making sure to detail that yes, I had a guest stop by and oh-by-the-way he needed a homework assignment.

Mrs. Ellery smirks like she's caught me in something big. She has no idea that Bren's going to be thrilled that I'm actually making friends after the Mini incident and the thrill will mix with the anger and that will leave . . . I don't know. I highly doubt it's going to get me thrown into convent school like Mrs. Ellery is hoping.

The older woman bangs out of the house and I lock the door behind her, setting the alarm even though it takes me two tries. My hands won't stop shaking. I drop the knife into the sink and dial Carson. He doesn't answer and I don't leave a message, but, sure enough, a few minutes later, he calls me back.

"What?" Carson snaps.

"Are you even *using* that tracking app I put on Baines?"

"Maybe. Why?"

"Because Baines was just here and his tattoo matches the one I showed you in the pictures. *He's* holding up Lell's head, not Kyle."

"Are you sure about this?"

I rub one clammy hand through my hair. "Definitely. I saw it. He knows I saw it."

"Good. We can use that."

"There is no *we*, Carson. He was here to kill me." That may not be exactly true, but it feels true and saying it out loud makes tears cram the corners of my eyes. "He must have known all along. He recognized me in the woods. He saw me at the party. This isn't about your glorious career anymore. People are getting killed."

"Have a little patience, Wick. This can lead us to something even better. There has to be more to what's going on, and if we play it right, Bay could end up sharing a cell with your dad."

"And more people could end up dead."

On the other end, someone says something to Carson. "I'll call you later," he tells me.

Only he doesn't and I spend the next hour pacing through the house, trying—and failing—to get a handle on what I know.

One. Kyle's the favored choice for being the murderer. Lell was his girlfriend. He had rage issues. He was paranoid.

Two. Jason could be the killer too, right? He was in the pictures. He was there. But why would he kill Lell? To prove something to my dad? To the other dealers? If he's sending a message, it feels like he's using the wrong people.

Which brings me to Three: Remember me? That's a message too . . . but for what? Is it a message from Kyle to the people who wanted to put him away? Or is it a message from Jason, a command to remember how powerful he's become? I have no idea. I don't know what to think about any of this.

I end up in my bedroom again, watching the security camera feed of the front yard. It's empty and that's good. My stomach stays knotted though, and no matter how long I glare at my computer screen, waiting for inspiration to hit, it doesn't.

I need something to take my mind off everything . . . except then I think of my mom. I could rewatch some of the interviews. I haven't touched them since finding out she was murdered. There really didn't seem like much point anymore.

I don't know what I'm supposed to be getting from watching them anyway. I seriously doubt they're supposed to provide distraction. I'd be better off sticking needles under my fingernails. All they do is upset me and they shouldn't—*at all*. They do though and I have to realize yet again that I'm not over what happened. No matter how much I want to be.

Norcut and Bren think I need more time to heal. Such bullshit. Yeah, time heals all wounds, but it leaves a scar and that becomes your pain's new face.

I'm sick of it . . . and I can't leave it alone.

I leave the security feed still running on one monitor and open the DVD file listing on my other screen, selecting the last interview. My mom appears and I hit play, tucking both knees under my chin to watch.

It's the usual back-and-forth until someone says, "I'm tired of your shit. Give me something useful."

I sit up a little. This is a new voice. Hard. Male.

Bay's.

The judge sounds like she's the bug and he's the boot, but my mom smiles. "You don't like my stories."

"Not particularly. Tell me what you know."

She shifts in her chair. "I don't know anything. That's what I keep telling you."

"Bullshit."

My mom looks at him, shrugs. For a heartbeat, she's

staring at something no one else can see, then her eyes refocus. "I love him and I hate it. How about that for what I know? Here's the deal with love: You can't control if you get love, but you can control if you give it."

I like that. I've heard the quote before, just never wrapped in her voice and, somehow, that makes it even better. I like how she said it, that she carried the words around, which says more about her than it does about whoever she's quoting.

Then I hear the downstairs door open and both my feet hit the floor. I stop the video and, barely able to breathe, I hover, hoping hoping hoping that I'm hearing things.

The alarm starts to beep.

I run to the top of the stairs and see shadows moving in the foyer below, drawing closer. For a terrible moment, I think I'm about to be finished, and then I realize it's worse.

Because Lily just came home.

And she's covered in blood.

This is my fault. Mine. Joe didn't decide to send someone after me. He sent someone after Lily. That's how this stuff works, but I still want to break something, scream. I take care of my sister instead.

There's a lot of blood, but the cut is shallow, skimming across her forehead before veering into her hairline. I don't think it will even need stitches, but Lily's still shaken.

So am I.

I dab a wet washcloth against my sister's skin. "Head wounds are always so dramatic."

"No kidding," Mina adds, and I cut a quick glance in the other girl's direction, gauging her reaction. Lily's little friend is looking a bit green around the edges and some of my sister's blood is smeared across her cheek.

"Here," I say, offering her a clean towel. Mina dabs at her face, eyes still pinned to Lily. "Anyone see you guys?" I ask.

Both girls shake their heads. Well, that's helpful—less people to explain the injury to—but I'll still need an excuse for Mrs. Harrison and Bren.

Like she's reading my mind, Lily pats my hand. She's trying for reassuring even though both our hands are cold. "'Sokay, Wick. I'll tell Bren I didn't pick my feet up." Her eyes meet mine and I know that's my cue to laugh. Too bad I can't even bring myself to smile.

I grab the Neosporin instead. "You can't go back to the Harrisons' in those clothes. Both of you need to clean up."

Lily nods. "Mina, you can borrow some of my clothes. We'll wash your stuff here."

"Won't my mom know?"

"Not if you don't tell her."

The other girl's mouth wads up as she considers what my sister's telling her. "What if my mom doesn't recognize the clothes and gets suspicious?"

"Tell her you borrowed them from me, okay?"

Mina nods. "Yeah. Okay." She heads upstairs, leaving Lily and me to stare at each other. That was nicely done. I don't know whether to be proud of my sister or worry that she's turning into me.

"So tell me what really happened," I say.

Lily holds up one finger, waiting for Mina's footsteps to cross the upstairs hallway. There's something about the way my sister's holding her mouth tight that just kills me. She looks so much like our mom it makes guilt pry into all my corners.

"I don't know what happened," she says at last. "Not really. It was all just so fast and then—" Lily looks away from me, scrubs one hand at her eyes. "I thought this was done, Wick. I thought we were safe."

We were until I screwed it up. I shake my head, concentrate on working the Neosporin into her cut. Not entirely true. We've never been safe, but I've always kept it so Lily thinks we are.

"Tell me what happened," I press.

"He came out of the woods. I didn't see him."

I stroke her hair, making soothing noises. Peachtree City is known for its bike paths—something like ninety miles of trails through the surrounding woods and golf courses. Some paths are used more than others and some paths are more overgrown, making them ideal hiding spots. Between cheerleading practice and school, Lily's schedule can be calculated almost to the minute. It would've made finding her easy.

Lily tries to touch her cut, winces. "We were walking home and then he was there and . . . and . . ."

"Did he say anything? Do you remember what he looked like?"

"He said Joe sent him." My sister's eyes go flat. She swallows and looks up at me. "He had me by my collar and Mina was too scared to run and when he brought the knife down . . . I kneed him. Really hard. You would have been proud."

I smile. "I'm already proud."

"I'll tell Mina she can't say anything. I'll say it was because of my dad and it's a secret and I'll get taken away if she tells."

"That doesn't make any sen—"

"It will to her. She doesn't know life like we do."

"True."

Lily wraps both arms around me and I hold her tight, feeling her shoulder blades press through her shirt.

"I miss Mom," she mumbles. "I miss her so much. I'm never going to get over that, am I?"

I hesitate. "No. Probably not."

She sniffles, curling tighter against me. "Why's Joe doing this? Is it because you won't work for him anymore?"

"Yeah." And a few other things that I should tell Lily and I don't because now she's smiling up at me like I'm a hero.

"I'm proud of you too," she says. "I was lucky. You think if he comes after me again I'll be that lucky once more?"

No. I kiss Lily's forehead. "You'll never have to be that lucky again, Lil. I'll make sure of it."

Mina reappears in Lily's clothes. She's moved past worrying about whether her mom will notice she's changed and is now worrying about whether they're going to be late for dinner. I'm starting to have serious concerns about if the girl will be able to keep her mouth shut.

Judging from Lily's scrunched expression, she agrees.

"I love you," I say, hugging my sister hard just before they leave. With the fresh clothes and cleaned cut, she looks so much less . . . horrifying. I never want to see Lily like that ever again.

"I love you too," she says, wrapping both arms around my neck.

"C'mon, I'll drive you."

Lily shakes her head. "Better if we walk." She slips a glance at Mina. "Gives me more time to talk to her."

"Talk in the car. You can't go anywhere by yourself now, Lil. It's not safe."

"So how's that work? You're just going to shadow me for the rest of my life?"

She's too young to sound so bitter, and another pang of guilt chokes me. I grab my keys. "We'll figure it out later. Just get in the car."

I call Mrs. Ellery to explain where I'm going as both girls pile into the Mini. Thankfully, the old bat doesn't give me any crap and I drive them back to Mina's, not leaving the driveway until Lily walks into the house and closes the door tight behind her. Milo's wrong. The past isn't dead. The future is. Everything we've done creates everything we will do.

Maybe this was always going to happen.

I'll have to be fast though. Business hours are only for another few minutes. I pick up my cell phone and I don't even have to search for the number because it's still in my

Recent Calls list. The line rings so many times, I think they've left for the day, but then the receptionist picks up. "Fayette County Jail, where can I direct your call?"

I angle the phone against my ear. "I need to make an appointment to see inmate Michael Tate."

I get the same guard as before, and as we walk into the Rainbow Visiting Room together, I try to gauge if he thinks it's weird that I'm here again.

Or, worse, if he thinks it's weird that I'm here for a totally different person, like weird enough to remember it for a jury.

Because if Michael does end up doing this—and if I'm going to tell him what happened, I should, at minimum, be able to say what *this* is and I can't—I want to make sure I'm covered. It can't get traced back to me. But the guard leaves without a second glance and I'm alone.

A few minutes later, Michael appears, and when he stands on the other side of the Plexiglas, he smiles and smiles.

All I can think about is how Carson said our smiles are the same.

"Hello, Wicket."

I swallow hard. "Michael."

My dad's eyebrows rise like he finds the greeting amusing. I don't care. The last time I saw him he nearly dislocated my shoulder and he's in jail because Griff helped catch him. He doesn't scare me anymore.

Maybe if I say it enough, I'll believe it.

Michael settles in his chair, palming what's left of his blond hair. The jail buzz cut makes the lines of his skull stand up in blunted ridges.

"What do you want?" he asks.

"Did you get my present?" Specifically, did he get a dented Samsung Galaxy loaded with the enhanced security video footage file from my computer? Stringer said he should have. Stringer will say a lot of things for two hundred bucks.

"I did. Where'd you find that?"

"Friend gave it to me."

Michael's eyes wander to the guard watching us. "Some friend."

You have no idea. "I wanted you to see it because"—I hesitate, trying to choose my words carefully—"because what happened wasn't an accident. It wasn't a choice. Mom did it because she had to, because Joe Bender made her."

Michael goes still. "You sure about this?"

"I reduced the blur in the video, and enlarged the image. You can clearly see them. It happened. It's him."

My father is silent for so long I think he doesn't care and I'm useless again. His eyes stay low, tracing some invisible word scarred on the tabletop in front of him.

"Who was with him?"

My mouth goes dry. I said *them*. I slipped.

"Some junkie he found to help him," I lie. Inside though I'm freaking. It's not like me to make that sort of mistake. I want him locked up, not dead.

Right?

Of course not. That isn't me. I don't want anyone to die. Only that's a lie now, isn't it?

"Why're you telling me?" My dad's eyes lift, meeting mine, and I have to struggle not to shudder.

"Because you need to know." I flex my hands under the table, rubbing sweaty palms against my jeans. Something wordless and urgent sits in my chest. I curl around it. "And because I want to know what you're going to do about it."

Michael smiles again and this time I do shudder. Maybe from fear . . . maybe from anticipation. I want Joe to pay and I know the look Michael has now. It's promising me mayhem.

"I'm going to take care of it, Wicket," he says. "Trust me."

When it comes to this, I do. I walk to my car not really feeling light or giddy.

Or guilty.

Instead, I'm just . . . centered? I don't know what it is, but I like how it feels beneath my bones, and when Bren calls the home phone and gets forwarded to my cell and I tell her I'm fine, for the first time in ages, I'm not lying.

I'm barely home when another text message comes through from an unknown number.

What else do you have?

Hello to you too. Carson must have got himself another burner phone. I dump my bag and sit down heavily on the floor. What else do I have? Um, nothing.

Nothing won't fly with Carson. I need something he can't reach himself. Something good.

I rub my eyes hard and, in the dark, I see my sister. My perfect, blond sister. Huh.

Chelsea was a blonde. Lell was a blonde. They were close in age . . . could that mean something? It might if I didn't know Chelsea was probably killed over leveraging Lell's pictures, so that leaves . . . Lell.

And suddenly, what Jason said before he passed out at

the carnival party comes roaring back to me: "Looks like Lell." If she was his first kill, it all starts with her, and whatever he started four years ago is finishing now . . . hmmm.

I double-check the security system and go upstairs, powering on my computer. After a few moments of waiting, I open Google and type in "Lell Daley Peachtree City." Several listings appear. Since the body's discovery, there's been a fair amount of news coverage and it's all pretty much saying the same stuff: local girl, tragic end, who could have done such a thing?

I click through the articles, finding nothing useful—no background revelation, no big clue. Unsurprising really. It's not like any of the local papers are going to make some amazing, case-breaking reveal. I finish one article, scroll to the top . . . and see Lell's picture grinning out at me.

I've seen this one before, but where?

Oh, yeah, Carson used it at his press conference and it's easy to see why. Lell's smile is stretched wide as it can go. She's leaning into Kyle, who's squinting into the sun. They look so happy.

I spend so much time staring at her smile that I almost miss the other arm linked through Lell's. Kyle is on her left. Someone else is on her right. I click on the picture, enlarging it. It's a man's arm. You can tell from the size of the forearm and the size of the watch. Judging by how he's holding on to Lell, they must be pretty tight.

So who is he?

I skim the article once more, looking for any information on the picture and there's nothing . . . except for a line about how Lell's mom took the photo a few weeks before the girl disappeared.

I wiggle my mouse, thinking. If Mrs. Daley took the picture and gave it to the press to use, she would probably remember who the other guy was, right?

Only one way to find out.

I open a new tab and start searching for Reichelle Daley's address.

Reichelle was an easy find. Even after Lell left, she never moved from our old neighborhood, and as I study her trailer through my windshield, I wonder if it was because she was waiting for her daughter to come back. The single-wide is at the end of a shallow cul-de-sac, its plastic shutters faded from yellow to tan, the edges of the metal siding peeling away from the frame.

When I knock on the door, the whole side porch shakes underneath me and, briefly, I think I'm about to cave through the boards.

I sigh. This better be good. I bet Mrs. Ellery is phoning Bren even as we speak. "Mrs. Daley?"

The plastic door opens and a woman in a stained sweatshirt and leggings stares at me through the screen. "Yeah. Who're you?"

"Wicket Tate. I used to live on Sycamore."

"And?"

"And I wanted to talk to you about your daughter."

A pause. She studies me. "You look like Lell."

I give Reichelle a tight smile, the skin along the back of my neck tingling. There is definitely something here. I just have to find it.

"I'm really sorry for your loss, Mrs. Daley." I hesitate, chew my lower lip for a beat. "Do you think I could ask you a few questions about her?"

"Why?"

I blank. *Because I'm doing a report for school? No. Because I work for the school newspaper? Not likely.*

"Because I knew Kyle and I think he killed her." Nowhere near the truth, but her eyes focus at the words and I know I've said what she wants to hear.

"I think he did too." Reichelle pulls open the screen door, motions for me to come inside. "I'd rather talk to someone from the neighborhood than those damn cops anyway."

I follow her into a cramped living room that smells like the inside of an old lady's purse. It's musty and stale, and when I breathe through my mouth, I can feel the dust hit my teeth.

"How did you know Kyle?" she asks, disappearing into the kitchen for a long moment.

"School. He was older. There was this outreach program and . . ." And I don't need to go any further because Reichelle's not listening. She shuffles into the living room and drops onto a worn corduroy couch, regarding me with flat eyes.

"You hungry? I got casseroles if you are."

"No, thank you."

"That's what I should have said. Everyone's treating me like I'm some sort of invalid. They keep bringing me food because they think I'm too busy crying to eat. No one understands that I already did my crying, cried all I cared to when Lell ran off with that boy."

"I had heard you were happy."

"I was." Reichelle nods hard, her gray hair fanning around her face. "I *was*. For a little while. Because that was the last I saw of her. Thought she had ditched me for her amazing new life with that rich boy. I cried then. Did for months actually. Haven't cried now. Don't know why that is."

Because grief is a funny thing. It ambushes you when you least expect it, and even though I should probably say something comforting here because I have an idea what she's enduring, I say nothing.

I clear my throat, but my voice still sounds like Minnie Mouse. "I wanted to ask you about a newspaper picture I saw—the one you took, where Kyle and Lell are smiling at the camera."

"Yeah." She lifts one shoulder. "What about it?"

"You can see another person's arm in the picture. Do you happen to remember who else was there?"

"Of course I do. It was Jason Baines."

They were all friends. Jason and Lell grew up together—just minutes away from me—and when Lell caught Kyle's attention sophomore year, they all started hanging out. Lell was Kyle's first love. Jason was Kyle's first dealer.

"Did you tell the police that?"

Reichelle stares at me like I'm an idiot. "No. Why would I tell them? What good would it do?"

"What if Jason was involved?"

Reichelle stiffens. "You know how much that boy cried when Lell left?"

I shake my head slowly and Reichelle relaxes a little, slumping into the couch cushions. "He still keeps an eye on me, makes sure the grass is mowed and stuff. I don't care what people say about him. If you're one of Jason's people, he takes care of you. He takes care of me. He makes sure his people take care of me."

I nod like I understand. All I can think of is Joe though and how I took care of him. Does that make me one of Jason's people?

My phone vibrates. Another text coming in. Bren? I check the screen. Carson.

Dental records identify body as Kyle Bay

I read it once, twice. That can't be right. That would mean . . .

"I think Jason loved her," Reichelle adds, and I have to force myself to meet her eyes even though all I can think about is, if Kyle's dead, who beat up Ian?

"I wish Lell'd loved him the same way," she continues. "You never want who you're supposed to though, do you?"

No, you don't. I'm shaking now. It takes everything I

have to push to my feet. "Thanks for your time."

A shadow falls across us.

"Absolutely, I want to thank you, Mrs. Daley." Jason stands in the doorway, grinning, and fear licks up my spine. He looks at Lell's mom like she's done something amazing.

She looks away. "You're welcome."

"I can't tell you how much I appreciate this." Jason steps into the room.

My legs turn to lead. "Appreciate what?"

"This." Jason holds up a Taser, fires it at me.

And my whole body goes up in flames.

I wake to pain. The skin on my chest feels scorched, and when I shift, bile surges into my mouth, gagging me.

"I wouldn't move if I were you."

Jason.

I jerk to my knees, swinging—and puking. The force of each heave brings my nose inches from the Oriental carpet under me. Four more retches and I manage to sit upright, push a shaking hand across my damp mouth.

And want to scream.

I'm in Bay's living room again and Jason's standing over me. "Told you not to move," he says, his eyes inching across my face. "Probably my fault. I Tasered you longer than I should have. It just felt so damn good."

I glare at him, coming aware in a horrible rush that we're not alone. Someone heavy is lying next to me. It stirs, moans. I look down and swallow hard. Judge Bay.

Jason kicks him. "Had a change of heart yet, old man?"

"Go to hell."

"Please, Dad."

I sit straighter, the edges of my vision sparkling, but my brain is starting to clear. A few feet away, Ian kneels on the floor, his battered face turned toward his father.

"Just do what he wants," Ian whispers.

"Exactly." Jason steps in front of Bay. "Listen to your son. Transfer the funds and I'll go away forever."

Money. If it's about money then why am I here? My stomach hits bottom again. This is already bad, but it feels . . . worse. Or like worse is coming.

Slowly, I shift my knees under me, studying the room from the corners of my eyes. The furniture has been pushed close to the walls, leaving the four of us on the expansive, pale carpet. Ian is whimpering, Bay is swearing, and Jason looks like he would enjoy taking each of us apart.

I watch his hands. The dealer's knuckles are so white I'm wondering how he can even feel the Taser—and that's when I see something move outside the window. A shadow separates from the dark. I blink, blink again.

Not a shadow. A person.

It moves to the right. Not any person. *Milo.*

Relief turns my bones mushy.

Until Jason punches Ian. Once. Twice. Three times. The poor kid's scream bubbles in his mouth, drowning on blood.

"Please, Dad." Ian's voice climbs higher, cracks. I cringe, eyes still on the window, praying for Milo to reappear. *"Please!"*

Next to me, Bay stiffens. "Stop sniveling!"

It makes Jason pause, fist raised. He looks at the judge with a smile meant for murder. "I remember that. I remember you saying that to her—"

"Who?" Bay's scooting backward now, pressing into me.

"My mother," Jason says. "You remember Tabitha, don't you, Bay? You screwed her enough. You screwed her enough to get me."

Underneath Jason, Ian makes a gagging noise of disbelief and horror. "Dad?"

"There's no proof. She was unstable and whored around and there was never any proof—"

"I'm the proof!" Jason screams. "Remember me? The son you ignored? I'm the proof! You assholes just use people like us and throw us away. You did it with my mom. Your son did it with Lell."

"He loved her," Bay whispers. It's so quiet none of us should have heard it. "Kyle shouldn't have, but he did."

"It wouldn't have lasted." Jason steps closer, leaning down so his face is only inches from Bay's. "It never does for your kind. Did you enjoy being blackmailed? Did you enjoy being scared? Because I enjoyed doing it to you. I really did."

Bay's face goes purple. "You'll never get a dime from me."

Behind him, Ian pushes to his feet and sways. My heart

leaps. If he's going to fight, I'll have to help. I'll jump on Jason's back or—

"Fuck this." Ian wipes the blood from his face and pulls a Taser from the small of his back. "I've had enough of your hysterics. Let's just kill him here and make it look like a robbery. I'll inherit everything and you'll get half, Baines."

"You're working with *him*?" The judge's question slides into a howl.

"Surprise," Ian breathes, and cocks his head like he heard something, feels something.

We all do.

First comes the pressure. It's so dense I feel it in my head, my chest, my *bones* . . . then comes the sound—glass shattering, drywall cracking—and the explosion shoves me forward. I hit the floor, face-first, my skull full of white light.

So that's where Milo went. Almost makes me smile.

Dimly, I'm aware of another explosion, a smaller one. Wait. Was it smaller? Or does it just *feel* smaller? My ears won't stop ringing. It's hard to breathe through the sudden smoke, but I haul ass anyway, grabbing for Bay.

He's already gone.

Jason kicks off the floor, running after him. I spin the other way and someone grabs my ankle, taking me to my knees. Ian. I lash out with my foot, connect with something soft. I ram my heel into it again. And again.

My ankle breaks free. I run for it, sneakers crunching on bits of glass. If I can get into the back garden, I can loop around to the road. I can do this.

"Wicket!" Ian screams.

I run harder, shouldering open what's left of the French doors and spilling onto the outside patio. My lungs burn. My eyes burn. I hit a wooden chaise lounge with both shins and crash to the ground.

Then I hear a siren wail. *Cops.*

It's to my right. Toward the main road.

Fastest way to get to them is across the front lawn and down the driveway. I stab one hand under me and push myself upright, racing down the stairs, cutting across the side garden . . .

Stopping dead.

Ahead of me, two figures grapple on the front lawn. There's a pop of light and a scream. Bay? Jason? I can't tell. Someone goes down, thrashing. Shit. I'd have to get past them to get to the road. I won't make it. That leaves . . .

The woods.

I could cut through the woods like I did before. If I run straight through, I could catch the cops on the other side. Between the underbrush and the darkness, I'd have coverage.

Of course, so would anyone else who's out there.

Fuck it. I sprint for the trees.

I'm almost there when I hear a snarl behind me.

"Got you now, bitch."

Ian.

I push myself, breaking through the trees with both arms outstretched. My feet hit the dead leaves and I have to force myself to count how many seconds pass before he joins me.

Three . . . four . . . five . . .

He's in.

I dive to my left and hit the dirt, tucking myself behind some brush like an animal. It might be appropriate actually. I feel like I've been run to ground.

"I know you're close, Wick." Ian walks a few feet ahead of me. "I can hear your breathing."

No shit. I'm struggling not to hyperventilate. I mash my shirt against my mouth, trying to smother the sound, and my elbow rams into something hard.

A broken-off branch.

I run my fingers over it, feeling the sharpened edge. Not a Taser, but it'll have to do.

Ian shuffles closer, kicking the smell of dead leaves into the air. "Come on out, Wick. You did this before with Jason, remember? He told me all about it."

The close-pressed branches and the ringing in my ears play hell with Ian's voice. I can't tell where he is. To my left? I think? I ease myself into a sitting position, look around. Not good. I went too far. I'm pinned by brush on one side and Ian on the other. I need to stand. I can't get a good swing if I'm lying down. But if I stand, he'll see me.

If I stay, he'll *find* me.

I push to my feet, staying close to a tree trunk, and pan the shadows, holding my breath until it's a pinch in my chest.

"Come on, Wick."

There. There he is. Ian's a few feet away, bent in half as he looks for me under a log.

"I know what you are in the dark, Wick. That's what made it so good. I saw you standing over Baines in the study. I saw your expression. You enjoy power. You're like me."

"Bullshit."

Ian straightens, hunting for the direction of my voice. "Liar."

I press to my right, deeper into the woods, but I need a better position, one where I won't get slowed down by brush when I run.

"I saw you through the window," Ian continues. He moves faster than I do, not worrying about the noise. He's getting closer.

"We both play weak because it suits us," he says. "It's not because we are. Predators keep excellent cover. Too bad we recognize each other."

"I'm not like you, Ian."

"Shitty attitude coming from a girl who stinks of fear." He inhales a long, deep breath. "You bitches all smell like it in the end."

I push through the last bit of undergrowth. Ian's maybe fifteen feet away. There's no way I'll outrun him.

"Don't feel like talking anymore, Wick?"

I lift the branch to my shoulder. "Why'd you kill Lell?"

Ian's head lifts, twisting back and forth as he hunts for me. "Lell was like me too—like us. She denied it until the end of course. I knew she wanted my brother for money. Baines knew Kyle wanted Lell for the moment. We were all friends and I . . . used that. I whispered to Baines all about how he should do something. And then he did—he killed both of them."

Ian pauses, taking a deep breath of night air. "I'm good at that, getting people to do what I want. Chelsea was like that too. She wanted money, power, to *get away* from here, and once she found those pictures, she saw her ticket—at my expense. She was my first and, God, how I enjoyed the cutting. Almost as much as I enjoyed burying Kyle. You want to know the best part?"

No. I almost say yes though because he's drawing closer and, one way or another, this is going to end.

"The best part was that our father believed it was Kyle. By that time, he hated him so much it was easy getting him to believe his son killed Lell and took off."

I shift behind another tree and a branch pops under my foot. Ian tenses.

And comes closer.

"I talked him through it," he continues. "Just like with Baines, I explained how it had to be, and do you know what my father did? Nothing. Instead of searching for his son, he helped cover it up. It all made too much sense after all of Kyle's blackout rages and the doctor's warnings. People see what they expect to see—of all people, you should get that."

I do and I ease back another step, feeling with the toe of my sneaker now, easing it into the leaves to minimize the noise.

"And then I got to thinking," Ian says, and I can hear the smile in his voice. "Because now that Kyle was out of the picture, I was set to inherit everything and what would happen if I were to . . . speed things up?"

He'd be free of Bay. I swallow and my throat catches. "And the 'remember me' thing?"

"I thought it was a nice touch. Remember the girl you buried. Remember what you *did*. Dad knew someone else knew. He started to melt down and I got to watch. I broke him like he kept trying to break me."

Ian pauses, scanning the woods. He's looking . . . looking. . . . He freezes. He *sees me*.

"This is going to happen, Wick."

Yes, it is. I clench the branch harder, force myself to wait, will my hands to stop shaking. They don't. I'm a breath away from crying. I don't trust myself to breathe. I'm afraid I'll sob. Then Ian moves sideways and I think I'm wrong. He hasn't spotted me at all. We're close—close enough to touch—but he's looking toward the road, like he thinks I'm heading there.

Wait for it. Wait for it, I think. *You know how to play the role of prey.*

And suddenly it's like Todd and my dad are both here, whispering my name. Ian leaps toward me and I swing the branch.

Connect.

His screams fill the air. I raise the branch again, start to bring it down, and pain courses through me, flying down my nerve endings.

It stops.

I'm facedown in the dirt now. Somewhere I can hear a low whimper and it takes me a second to realize it's me. A fist knots in my hair, yanking me onto my back, and Ian crouches down, pinning my shoulder with his knee.

Getupgetup! Don't let him get on top of you. You won't get up again.

Too late. I want to laugh as he sticks his face close to mine, stares into my eyes. *I am always too late.*

There's a bite of pain on the side of my face. *What*—a blade. He's pressing a knife into my cheek and blood runs down in a warm wave.

Ian rubs his thumb against my lips. "This isn't the way it was supposed to happen, Wick. I thought we could've had something good together. I get you—even if you don't want to see it."

My hands scrabble in the dirt around us, finding nothing. No rocks. Not my damn branch. There has to be something.

Then Ian's hip touches mine and I feel the Taser's hard plastic corner.

"What do you think, Wick?" Ian draws the blade down toward my mouth. "Should I give you a smile before I go? Or can you smile for me all on your own?"

I can. I do. I smile at Ian as my fingers close on the Taser's handle. I twist it up *hard*, pressing it into Ian's stomach and holding down the trigger until the cops follow our screams.

What's worse than sitting in a cop car? Sitting in an ambulance.

Where the hell is Carson? I shrug off the blanket the EMTs gave me. Yeah, I haven't stopped shaking, but wearing it around my shoulders makes me feel like a flood victim.

"Miss?" The EMT stops checking my pulse and glares at me. He looks familiar. Name on his shirt says Morris. Huh. Either I hit my head way harder than I thought or this is the same EMT from five months ago.

"If you could just hold still?" Morris asks through gritted teeth.

"I'm fine. Really."

"You're not fine. You might be after they get stitches into your cheek. I doubt it though. Your pupils are uneven. You're probably concussed—"

"I feel okay."

"You Tasered yourself."

"And also the bad guy." I give Morris a stinging, bright smile and he ignores me, dumping extra bandages into a plastic tub he shoves under one of the bench seats.

"Stay put." He points a finger between my eyes. "The detectives are going to want to speak with you before we go to the hospital. Do. Not. Move. Understand?"

Definitely the same guy from last time.

I roll my eyes. "Fine."

Morris's hands flex once before he walks to the front of the ambulance, leaving me to stare at the gathering crowd and debate my next move or, rather, lack of moves. I have no idea how I'm going to explain this to Bren. None. Next to my thigh, something buzzes.

What the . . . oh. That's right. Morris put his cell down while we were washing the blood off my face . . . only that's Milo's number flashing on the caller ID.

I look up, searching the faces on the other side of the police tape. No Milo. I rub one hand along the back of my neck. Now really isn't the time for a heart-to-heart— especially on someone else's cell.

The call rolls to voice mail and, seconds later, Milo calls again. I stick my head around the side of the ambulance. Morris is nowhere in sight.

I pick up the phone, sliding the pad of my thumb along the screen to answer. "Neat trick."

"Isn't it? I'll teach you how to do it if you like."

"Maybe. It's almost as neat as figuring out I was at Bay's house."

"I just wanted to make sure you were okay."

"Apparently I have another concussion . . . and I may need stitches."

"Jesus, Wick—"

"How did you know I was at Bay's?"

Silence.

I grip the cell harder. Surely, he didn't . . . *"Milo!"*

"I put a tracker on your car, so when the skeevy-looking guy drove it, I knew where you were." The words rush from him, piling up in a messy spill, and even though I expected them, they still sting. "I'm sorry, okay? Really sorry. It was shitty, but I wanted to see if it worked and I wanted to see you and—and we could talk about my total lack of boundaries if you would let me take you to dinner."

"That would be like giving you permission to stalk me." I check for Morris again, spotting him near two cops, everyone gesturing with their arms. "Where'd Jason leave my car anyway?"

"Not far. Other side of the woods. Shouldn't be long before the cops find it."

"Goody."

Milo makes a strained noise. "Look. I fucked up, okay? But this worked out really well for you."

"I wouldn't say 'really.'" I could say way worse. Without that explosion . . . I start shaking harder.

Milo takes an uneven breath. "I feel worse that I left

you, Wick. After the blast, I tried to find you and I couldn't and the cops were coming and I had residue all over my hands and I couldn't afford to get caught."

"I understand." And, surprisingly, I do. I get it. I would've even told him to run. We're the same like that. "I wouldn't have wanted you to get caught . . . and I'm sort of glad you stalked me. The bombing was . . . nicely done."

"So does that mean we're dating?"

"I'm hanging up, Milo." I do too, but not before I hear his laugh, liquid and hot, in my ear. It stays with me as I erase Morris's Recent Calls list, lingers as I walk around the back of the ambulance.

All three EMTs are with Judge Bay, and neighbors are drawing closer to the police lines. It's hard to recognize any faces. I probably don't want to anyway. Until my eyes snag on a familiar shape. For a second, I think it's Milo. It's not.

It's Griff.

And I'm two strides toward him before I even realize I'm moving. I duck around two police officers heading for the judge and, for once, know everything I need to say to Griff. I can make this right.

You came, I will say. Always, he will say. I'm sorry, I will say. We'll put this behind us, we both will say because I'll tell him the truth about everything. Only I get closer and none of that comes out because, when I reach for him, my fingers circling his bare wrist, Griff jerks away.

"Don't," he says, and I freeze. "I had to see if you were okay. That's all."

"I'm okay." It's a whisper and I want it to be more. I

clear my throat in a sharp cough and Griff's eyes waver. I thought he was looking at me. He wasn't. Griff was staring at the gouge on my face. He's *still* staring at the gouge on my face. "Thanks for coming."

The skin along Griff's throat tightens as he swallows. "I want to hold you and I can't."

"You can."

"I can't. If I touch you once, Wicked, I'll have to touch you again."

"Griff—" His eyes lift to mine and something inside me pitches sideways . . . cracks.

"Bye, Wicked."

No. No. No. A million *no*s and I can't breathe even one. Griff steps away as a hand snatches my shoulder, spins me around.

"Miss, I need you to stay put." It's another officer. He props me up by my bad arm and pain makes the world stumble sideways.

"I can't. I—I need Detective Carson." I tug myself from his grip. "Is he around?"

The officer shakes his head. "No."

"Will he be here soon?"

The guy hesitates. "They can't reach him."

"Can't—" My stomach plummets into my feet. You can always reach Carson. Always. There's only one thing that would keep him away from watching Bay's destruction: his own.

Behind us, someone calls for the officer. "Just a little

while longer," he promises, walking away. Leaving me alone again.

It bumps my heart into my mouth. Milo's plan to tank Carson. If it worked, Carson's storage unit will be packed with ATF agents busy tracing their leads to him. Considering the detective's already missing, I bet he knows. He knows and he's running.

If I could get to Carson's house before the agents do, I could steal back my desktop and the footage of Griff. I bite down a laugh.

I could steal back my *life*.

Revenge looks like this: It's stealing Morris's EMT jacket from the hook in the ambulance and walking from the crime scene like I was never a victim. It's finding my car before the cops do and using the spare key—the one I never thought I'd need when Bren stuck the magnetized box to the Mini's undercarriage—to drive away.

It's walking up Carson's muddy driveway in the dark, wanting to laugh.

I should be shaking and, instead, I'm smiling. It feels hard, like something carved with knives.

No more Carson. It's done.

Or it will be once I finish this. Steal my computer. Wipe the detective's. I'll be free. Griff will be free. The possibility is a sharp and brilliant pang. He'll be safe. We both will.

Doesn't take long to reach the house. It sits, still and

black, in the moonlight and I have to force myself to wait when all I want to do is run across the yard cheering.

Gone. Gone. Gone. Carson's gone.

I skirt the yard, staying close to the tree line, until I reach the rear of the house. If his alarm is set, I'll have maybe twenty minutes before the police show up. That's fine though. I need less than ten. I tug on the latex gloves I stole from the ambulance and I pull the Mini's tire iron from underneath my hoodie, taking two running steps and smashing the door's side window.

Nothing. I jam my hand through the opening and pop the locks. Best to assume it's a silent alarm and hurry. I stumble through the unlit kitchen, making it to the living room by feel alone. My hip grazes the worn couch. Two more strides and my shin rams into Carson's computer desk.

Bingo.

I drop to my knees, one hand groping for the CPU, the other grabbing my bootable jump drive from my bag's pocket. I plug it into Carson's computer and punch the power button, tilting the screen down. It makes it hard to see what I'm doing but doesn't throw much light into the room.

After a minute, a blue menu appears. The command prompt blinks "boot:" and I quickly type "autonuke." The screen jumps to black, a progress bar appearing at the top. The computer clicks and whirs as the hard drive begins shredding all its data. By the time the program finishes, the computer's information will be completely unrecoverable.

Lights twirl across the room.

I lift my head, see a car easing up to the house. A man gets out.

Carson's home.

I wait for him in the dark. Two days ago, shadows this thick would have suffocated me. Now . . . it feels fitting. Right.

Which isn't to say I'm not thinking about my options. If Carson comes through the rear door, he'll see the broken glass and know I'm here. If he comes through the front, I could leave through the kitchen. The detective won't know I've been here until I'm way gone.

I watch him linger in front of the still-running car, his shadow stretching through the window and into the room.

Almost to my toes.

Carson moves, a quick, jerky walk toward the porch. Perfect. He's coming through the front door. For every step forward, I take a step back, my stomach sinking. No time left to search for my computer, but at least Griff will be safe.

By the time Carson's opening the lock, I'm almost to the kitchen. The door swings open and I pause, waiting for his movement to cover the sounds of my own.

"Wick?" My name is soft, urgent, and nothing like Carson. It stops me dead.

"Wick?" the detective whispers. "If you're here, you need to run. They're coming and you can't be seen here. They're looking for me."

No shit. I want to move, but my legs have turned to lead.

"Believe me," I say at last, watching his head twist side to side as he tries—and fails—to locate me in the dark, "I am *so* gone. I had a few things to finish first though."

"My computer?"

I don't say anything.

"Will they be able to find anything on it anymore?"

Again, I don't say anything and Carson nods, hearing everything. By helping Griff, I've helped him. On the one hand, it's a steep price. On the other . . . there is nothing I won't pay for Griff to go free.

"Then let me repay the favor," Carson says, taking three heavy steps into the room. The detective uses his cell to cast a small patch of light on the shelves and, as I watch, he removes several rows of books. They were hiding a safe.

"No point in keeping them anymore." Carson cradles the desktop and a VHS tape against his chest, carrying them toward me. I'm about to tell him not to come any closer when he stops, puts the both of them on the carpet between us.

"There. Now we're even." The detective retreats to the front widows, scanning the yard.

We are not even, but I decide not to argue. I tuck the desktop under one arm, tossing the tape into my bag. "Thanks."

"Joe Bender was shivved a few hours ago. Any idea why that would happen?"

I turn to go. "Karma?"

"More like something you did."

Suddenly, I wish there were light. I want to see the detective's face. He sounds . . . pleased? I can't tell.

"They had to Life Flight him to the hospital," Carson continues.

Something inside me squishes flat. "So he made it?"

"No." The detective pauses to let me digest this, or maybe he's hunting for some sign that I'm thrilled.

That makes two of us.

"I know you were involved, Wick."

"Prove it."

"I don't have to. You've never visited the jail and, suddenly, you're there *twice*. And then one of them dies. You want to tell me that's not connected?"

"Prove. It."

"I can't, but other people will have noticed." The detective's shoulders round, and in the glow from the headlights, he looks close to collapsing. "There are some things you need to know before I go."

I don't care. I *don't*. My stomach squeezes uneasily and Milo's smile lights up my head. "Where are you going?"

"Can't tell you. Hell, I don't even know yet."

"What happened?" The words escape before I can smother them.

"I had this storage locker, kept some of my . . . information in there. Someone called in a bomb threat and the next thing I know they're running dogs by all the units, looking for explosives. Guess where they found them? My locker. My fingerprints. My stuff. And I had it all under a fake name. How do you think that will look?"

"Not good?"

"Not good," he echoes, and his laugh sounds rotten. "Damn right it's not good. The stuff in the unit is mine, but the explosives—" Carson shakes his head hard. "I've been set up. I can't prove it and, even if I did, there's the matter of the other . . . *things* in the locker. I had information from other sources, information on other cases. Once the ATF tracks it to me, I'll be put on administrative leave pending the investigation's completion. Everyone will act like I'll be back and we all know I won't be. I'll never work again."

And all those other "sources" like me will go free. Red-hot satisfaction rolls through me. It's round and hard as pennies. I want to spill it over my fingers, roll around in it until I come up drenched. Milo was right. I am impressed.

I'm fucking thrilled.

"You need to know about who's been watching you, Wick. There are other people who want to use you."

"No shit, I'm talking to one."

"I'm not like them. I mean . . . I have used you, just not like they would. I know they've contacted you. You need to ask yourself *why* they're doing it now." Carson pauses, waiting for my response, and when there isn't one, his shoulders sag. "We were doing real work, Wick. I was going to make you a hero."

Except Carson decided who was worthy and who was evil—and I'm not sure which is worse: Carson thinking he's a good guy or the idea that other people are hunting me.

"What else do you have?"

"Nothing. I swear it."

I start to leave. "Good luck with running."

"Wick."

I don't know what I'm expecting when I turn around, but it's not the hunched figure standing in front of me.

"Be careful," he says, his voice a flattened nothing. "One day you'll look back on this and you'll remember how good it was. We were a team."

"We were never a team, Carson."

He lifts one shoulder in a halfhearted shrug. "Then you'll remember me telling you this: They're coming for you, and without me, you'll have nowhere to hide. It's just beginning."

"You're wrong, Detective. It ends tonight. It ends just like this." And I walk out the door.

What Happened After

By the time I leave Carson's, all hell has broken loose. The cops are pissed I disappeared. The EMTs are pissed I disappeared. Bren has left me four voice mails because, due to someone's infinite wisdom, she was notified and she's pissed I disappeared.

I drive straight to the Fayette County hospital and plead a head injury.

Ten minutes later, I'm admitted. Twenty minutes later, the cops I ditched show up.

You'd think we'd all be happier to see each other.

Not.

The doctors keep me overnight in the hospital, and when I wake up, it's so quiet, I think I'm alone . . . then I see Bren. My smile has never hurt so much and it is *so* worth it. She's worth it. I escaped. It's over.

But when I reach for Bren, she recoils.

"What are you?" she breathes.

My skin crawls. "Nothing."

"You're lying."

We study each other, Bren using silence as a leverage that will never work on me. I know how this game is played. I'll wait. Even if the silence drowns us.

Bren touches her fingertips to her lips, chin. "You didn't find him on a hunch, did you?"

She should be talking about Bay or Ian or Jason. She's not. She's talking about Todd.

"You tracked him down," Bren continues softly. "You hunted him."

Him. Her husband still turns soft in her mouth, like Todd's living under her tongue.

Stick to the story, Wick. That's what is in the police report. That's what you have to say. But, right now, I can't say anything. For the first time, I want the words and I don't have them. I want to explain and I can't.

I look at her. "He deserved it, didn't he?"

"Yes." The word escapes on a hard exhale. Bren stands up, starts to pace.

"It isn't like what you're thinking."

"Then what's it like?"

I study the blanket . . . the hospital ID tag. Now is the time to say something and I have nothing.

"That's what I thought," Bren says, and I feel her take one step back. Two. Her breathing has gone shallow and loud. "Then it's true? That you've been entrapping people online? You've been breaking the law? Why would you do that?"

How could I *not*? I don't say that though. How do I explain that I lived in the dark so they could stay in the light? How do you explain that?

You don't.

So I let Bren think I'm deranged. Damaged.

It might be pretty damn close to the truth anyway.

As long as we're on the subject of truth, Ian and Jason came clean the night they were arrested. Technically, Jason confessed first: why he killed Lell (to save her from Kyle), why he killed Kyle (to keep him from Lell). His love and his hate seem so sound-bite tidy when the police explain it like that. Everyone nods and I have to struggle not to gag.

The boys partnered with each other for the money—and also to get revenge on the father they hated. Kyle, for all his imperfections, was the judge's favorite child, the one who would inherit everything, the one who was openly praised, the one who was *noticed*.

Jason was at the party to see Ian when I roofied him, a mistake that made Jason see me as a loose end and Ian see me as his own. This actually came up with the cops—how I roofied Jason. He told them all about it and he might've had something there too since Ian backed his story, but Bren swore I never left her side during the party. I still don't know if she lied for me or if she just didn't remember. Either way, Ian won't see the outside of a prison cell until he's old enough to retire and Jason won't be too far ahead of him.

Bay lived. For a while, we were a few doors away from each other at the hospital. Then he was transferred to a rehab center with promises that he should be able to go home soon. As far as I know, he never did. The house was repaired and went up for sale. He retired—effective immediately—from his position. He moved. No idea where. I guess I could find out if I wanted. I like pretending he disappeared though. It's almost as good as pretending the whole thing never happened.

In the end, Bren checks me out of the hospital once both doctors (the first opinion and the second opinion) say I'm good to go. We go home and nothing's the same. Part of me mourns it. Another part of me thinks everything is just so much easier now. There's less need to include me. Less pressure to be perfect.

Less notice when I slip away.

I don't remember who I am anymore, who I'm supposed to be. Sometimes I go back to my old neighborhood and stare at our house. I'm not sure how I went from the girl who lived there to the girl I am now. Did it happen when Carson started blackmailing me? When Todd preyed on Lily? When Tessa jumped?

Or when my mom did?

I don't know. I don't know that I'll ever know, but I do understand this: I'd struggled to survive for so long, I didn't recognize when I was safe. I won't make that mistake again.

Funny how safe brings me to Milo, isn't it? The boy has a thing for explosives. How does that make anyone feel safe? Milo knows something's wrong and even though I don't tell him . . . well, I'm sure he's figured out things aren't so great at home. I think it makes him try harder with me. Some days I'm grateful because it makes me feel like I'm still here. I still exist.

Other days . . . I wish he wouldn't because this isn't who I want to be.

Naturally, Milo disagrees. He thinks we're brilliant together. I think we're dangerous. We're too alike. There's nothing noble, nothing good about either of us.

Except it *feels* awfully good when we're together.

What else? Oh, Carson's still gone. No one knows where he went. Agents from the ATF and NSA are searching for him and he must have better skills than I would have given him credit for because they're coming up empty-handed.

It's an interesting development—not interesting enough to keep my days from stretching into one long smear though. I open my hacking-for-hire business again. Not because I have to; because I need it.

I need something to distract me from Lily's anger, Bren's watchful eyes, and the voice mail from my dad. He called one day while I was in the shower, left a message saying, "You owe me." The old Wick would've puked. The new Wick . . . well, I replayed the voice mail twice and thought, *Maybe. He'll have to catch me first.*

Tough words considering it kick-started another round of insomnia. I'm barely sleeping and, when I do, I dream of

Joe. I wake up at two or three in the morning drenched in sweat, skin slippery as blood. I don't feel bad—I don't—but his murder left a stain.

I just need some time for everything to settle. Only it doesn't, because I come home from school one day to find Bren waiting for me in the living room. There's a guy with her, and even before he turns around, I know him. Maybe because part of me has been waiting for this.

Officer Hart—only it isn't "officer," is it? That suit and tie look like Fed—stands next to our couch, and when I step closer, he comes forward, ready to shake my hand.

"I'm so glad to meet you, Wicket. Your mom's told me all about you."

I glance at Bren and my eyes snag on her hands. They're clasped in front of her chest like she's praying . . . or holding herself down.

"Wick," Bren begins. "Considering some of the . . . difficulties you've been going through, Dr. Norcut recommended we contact Mr. Hart. He runs a program for at-risk youth, for teenagers dealing with loss. We want you to go. We think you need the help."

She's sending me away? It nearly kicks my legs out from under me. I straighten. "I think I'm doing fine."

Bren's mouth thins. "I'll give you two a moment then." She pushes off the couch, pawing her eyes. My skin goes hot then cold. She's . . . *leaving me*.

Like an idiot, I open my mouth, snap it shut. That won't work. I don't know the words to bring her back even if I can name all my feelings—another gift from Norcut. There's hurt and horrified . . . and hate.

I face Hart. This feels like a game, and when I see the way he grins, I know somehow I've lost.

"I was so looking forward to meeting you properly, Wicket. You have exceeded every expectation we could dream of."

"Oh yeah?"

"We want to help you. We've seen what you can do, how determined you can be when properly motivated." He lifts his brows like my biological mother is a punch line he's waiting for me to get. "What you did with those video clips of your mother? Excellent job. I've enlisted dozens of kids over the years. Your results were the best."

The best? My throat closes. I did an excellent job by following their clues? Or by taking down Joe? I'm not sure, but, suddenly, I feel very used . . . and afraid. What did Carson say? That he was protecting me from people who were worse? So that means . . . ?

"No smile?" Hart sighs and his eyes pull at the corners with some emotion I won't name. "Let's be friends. We're the good guys, Wicket. Trust me."

Acknowledgments

At this point, I feel like I am thanking the usual suspects, but there's no way I would be here without any of them, so here we go.

As always, I'm indebted to my long-suffering agent, Sarah Davies, who routinely pulls me back from the edge even when—especially when—I cannot do it myself. A big thank-you to both my editors, Karen Chaplin and Jessica MacLeish, who are beyond gracious with their time and their feedback. I know darn well my timeline issues make you both twitchy. Next book, I promise to use a calendar, but we all know I'll probably forget again . . . and then you'll have to fix me again . . . and then I'll break out the calendar again . . . and forget it again—and you know what? Let's just leave it at: thank you for putting up with my digressions.

All of them.

You know who else puts up with me? Alana Whitman, Olivia deLeon, Margot Wood, and Aubry Parks-Fried. Thank you for everything, ladies. I so so so appreciate your expertise and input over the past two years.

And, of course, a very sincere thank-you to Joel Tippie for the exceptional covers. They are beyond beautiful.

Another big thank-you to the Doomsdaisies, who make me look way cooler than I am—especially looking at you, Cecily White. Thank you to Pintip Dunn and Stephanie Winkelhake for talking me through, well, *everything*, and particular thanks to Meg Kassel and Sally Kilpatrick, who saw every incarnation of this novel, and I do mean *every* incarnation. You ladies are so gracious. Thank you.

Huge, huge, huge thank-you to Natalie Richards, who has toured with me, critiqued with me, and pulled me out of the fetal position more times than I can count. Or want to. I'm a better writer because of you.

An equally enormous thank-you to my husband, Boy Genius, for all the website stuff and editing stuff and making sure there's food in the house stuff. For everything, basically. And another thank-you to my parents. I wouldn't be here without your unwavering support.

I would also like to thank Kari at *A Good Addiction*, Shay at *Shaytastic Books*, and Alex at *Peace, Love, and Fangirl* for all the beta reads and feedback. I am crazy lucky to have you guys.

Speaking of lucky, I want to particularly thank Ashley at Nose Graze and her husband, Peter, for their technical expertise. I know how slammed you two are. I really appreciate you taking the time to answer all my questions.

Another thank-you to Natalie C. Parker, who is not only an amazing writer, but also does an amazing critique. And thank you to Abra Schwartz for letting me steal one of her observations. She knows which one.

Bottom line, *Remember Me* is so much better because of all of you. You took time away from your writing and your lives to help and I cannot begin to tell you how much you mean to me. Thank you.

And, last but not least, thank you to all the bloggers and librarians who have been so passionate about the Find Me series. You guys are amazing. It's been a total privilege.

Keep reading for a sneak peek
at *Trust Me!*

```
        ·/ ^*r.
     unti1l#*%:
  .URRUU\r9E"%:
%p")*(r"  )%pi:
 ."i      )%pi:
          ^#P.
          1#f%:
          SR"%i
          t//:·
         ·"u#:
          ·#P.
          1#f%:
          SE"%i
         )%pi:
          )%pi:
          SE"%i
p")*(P.P)%pi%pa"r#p'
p")*(P.P)%pi%pa"r#p'
```

Is it still kidnapping if your mom lets them take you? Because it definitely feels like kidnapping—no matter how many times Agent Hart smiles at me.

"C'mon, Wick," he says, rebuttoning the front of his suit jacket because I won't shake his hand. "I promise you'll like where you're going."

Doubtful. That smile snakes chills up my spine. "Bren?" I call, wincing when my voice cracks. My adoptive mom left me with Hart so we could "talk," but I'm *so* done talking. "Bren?"

Bren appears in our living room doorway, my duffel bag—already packed—in one hand. It kicks all the air right out of me.

"How long have you been planning this?" I whisper.

"It's not like that, Wick."

It *is* like that or she'd be able to meet my eyes.

"You'll like it there," Bren continues, her free hand going to her reddening neck. "Mr. Hart's program is specifically designed for teenagers dealing with loss. He can keep you safe—keep you out of trouble."

"I'm not *in* trouble."

Yet. The word hangs between us and Bren takes a deep breath. "Your therapist thinks it's for the best."

"We've been watching you together, Wick," Hart adds.

I flick my eyes to him, force myself to hold his gaze. The way Hart grins looks like a toothpaste ad, but I can hear the threat simmering underneath. He's daring me to challenge him.

What if I did?

What if I told Bren everything? I could tell her how it all started when Hart gave me the videos of my mother informing on my father, how the informing led to my mother's murder, how I found that murderer and made him pay.

I could tell Bren that I used to track down cheaters for money and that Detective Carson blackmailed me into working for him. I could tell her that my nightmares are so bad I'm afraid to sleep.

I could tell her I spent so much time being scared, I didn't know what it felt like to be safe until it was too late.

Hart steps closer. "We know how much you've been struggling. Your therapist thinks your PTSD stems from what happened with your foster father."

I stiffen. My foster father is better known as Bren's husband, or ex-husband, Todd. He raped a childhood friend of mine. It drove her to suicide; then he switched his attention to my sister.

And then to me.

I caught him before he could hurt anyone else, but the way I did it wasn't exactly legal and I attracted Detective Carson's notice. He threatened to tell Bren everything if I didn't work for him. I agreed. After the damage Todd's crimes did to Lily and Bren . . . well, how could I *not* have agreed? He was going to ruin what was supposed to be the rest of our lives.

I lift my chin a little higher. "Yeah, so?"

"Looking Glass," Hart says softly, "is a very special program. We can help you get back your control, your life. It's designed specifically for teens with your computer talents. You'll be safe there. I'm asking you to trust me—just for a little while."

I stay still.

"We really need to get going, Mrs. Callaway," Hart says, turning that full-watt smile on my adoptive mom. There's something plastic about him. It's the way his chestnut-colored hair doesn't move, how his shoes are shined. Hart's like a Ken doll come to life except for the bulge at the small of his back. Is that a pistol?

Hart's careful to always face Bren so she won't see it, but I do. What kind of counselor needs a gun? This isn't good, but if I tell Bren, what happens? Will he tell her everything he knows about me? That's worse.

"I want to get Wick settled before dinner," Hart says. "She'll need to meet the other teens, see the facilities—"

"What about Lily?" Saying my little sister's name conjures tears in my eyes and I force my chin higher. "How am I supposed to say good-bye?"

Bren focuses on her feet. "I'll tell her what happened."

She's really going to give me up. I blink; blink again because now my eyes are stinging. I know how this works. I've been through enough foster homes to understand how to leave. I knew this wouldn't last.

But I didn't know how much it would hurt. The pain is incandescent. I feel like I could walk around it, sling it across my shoulders, and carry it. Bren was supposed to be forever and I was stupid enough to believe her.

"Please, Bren. Please don't do this." The words shoot from me before I'm even aware I'm saying them. "Please don't send me away."

For the first time since Hart arrived, Bren looks at me. "It's for your own good, Wick. It's not just the . . . *acting out*." Her voice drops into a whisper and she edges closer. "It's not safe for you here."

My heart double thumps. "What are you talking about?"

Bren's eyes go past me and straight to *him*.

I step in front of Bren, block her from seeing Hart. "What aren't you telling me?"

"Show her." Hart again. He appears at my side, those shiny shoes quiet as cat feet on the carpet. "Be honest with her, Mrs. Callaway."

Bren does as she's told, but not before I see her wince. Was that "honest" dig supposed to hurt her? Because it did. I glare at Hart and Bren touches my arm.

"That boy you caught—the one who was trying to murder his father—he's dead." She passes me a police report. It's pages and pages of tiny font, but two words stand out: Jason Baines. He was a rising star in my father's drug ring and damn near killed me.

I shrug. "That's horrible, but it doesn't mean anything."

"Good point," Hart says. "I mean, people get shivved in jail all the time, right?"

I don't look at him. Can't. He put the slightest emphasis on "shivved" and now I know he knows about another shivving—one I helped make happen. I'm not ashamed I helped my father kill Joe Bender. I know what Joe did to my sister and what he was going to do to me when he was released from jail.

I am, however, scared for Bren to find this out.

"It isn't just Jason who's gone," Hart continues and there's the flutter of paper as he takes the report from Bren. "It's every single person who worked for your father. They're disappearing and—"

"Michael," I say.

Hart's brows twitch together. "I'm sorry?"

"*Michael*. I would prefer you call him Michael, not my father."

Hart nods. "Fine. This is just the beginning. They will come for you, Wick."

I flinch and Hart sees it. I hate that. Now he knows his words just climbed under my skin to simmer.

"'They'?" I roll my eyes. "Could you be any more vague?"

"Stop it." Bren thrusts herself between us and braces both hands on my shoulders. "I *know*, Wick. I know what you did to catch Todd was illegal and dangerous and—" Her voices catches and she has to swallow twice. "Mr. Hart says you've attracted some attention because of it. When your father went to jail, he left a vacuum. There are others who are going to take his place and they'll want you to help them do it. Mr. Hart says that's why Detective Carson kept coming around. He says you *will* be a target. He's very sure you're in danger."

That's because he's lying. I'm not a target. I'm not in danger. No one knows what I did for Michael. And I start to say so, but Bren cuts me off.

"I forgive you, Wick. I understand. When it came to Todd, it was my fault. I didn't protect you. You had to save yourself, but this time, I'm saving you."

"Bren, I—"

"Just *try*, okay?"

I nod. Honestly, when it comes to Bren, it's kind of automatic for me. I always agree because it's easier than telling her the truth. She can't even talk about the hacking I did to catch her husband, Todd, before he attacked another girl. And if she can't say any of that, what would the rest of the truth do to her? Once you learn something about someone, you can't unlearn it. And I'm not sure I want to find out what would happen. She's giving me an opportunity here. We can cover this up, pretend it never happened. I'm good at that.

"The point is," Hart says, rubbing one palm against his jaw, "you're prey now. You can't stay here. It's not safe for you and it's not safe for them."

My stomach lurches sideways. *Them.* Bren and Lily.

"If you come with me," Hart continues, "I'll make sure they're protected."

"So I go away forever?"

"No!" Bren tugs me closer, eyes glassy and bright. "Just for right now. Just until we decide what to do."

"Beyond the obvious benefits of keeping you alive, I'm offering you an opportunity." Hart takes the duffel bag from Bren and slings it onto his shoulder. "You have so much potential. Let us help you reach it."

Chills again. They crawl all over my body. Hart's acting like a friend, but he can't be. There's no way. Hart gave me the videos of my mom, said he wanted to see what I could do with "proper motivation."

Know what I did? In the course of six weeks, I brought down a pair of murderers, I discovered who my biological mother really was, and I saved my sister and myself.

I also helped kill someone.

Joe Bender was my father's right hand and my once-upon-a-time handler. He would've killed me, my sister, maybe even Bren, but I got to him first. I used Michael to take him down and Hart knows it.

Thing is . . . to blow Hart's cover, I'd have to destroy my own.

"Promise me you'll try, Wick." Bren's eyes are huge and shining. Her fingers link in mine, squeeze. "Please? Just do what Mr. Hart says and then come home to us."

I open my mouth . . . close it. Bottom line, everything started when Hart brought me those videos and now he's finishing it. If I go with him, I don't know what will be waiting for me and that's terrifying.

But telling Bren the truth? That's worse. Even if she didn't haul me straight to the police, she'd hate me. I'd trade the truth of what I did for my hope that she'll let me come home. If Bren doesn't know and I play Hart's game . . . maybe I could come back? Maybe we could be together again. I could be with my sister, my friends.

"I'll visit you soon," Bren whispers and tucks a strand of hair behind my ear. I have to fight not to lean into her. If I do, I'll fall apart. "I didn't keep you safe enough before. I'm making up for it now."

"It wasn't your fault—"

She leans close, touches her forehead to mine. "Letting him take you is going to kill me. That's how I know how lucky I am—because I'm losing so much right now."

"Mrs. Callaway?" Hart's trying for polite and failing.

His smile is gritted. "We really need to go."

Bren nods and follows us to the front door. She opens it, and briefly I'm blinded by sunshine. It's a beautiful day. The neighbors are out; one of them waves to Bren, but she doesn't notice.

Hart's hand goes to my shoulder. Like we're good buddies. Like this is fun and I can't feel the way his fingers tighten.

I swallow and my throat click-clicks. We're off the porch now. In the open. Panic flares in my chest. If I ran, could he catch me?

I slide him a sideways glance. Hart's considerably taller than I am. He looks fit too. If I ran, he *would* catch me.

And if he didn't catch me, where would I go?

My entire life is tied up in the computer in my bedroom—my viruses, my customers, my bank accounts. How freaking ironic. I've prepared and prepared for the day I'd have to disappear, and now?

My hands roll into fists.

"Promise me, Wick," Bren whispers.

"I prom—" Hart jerks me forward, steering me down the sidewalk. There's a town car waiting at the curb and beyond the town car . . . there's a dark gray Ford headed my way.

Milo. Panic makes me stumble. Our date. We were supposed to meet and now—oh, God. *Milo.*

His car coasts closer and the hum in my ears grinds into a roar. I want to scream for him to gun it. To run.

But then Hart will know there are others and he'll come for Milo too.

I force my eyes forward, focus on the house across the street, and one second . . . two seconds . . . Milo's car rolls into my line of vision. I watch him.

He pretends to watch the road.

Our eyes only meet once.

Once is enough. Milo drives on, dragging something from me as he passes. It limps behind his car and makes a left at the corner to follow him.

"Is everything okay, Wick?" Hart asks. He's watching me so closely. Did he see? Does he know? He isn't saying anything. What does that mean?

A driver in dark shades pops out of the car, takes my bag, and tosses it in the trunk.

"Nice ride," I say as Hart opens the rear door for me, our reflections stunted in the glass. "But I thought kidnappers preferred panel vans?"

Hart laughs. It's a buttery sound like something that belongs to talk show hosts and sitcom dads. "Smile, Wick. This is going to be fun."